SOLDIER OF FORTUNE (

By David Pilling

More Books by David Pilling

Leader of Battles (I): Ambrosius

Leader of Battles (II): Artorius

Leader of Battles (III): Gwenhwyfar

King's Knight (I)

The White Hawk (I): Revenge

The White Hawk (II): Loyalty

Folville's Law (I): Invasion

Caesar's Sword (I): The Red Death

Caesar's Sword (II): Siege of Rome

Caesar's Sword (III): Flame of the West

Robin Hood (I)

Robin Hood (II): The Wrath of God

Robin Hood (III): The Hooded Man

Robin Hood (IV): The King's Pardon

Nowhere Was There Peace

The Half-Hanged Man

Co-written with Martin Bolton

A World Apparent Tale (I): The Best Weapon

A World Apparent Tale (II): The Path of Sorrow

Follow David at:

www.pillingswritingcorner.blogspot.co.uk

www.davidpillingauthor.com/

Or contact him direct at:

Davidpilling56@hotmail.com

Author's Note:

This tale is an indirect sequel to an earlier novel, The Half-Hanged Man. They can be read together or as stand-alones

Glossary

Chevauchée - An organised system of plundering and devastating enemy territory

Bascinet - type of open-faced military helmet

Destrier - Medieval warhorse, ridden by knights and men-at-arms

Rouncy - a common, all-purpose horse used by poorer soldiers, and as packhorses

Routier - French term for a mercenary soldier

Sipahi - Freeborn Turkish cavalry, split into feudal and household troops

Springald - A device for hurling large bolts, and less often stones and Greek Fire

Tulwar - Type of Turkish sword, usually with a curved blade

Verderer - a forest official, responsible for protecting and administering parks and forests

Constantinople, May 29th 1453

One cannon-shot decided the fate of the city. The ball tore into the battlements, ripped through the ancient stonework and flung up a cloud of debris.

Part of the debris hit Giovanni Giustiniani, a young Genoese mercenary captain. His finely-wrought armour, already dented and battered by Turkish blades, offered little protection against the hail of shattered stone.

The force of the blast knocked him down. His bloodied sword dropped from his hand, and he fell onto the walkway, half-buried under the rubble.

Two of his soldiers rushed to their captain's aid. One knelt beside the body and sought frantically for a pulse.

Giovanni was still conscious. "Get me out of this," he murmured feebly, "back to our ships."

His voice was almost drowned by the thunder of cannon and the frenzied screams and war-yells of Turkish janissaries. The Sultan's elite infantry swarmed about the walls, flung into battle in a titanic effort to overwhelm the stubborn defenders.

Between them the soldiers managed to drag Giovanni clear. More Genoese ran to help. Four of the strongest lifted his body and carried him down into the city.

Too late, they realised their mistake. In the weeks since the siege began, Giovanni had fought like a lion, and become a symbol of resistance to soldiers and citizens alike. So long as he lived, there was hope.

Now a great cry of panic and terror rippled through the streets as news of his fall spread like fire. The few Genoese left in defence of the Gate of San Romano, where Giovanni had made his stand, abandoned their posts and fled for the harbour. There galleys waited to carry them to safety.

San Romano was the weakest part of the city defences. Pounded for days by Turkish cannon, much of the wall was already flattened, the gaps shored up with mattresses, baulks of timber, piles of loose earth and stone - anything the defenders could find.

The Ottoman Sultan, Mehmed the Second, rode close behind his janissaries as they flooded towards the gate. A brave man, he had no fear of the occasional pot-shot aimed at him from the walls. He kept a sharp eye on the Gate of San Romano. Once the courage of the Genoese was broken, Constantinople would be his.

Mehmed saw the gate abandoned, and beckoned to one of his officers, a huge black-bearded jannisary named Hasan.

"Hasan," he said, "take your company forward and secure the gate. The first man to raise my flag on the battlements shall win his weight in gold."

Hasan and his men greeted the Sultan's promise with a cheer, and stormed towards the broken, shell-pocked ruin of the gate. They met no resistance, and swept on into the streets. Hasan himself was the first man onto the battlements. There he cast down the banners of Saint Mark and the Greek Emperor, and raised the Ottoman standard in their stead.

Everywhere the resistance of the defenders collapsed. Final disaster struck when the Turks overran a small sally-port, the Kerkoporta, and set up their flags on the tower. Seeing this, the last defenders scattered. The Greek soldiers ran to their homes in a vain effort to save their families, while the Genoese and Venetian mercenaries made for their ships in the harbour of the Golden Horn.

The hapless citizens fled like sheep before the onslaught of the Turks. Bells and tocsins rang through the city, heralding the death of Constantinople. A few wretched souls preferred to jump from the walls rather than die on Turkish swords, and so committed suicide.

One man did not run. Constantine the Eleventh, last of the Emperors who had ruled the city for over a thousand years, reached the Gate of San Romano in time to see it overrun by the enemy.

A gaunt, sad-eyed figure, stooped under the weight of history, Constantine knew his time had come. "The city has fallen," he murmured, "but I am still alive."

He unclasped the brooch at his shoulder and let his purple cloak fall to the ground. Then he removed the imperial diadem from his head, let that fall too, and all the other jewelled ornaments on his person. Now he looked like a common soldier, and would die like one.

Constantine drew his sword and charged at the mob of janissaries clustered about the gate. His escort, all that remained of the famed Varangian Guard, followed. Big men in thick steel plate, armed with double-handed axes, they would fight to the last beside their master.

"Is there no *Christian* here?" Constantine shouted as he laid about him, "no Christian to take my head?"

His sword drank deep of Turkish blood, while behind him the Varangians wielded their axes with lethal skill and savagery.

3

The janissaries reeled under the furious assault, and then closed in again, eager to stamp out this last ember of Greek resistance.

One by one, Constantine's guards were slain, until a mere handful of survivors fought around the sacred person of the Emperor. The last of the Varangians chanted prayers even as the halberds and sabres flashed down to make an end of them.

At last Constantine was alone among his enemies. His sword lodged in the guts of a janissary and twisted out of his hand. Sharp steel bit into his flesh. Clubs, tulwars and halberd-butts rained down on his head.

The Emperor fell, and the tide washed over him.

Constantinople was given over to the horrors of the sack. Mehmed wisely allowed his troops to spoil and plunder for the traditional period of three days, knowing that to prevent them was impossible.

"I have come to conquer, not destroy," he told his generals, "send an advance guard of janissaries to protect the Hagia Sophia and the Church of the Holy Apostles. I wish to preserve them for our use."

It was done, and companies of his soldier-fanatics sent into the heart of the city to defend these buildings from harm. Mehmed planned to convert the Hagia Sophia, the enormous Orthodox church that dominated the skyline of the city with its great dome and four tapering spires, into a grand mosque. The Church of the Holy Apostles, meanwhile, would provide a seat for the tame patriarch he appointed to control his Christian subjects.

The rest of Constantinople was allowed to suffer. Mehmed's soldiers ran wild, as soldiers do in the wake of a

4

victory. They broke into shops and houses, fought each other like mad dogs for plunder, subjected the terrified and helpless citizens to every kind of abuse. Women were raped, children butchered before their eyes, menfolk slaughtered or enslaved. Old men, monks and priests were among those taken into miserable captivity. Those who dared to resist were murdered.

Many of the citizens fled to the churches for refuge, but the Turks cared nothing for Christian laws of sanctuary. They used rams to smash down the doors and poured inside to loot and kill. Shrines were violated, holy icons and vessels burned, broken up or simply hurled aside like so much ornamental rubbish. More valuable objects, such as chalices and cups made of precious metal, were taken as spoil or to be melted down.

Murdered priests were defiled, garments embroidered with gold and studded with pearls and gems ripped from their bodies, to be cast into great bonfires or auctioned off to the highest bidder. Sacred books and texts were also tossed onto the flames, or else trampled, torn up and thrown about as playthings.

The morning of the third day dawned red and heavy over the ruin of Constantinople. Mehmed, who until now had closed his eyes to the atrocities his men committed, was overcome by guilt.

"Enough!" he cried, "let be, let be. What a town was this, and I have allowed it to be degraded. No more!"

He sent more troops into the city, to clear out the looters and punish those who refused to obey with mutilation or death. His men marched purposefully through streets littered with corpses and heaps of discarded plunder. Blood flowed like rainwater in the gutters, and the stench of death hung in the air like a poisonous fume.

When all was safe, Mehmed entered his conquest through the Adrianople Gate at the head of his household guards. Heralds went on foot before him to proclaim a general amnesty to those citizens who had managed to avoid death or captivity. If they emerged from their hiding places and bowed down before the Sultan, he promised to spare their lives and restore their houses and property.

The procession made its way down the great central thoroughfare called the Mese, preceded by the screech of trumpets and the clash of cymbals. Standard bearers advanced before the Sultan on foot, holding aloft Ottoman banners.

Mehmed himself rode at a stately pace on a snow-white gelding, his eyes fixed on the dome of the Hagia Sophia. He refused to look at the smashed windows and ruined, blood-spattered houses, the naked corpses of murdered innocents, the chaos and destruction and misery. All his life he had dreamed and schemed for this moment, the final victory of his people over the Greek state.

His heart swelled when the procession reached the vast central plaza of the Augusteum. The plaza was thronged with people, Turkish soldiers and Greek citizens, and the bronze gates of the Hagia Sophia stood open. They bore the marks of force, the locks shattered and the metal severely dented.

The citizens had been taken captive, chained together and forced to stand or sit in rows. Turkish officers moved among them, inspecting the miserable wretches like so many cattle brought to market.

A group of janissary musketeers, weary and hollow-eyed from the night's work, came before Mehmed to make their report. They salaamed before him, bowing deeply with their right palms against their foreheads.

"Most Sacred and Imperial Majesty," said their leader, "all these Greeks gathered in the plaza are your prisoners. They took refuge inside their great church, so we breached the gates with a ram. We have divided them according to the price they may fetch in the slave-markets."

"You did well," Mehmed replied distractedly. His eyes searched the ranks of prisoners for people of quality. Most appeared to be commoners, secular and religious persons of middling to low rank.

"Some few resisted," went on the janissary, "we slew all save one, a nobleman by his dress and bearing. He fought valiantly to defend a woman and her children, himself against five of our warriors, and cut down three before his sword broke. We thought he may be worth a ransom."

Mehmed looked with interest at the speaker. "Where is this man?" he demanded, "bring him to me."

The janissary bowed again. "At once, O Khan of Khans."

He vanished among the crowd, and returned shortly with two prisoners in tow. Both were male, and escorted by six burly halberdiers.

One of the prisoners was short and plump, and had the look of a clerk. He was fifty or thereabouts, with neatly trimmed grey hair. His plain white tunic, fringed with gold, was stained with the blood from a half-healed cut on his scalp, and his right eye was puffy and swollen. He had clearly been robbed, his outer garments ripped away, rings torn from his bruised fingers.

Terror flared in the little man's eyes when he beheld the Sultan, but he stood his ground and refused to make any

7

gesture of obeisance. Mehmed smiled at this pointless defiance.

"This one claims to be George Phrantzes," said the janissary officer, "our men found him hiding behind the altar with his family. His wife is very beautiful. Our men would have violated her, but the nobleman I spoke of prevented them."

George Phrantzes, a famed Greek historian, ambassador and courtier, and personal friend to the Emperor Constantine. This was a great prize indeed.

"Where is your master, Phrantzes?" demanded Mehmed, "does he live?"

Phrantzes went red as he worked up the courage to speak. "I know not," he replied in a shaken voice, "nor would I tell if I did. This I do know. Constantine would never allow himself to be taken alive, and paraded through the streets of his own city as a trophy of war."

Mehmed looked at his companion. "This is the nobleman, Your Majesty," said the janissary, "he is old, but has the strength of one half his age."

The second captive towered head and shoulders over the first. Mehmed expected a thickset warrior, and was surprised to find a tall, slender wisp of a man with a strangely boyish face, round and smooth and clean-shaven. His fine white hair was cut in a short military style, and his mild blue eyes and sensitive mouth gave him the look of a poet rather than a soldier.

A person of rank, certainly. He wore a combination of plate and mail armour, Italian if Mehmed was any judge, ruinously expensive and spattered with fresh blood. A single word,

'Avaunt', was inscribed in delicate letters on the breastplate.

The old man was bareheaded, and wore a yellow silk scarf about his neck. Taken in all, he looked like a foppish courtier who had accidentally strayed onto a battlefield.

Mehmed was not fooled. "Take off your gauntlets, Christian, and hold up your hands," he ordered.

He spoke in Greek. The other understood, and obediently stripped off his fine steel gauntlets.

Mehmed nodded to himself when he saw the Christian's hands. Killer's hands. Swollen and callused by decades of handling weapons. The nails were immaculately clean, but broken, and the fingers long and powerful, doubtless capable of snapping a man's neck.

"I'm told you slew three of my best warriors," said Mehmed, "single-handed, in the defence of a woman. That was a brave act. Your Christian troubadours will sing of it. Tell me your name and degree, so I may consider sparing the life of their owner."

"I am Sir John Page, O Sultan," the prisoner answered, "a knight of England. In my time I have been soldier, courtier, poet, outlaw, thief, traitor and play-actor. All the roles a man can play in this world, save priest, which never struck me as much in the way of pleasure or entertainment."

He spoke bad Greek with an unfamiliar accent. Mehmed knew of the English, that fierce and troublesome race who lived on a cold island in the North Sea and preyed on their neighbours.

"A mercenary, then," he said, "one of the pestilent crew who came with Giovanni Giustiniani to aid the Greeks in their defence of the city. I thought they were all Venetians and Genoese. Most of your comrades managed to escape the sack."

This was true. The small band of Western mercenaries had steered their ships out of the Golden Horn before Mehmed's fleet could close off the harbour, and taken their wounded captain with them. They would be at sea by now. Mehmed cared little, so long as they were gone.

"You chose to stay," added Mehmed, "why?"

Page shrugged his armoured shoulders. "For that, I must blame my conscience," he replied, "the accursed thing has ever brought me into trouble."

Mehmed laughed for the first time in many weeks, ever since the siege began. Only now, with the city secured and his enemy cast down, did he feel the burden start to lift.

He glanced to his left, where a gaggle of courtiers and imams and generals hovered anxiously, waiting for the Sultan to favour them with his attention. The final victory over the Greeks had been centuries in the making, and there was much business to attend to.

First he had to decide what should be done with his captives. The joy of conquest was still in his blood, and inclined him to show mercy.

Mercy, and something else. This Englishman had described himself as a poet, among other things. The seed of a whimsical idea flowered inside Mehmed's head.

"Tell me, Sir John," he said, "do you know the legend of Scheherazade?"

*

The Sultan meant to reside in Constantinople, the new capital of his empire, but ignored the old palaces of the Greek Emperors. Most had been pounded into rubble by his artillery, and he showed no interest in having them rebuilt.

He paid one visit to the shadowy ruins of the Boukoleon Palace, long-since abandoned by the Greeks and fallen into decay. Those who accompanied Mehmed saw tears glisten on his cheeks as he stood among the fallen stones, and heard him recite lines of verse from the poet Saadi:

"The spider weaves the curtains in the palace of the Caesars. The owl calls the watches in the towers of Afrasiab."

George Phrantzes and Sir John Page were among the captives led in the wake of the Sultan's retinue as he toured the city. Their hands were chained, but otherwise they were treated well enough. Phrantzes was devoured by grief for his Emperor and the fall of Constantinople, and worry for his family.

"My wife and children shall be enslaved," he sobbed as they traipsed down the Mese between companies of musketeers, "and made the playthings of heathen men. Have mercy, Lord Jesus Christ and Madonna Saint Mary, have mercy on my precious ones!"

Page was silent. He had been stripped of his fine armour, and walked in a padded silk doublet, yellow scarf and black and white parti-coloured hose. Even in chains, he cut a dignified figure, and smiled agreeably at his Turkish captors whenever they happened to glance at him.

Mehmed had not yet explained his mysterious reference to Scheherazade, though Page had some vague knowledge of the collection of Eastern folk tales known as the Thousand and One

Nights. Scheherazade, wife of the sultan of India, was forced to tell her husband a different tale every night, in such an interesting way that he spared her life.

Page had witnessed much cruelty in his time, and considered himself an expert. The Sultan's decision to let his prisoners stew a while, their lives dangling by the slenderest of threads, was an impressive piece of sadism.

He was surprised to find how much he valued his life, even though he had done his best to throw it away in the Hagia Sophia. Sixty years in this world was more than most career soldiers could expect, yet he wasn't quite ready to sample the next one.

"How can you remain silent?" cried Phrantzes, "are you made of stone? Do you have no wife or children of your own? What would they think, to see you in chains and doomed to die at the hands of the Turk!"

Page glanced at the little clerk in annoyance. Phrantzes had expressed no gratitude for the rescue of his wife from the janissaries, and his tears and hysterics shamed them both.

"My eldest son is a fat abbé in Normandy," said Page, "and might say a prayer for me if he ever bothered to raise his snout from the ale-pot. My other boys would probably laugh, and one at least would pay good money to see his father's head on a platter. As for my daughter..."

Page fell quiet again. He had no wish to speak of her.

Mehmed took up temporary residence in one of the Franciscan monasteries on the northern shore of the Golden Horn. There he started to plan his new palace, and the conversion of Constantinople from a Christian city to a jewel of

Islam.

Phrantzes and Page were lodged inside one of the cells, a plain, sparsely-furnished chamber with a vaulted roof, and a latticed window overlooking the Bosphorus. Two halberdiers occasionally looked in at them through a grille in the thick iron-bound door.

Page sat on one of the low benches and studied the window. The lattice was made of iron, and the casement too narrow to squeeze through even if the bars could be broken.

"Ah, well," he said, "it seems we must be discomfited."

He leaned his back against the wall, folded his hands behind his head and started to whistle an old crusader's lament.

Phrantzes, who had slumped onto the other bench, looked up from his misery. "I know that air," he said, "the *Chansons de croisade*. It mourns the loss of the shrines and churches of Jerusalem, and pleads for a fresh host of virtuous crusaders to rescue the Holy Sepulchre."

Page nodded. "This white head of mine is full of old songs," he replied.

"You chose a most fitting one." Phrantzes' red-rimmed eyes filled with tears again as he looked out of the window.

"That I should live to see this," he said brokenly, "the city of Constantine overrun by the followers of Mahomet. Her walls tumbled down, and her most holy churches defiled and converted into mosques. Her people reduced to slavery, while the rest of Christendom looks on and does nothing! Nothing!"

He wrung his plump hands. "My poor master pleaded to the West for aid, and what did he get? Seven hundred mercenaries, the scum of Europe, and a handful of ships. A few ragged hirelings, to ward off all the hosts of Islam!"

"My heart shall break," he added, "when I hear the cry of the muezzin ring through the streets of Constantinople for the first time. It shall be the end of days."

Page raised a finger. "Mind your tongue, master clerk," he said in a friendly tone, "I was one of those ragged hirelings. We kept twenty times our number of Turks at bay, and threw back Mehmed's janissaries time and again. If Giustiniani hadn't fallen...but there, it is useless to deal in maybes."

Phrantzes paled. "My apologies," he stammered, "I meant no disrespect, or to besmirch your efforts. You and your comrades did indeed fight like lions on our behalf. If a mere seven hundred could do so much, think what five thousand may have achieved - two thousand, even!"

"True," agreed Page, "Constantinople may have been saved for another generation, if the princes of the West had sent adequate troops and supplies. Yet it would only have delayed the inevitable. The city was doomed. Your master knew that. Some men walk with the shadow of death at their side. He was one."

His companion started to weep again, so Page rolled his eyes and tried to snatch some sleep. He had been a prisoner before, many times, and knew from long experience there was no use fretting. All a sensible man could was rest, think on happier days, and wait for his opportunity.

Phrantzes tapped his knee. "Sir John," he whispered urgently, "Sir John, wake up!"

Page slowly counted to five before responding. "Only a

fool disturbs the soldier at his rest," he said through gritted teeth, "what do you want, little man?"

He opened his eyes a crack. The clerk's moon-round face was uncomfortably close to his own, and crimson with excitement.

"There are two guards on the door," Phrantzes hissed, "and they mere footsoldiers. I saw you cut down three of the Sultan's finest in the Hagia Sophia when you so nobly defended my wife. If we lured the guards in here..."

Page nodded thoughtfully. "Perhaps if you feigned illness," he said, "they would come into the cell, and we could overpower them, take their clothes and escape in disguise. Then make our way down to the harbour and bribe a sea-captain to smuggle us out of the city. You had something like that in mind?"

Phrantzes nodded eagerly. "Yes! You think it possible, then?"

"No. I think it's absurd. Now be quiet and let me sleep."

He shut his eyes, so he didn't have to look at the clerk's dismayed expression, and folded his arms across his chest. Silence reigned in the cell for the next hour, until iron footsteps rang on the stone-flagged floor of the corridor outside.

There was a murmur of Turkish voices, and the scrape of keys in the lock. Page yawned, rose, and stretched until his joints clicked. Phrantzes pressed his short back against the wall. He looked on the verge of rage or panic, like a trapped animal.

"Peace," said Page, "don't do anything foolish. We can't fight our way out, and nothing will be gained from making them angry."

15

The nailed and timbered door swung open, and the halberdiers entered with a third man between them. This was a Sipahi officer in late middle age, squat and fleshy, with enormous strength in his heavy shoulders and long, powerful arms. He wore a mail hauberk over a gorgeous green and gold silken under-tunic that reached below his knees, and a tulwar hung in the red scabbard clipped to his thick leather belt.

Page was immediately wary. The officer's little eyes were like two shards of ice, and his mouth under the drooping grey moustache had an unpleasantly full and sensual look to it. A pale scar ran from his left nostril down to the edge of his jaw, and his mangled nose had been broken at least twice.

The officer stopped, and planted his feet wide apart. His eyes slowly raked the prisoners.

"I come from the Sultan," he said in thickly-accented Greek, "Mehmed the Conqueror has not forgotten you."

His thick fingers curled about the grip of his tulwar. Page carefully judged the distance between them. The officer looked strong, but slow. A sudden spring, a punch to the man's jaw, a snatch for the sword...

A halberd's point buried in his flesh. The guards looked watchful, alive to any sudden moves. Page willed himself to be calm.

The officer's plump lips twitched in amusement. "His Majesty's wisdom is only matched by his mercy. Neither of you are to die. At least, not yet."

He raised his free hand and snapped his fingers. A fourth man, previously unseen, darted into the room.

This one was a Turkish version of Phrantzes. He wore a

long black robe and a skull-cap, and had a sickly, pinch-faced look about him. Under his arm he carried a black dossier, a bundle of quills and a pot of ink.

The officer pointed a hairy finger at Page. "You," he snapped, "say you are a poet as well as a soldier. His Majesty intends to put your skills to the test. The Sultan wishes to know more of the Western arts of war, from one who has spent many years serving in Western armies. You claim to be such a one."

He grinned. "Let us hope you made no idle boasts. Both your lives depend on it."

The clerk wordlessly placed the writing materials on the little table in the centre of the room. Then he made a hasty salaam to the officer and vanished through the doorway.

"Write," said the officer, with a nod at Phrantzes, "write down the words of Sir John Page, and pray he spins a good tale. When you are done, my master shall have it read to him. If the story proves entertaining, you both shall live. If not..."

He ran a finger across his throat. "You have three days," he added, and showed them his back.

The halberdiers filed out after him, and the door slammed shut like the clap of doom.

"Scheherazade," remarked Page when the echoes had died away, "now I understand the Sultan's meaning. So I must tell him a story, and hope he likes it enough to spare us from the headsman."

Phrantzes approached the table. His hands trembled as they picked up the bundle of quills.

"We should tell him something...something that will appeal

to his warlike nature," he stammered, "the legend of Roland, or Arthur and his knights."

"No," said Page, "Mehmed is an educated man, and will know them already."

"What, then?" shouted Phrantzes, "should we treat him to a few of your bawdy soldier's tales? Some lewd rhyme from Chaucer? I can already feel the kiss of steel on my neck!"

Page rubbed his jaw. "Offhand, I can think of no better story than my own life. I am a soldier, which should appeal to Mehmed, and have seen service in France, Bohemia and the Italian city-states."

"Your own life?" Phrantzes sneered. "Modesty becomes you."

"This is no time for modesty. Take up your quill, and pass me that jug of water. I cannot describe the past sixty years with a dry throat."

The other man looked full of doubt, but did as he was asked. He gave the jug to Page, and dragged his bench up to the table. Then he sat and reached for a sheet of vellum.

When Phrantzes was ready, quill poised, Page took a long draught from the jug and started to talk.

1.

Know, O Shah of Shahs, that I was born in Sussex in England, thirteen hundred and ninety-four years after the birth of Our Lord. My mother was Margaret Daubeney, a widow and lady of the manor of Kingshook.

Her late husband, Sir John Daubeney, was not my father. He died of dysentery at the siege of Nantes, fourteen years before my birth, and left his wife alone and childless. She inherited his house and lands, and spent much of her time repelling offers of marriage from the young lords of Sussex.

"I will have a husband who loves me for myself," she used to say, "not for the sake of a dead man's acres."

My mother was proud, too proud for her own good, and never remarried. That is not to say she was always alone.

In the spring of the year before my birth a stranger came to Kingshook. He was a wandering mercenary, full of dark passions and secrets, his skin burned brown by foreign suns. All he owned in the world were the clothes he stood up in, the ring on his finger, the sword at his hip, and a packet of letters he never let anyone read, even my mother.

He was my father. Thomas Page, remembered in snatches of song as the Half-Hanged Man or the Wolf of Burgundy.

In return for bed and board, Thomas offered to knock into shape the handful of servants and verderers who guarded my mother's lands. In truth, they required little knocking - several were, like him, hardened veterans of the French wars - but she was happy for the excuse to keep Thomas in her house.

She was thirty by then, still beautiful, and lonely. Thomas was a charming, handsome brute, and my mother cared little for her reputation. She took him to her bed, and for some months they enjoyed each other.

I don't hesitate to call my father a brute. He used my mother quite shamefully, sated his lusts on her, ate her meat and made free with her wine, and then abandoned her. One morning in late summer she woke to find him gone from her bed, and her best horse taken from the stables.

He left her with nothing, no trace of himself save bittersweet memories. And, it soon became apparent, something more. Something unwanted. Me.

I was born the following spring, and named John after my mother's late husband. Her labour was not easy. More than once, so the midwives told me in later years, she called on Christ's mercy, and begged to be released from the pain. It still galls me now to think she preferred death over her child.

Christ spared us both. My mother's initial rejection of me passed, and I was happy enough, doted on by her and the servants. She kept my bastardy a secret from me until I was aged six or thereabouts, when my playmates in the local village started calling me the Wolf-Cub.

One of my earliest memories is of running home and demanding to know what they meant. My mother smiled - she had the warmest of smiles - sat me on her knee, brushed away my tears, and told me the truth of it.

"Dear son, I have lied to you," she said, "for which I must beg your forgiveness. Your true father was not Sir John Daubeney, as I have pretended. He was a sell-sword named Thomas Page, a man I loved for a time. He ran away before you were born."

Incredibly, she bore no resentment towards the man who deserted her. "You must not be ashamed of your birth, or your father," she went on, "he was a great soldier in his time, and performed famous deeds of arms in France and Spain. The troubadours still sing of him."

She spared me the gruesome final verse of Page's life until I was older, and more able to bear it. Thomas Page was eventually murdered by his great enemy, Sir Hugh Calveley, another famous English routier, and his corpse hanged in a cage from an oak tree on the border of Calveley's Berkshire estate.

I was fourteen, on the threshold of manhood, when I learned how my father died. By then I knew all the songs of his exploits, and was set on following in his footsteps as a soldier. I still hated him for deserting us, but took a certain pride in calling myself the Wolf-Cub, and letting others know I was the son of a ballad hero.

Now I shall end the account of John Page as a lad, and move on to the year of Agincourt.

2.

I have no glorious falsehoods to tell of my role in that most famous battle. While King Henry mustered his army at Southampton, and all the youth of England were on fire to join him, my mother lay mortally ill at Kingshook.

She had taken a fever during the summer, and it rapidly grew worse with the onset of autumn. I sent for a physician from Horsham, but none of his purgings and bleedings did any good. Consumed with grief, I swallowed my desire to join the king, and swore an oath to stay by my mother's side until the end.

She fought her illness with the courage of one whose ancestors had fought at Senlac, Northallerton and Crécy, and lingered well into the autumn. Henry's army was still camped outside the walls of Harfleur when she finally passed away in late September.

"Dear son, I must beg your forgiveness," she whispered at the last, "I have selfishly kept you here, beside an old woman's bed, when your duty lay with the king."

Weeks of watching her die had worn me away to almost nothing, and this final apology broke my heart all in pieces. "Madam," I said, clasping her fragile hand, "what is France, what is all the martial glory in the world, compared to you? I would give it all up, just to keep you alive another year."

Her wan face, racked with pain, twitched into the ghost of one of her old smiles. "Pretty lies," she replied, her voice a mere tremor, "meant well. You have been my only comfort in this world. Comfort me one last time. Swear you will find peace after I am gone, and be happy."

I swore, and she was quite mistaken: I would have made any promise, even to the Devil, to save her life.

My body is covered in scars, but no battle-wound ever equalled the agony of my mother's loss. The moment she breathed her last, I wept like a child, and had to be led away by three of her servants. They made me drunk, those honest men, drunker than I had ever been, until my well of tears had run dry.

I stayed on the manor, and felt honour-bound to help look after the estate instead of riding off to the wars. As a bastard, of course, I could not inherit. Thus I remained in Sussex, chained to a crumbling manor house and a few hundred acres of dirt, while other men won glory in France.

The news of Agincourt was brought to Kingshook by a breathless messenger who rode from Chichester to spread the word among the local villages. He was just a lad, his bright red hair bristling in the wind as he galloped up the lane to the gate, singing as he rode:

"Our King went forth to Normandy,

With grace and might of chivalry,

There God for him wrought marvellously.

Wherefore England may call and cry,

Deo Gratias!

He set a siege for sooth to say,

To Harfleur town with royal array,

That town he won and made a fray,

That France shall rue till Doomsday,

Deo Gratias!

Then went forth our king most comely,

In Agincourt field he fought manfully,

Through grace of God most marvellously,

He had the field and victory,

Deo Gratias!

I have heard the song since, many times, shouted around the campfires of any army or mercenary company with a fair number of Englishmen in their ranks. The first time I heard it, I was eaten up with envy, and stopped just short of throwing a stone at the lad's head as he reined in beside the gate.

"You are the bastard of Kingshook?" he cried. "The one they call the Wolf-Cub?"

I was both flattered and annoyed by his insolence, and gave a curt nod.

"Then rejoice, Wolf-Cub!" he cried, "for the armies of the French have been utterly smashed, and hundreds of their great men slain or captured! London is swamped with ransom money. An ocean of French gold, enough for us all to drown in!"

"Calm yourself," I said as he laughed and clapped his hands, "the King is returned safe to London, then?"

"Safe? My lord, His Majesty is not only safe, but exalted! He returned five days ago, and entered London on foot, dressed soberly, like the pious man he is. His knights followed, guarding all the Frenchies they captured at Agincourt -"

"Agincourt? Where is that?"

"It is what they call the battlefield, my lord, the field where our little army, ragged and half-starved, tore down the might of France! They say thousands of citizens turned out at Blackheath to meet the King, the mayor and the aldermen all in scarlet, the lesser men in red cloaks with parti-coloured hoods, and they set up a tower at Cornhill draped with a scarlet cloth, and around it were the arms of Saint George, Saint Edmund and of England..."

He gabbled on, describing in detail the magnificent reception the Londoners gave King Henry when he entered the city. The celebrations were all the greater, I suspect, because few had expected him to achieve much in France, let alone win such a resounding victory against the odds. There had been nothing like it since Poitiers, some sixty years or more in the past. Since then the English cause in France had met with little save defeat and humiliation, until Henry so gloriously redeemed our fortunes.

Great Sultan, I know not if the fame of Agincourt has reached your Eastern courts, though it still rings like a trumpet-blast through Christendom, some forty years on. Your Majesty may have heard that a little army of English and Welsh bowmen, confronted by a French host ten times their number, performed a miracle of arms on Saint Crispin's Day and defeated the enemy with great slaughter.

A miracle it was, but the chief weapon of the English was not the war-bow, six feet of English yew, capable of loosing an arrow a distance of two hundred yards. The bodkin-tipped arrows our men shot that day failed to penetrate the thick steel plate worn by the French knights and men-at-arms.

No, the saviour of England that day was something far more prosaic than holy saints or grey-fletched arrows: in short, King Henry owed his victory to mud. Acres of thick, cloying mud, knee-deep and soaking wet after days of heavy rain. Mindful of previous defeats, the French dismounted and tramped across the field to engage our army on a narrow front. Weighed down by their steel shells, they sank into the mud, and became hopelessly crowded together.

Picture, O Sultan, thousands of brave, misguided men drowning in filth. Meanwhile the rain hammers down and our half-naked archers, some with their breeks cut away to allow loose excrement to flow from their dysentery-ravaged bowels, tear into the baffled French with hammers and hatchets, clubs and knives and short swords.

That was Agincourt, perhaps England's greatest military triumph, as described to me by veterans and eyewitnesses of the battle. Poets and bards and troubadours transformed a vicious brawl in unspeakable conditions into a hymn to martial glory. I, who have seen and fought in more pitched battles than most, have learned to despise the flowery lies told of war.

At the time of Agincourt, I was still young, and as

overcome with the glory and romance of it all as any other Englishman who had never been within shouting distance of a battlefield.

I sent the red-headed boy off with a silver penny for his trouble, and spent the rest of the day listening to a dispute between two of my late mother's tenants. It was over a cow, I think. The silly beast had slipped her tether and wandered onto some neighbouring land, which caused the peasants to break each other's heads over their rights to her.

Such was the quiet, dull life of a minor country esquire. It might have been my lot forever, but for my cousin William.

Years passed. Once he had used the glory of Agincourt to milk his Parliament of funds, King Henry made ready to embark on another expedition to France. This time he planned to land in Normandy, his ancestral duchy, and conquer it in methodical fashion, one town and castle at a time. I was still chained to the land at Kingshook, and took no thought to joining the army before it sailed.

One warm midsummer day, I sat on the bank beside the little stream that ran through the orchard behind my house. This was a favourite spot of mine, a haven of peace and quiet, where I liked to study my reflection in the water.

I tried to read the eyes that stared back at me. Those eyes, and my slender, wiry build, were my mother's gift. The soft, almost girlish contours of my face were all (according to her) derived from Thomas Page. I found it hard to imagine that a hard-bitten mercenary could have looked so fair, more doe than wolf.

My thoughts fastened on him. He was a mercenary, a

freebooter and a base rogue who used and dishonoured an honest woman, stole from her, and finally deserted her. How much of the father lived in the son?

"Master!"

The voice of Peter Busket, one of my servants, broke in on my thoughts. I turned to see his thickset, greying figure, twisting his felt cap in his hands.

Peter had never looked so nervous in my presence. He was a naturally cheerful man, and always took a paternal interest in me. When I was a child, he placed my first wooden practice sword in my hand, and taught me how to handle a bow.

"Master," he repeated, "your cousin William is here."

I went cold. William was the son of my mother's brother, Sir Reginald Ulverton, the Baron of Steeping. Sir Reginald held a small castle at Steeping, as well five other manors, and had cast greedy eyes at Kingshook ever since the death of his brother-in-law. Sir John Daubeney had no close kin to leave his estate to, and before he departed on his final campaign made everything over to his wife.

"John!"

The voice of Peter Busket, one of the servants, broke in on my thoughts. I turned to see his thickset, greying figure, twisting his felt cap in his hands.

Peter had never looked so nervous in my presence. He was a naturally cheerful man, and always took a paternal interest in me. When I was a child, he placed my first wooden practice sword in my hand, and taught me how to handle a bow.

"John," he repeated, "your cousin William is here."

I went cold. William was the son of my mother's brother, Sir Reginald Ulverton, the Baron of Steeping. Sir Reginald held a small castle at Steeping, as well five other manors, and had cast greedy eyes at Kingshook ever since the death of his brother-in-law. Sir John Daubeney had no close kin to leave his estate to, and before he departed on his final campaign made everything over to his wife.

With no living kin or legitimate issue, Sir John's manor passed to my uncle, who in turn bestowed it on his son. William was fifteen now, almost a man grown, and I lived in fear of him taking up residence at Kingshook. Spoiled and indulged by his father to the point of ruin, he had already gained a dark reputation as a drunk and a womaniser. There was some talk of him violating the daughter of a local bailiff, though the matter was quickly hushed up. Enough gold, pressed into the right hands, can smother most evils.

"Fetch my sword," I ordered Peter, "and stand by while I talk to him. Is he in drink?"

Peter nodded. "Then fetch the grooms as well," I added. "If he has any brains at all, he won't try anything with witnesses on hand."

He ran to get my broadsword, while I composed myself and walked slowly to meet my cousin.

I could hear his voice, raised in drunken anger, before I reached the courtyard.

"Where is he?" William shouted. "Where is the bastard of Kingshook? Why does he hide?"

Kingshook Hall was an old-fashioned place, built in the time of Rufus and not much changed since. The grey, weathered stones had endured the buffets of centuries. They probably endure still, though I have not clapped eyes on the place for many years.

I paused by the stair to the door while Peter came running with my sword, snug in its leather scabbard. It had belonged to my maternal grandfather, and had a nick two-thirds up the blade - caused, the old knight always claimed, when it rebounded off a Frenchman's bascinet at Crécy. His sword was mine now, along with all the other bits and pieces of war-gear in the armoury.

I buckled on the scabbard and emerged to face William. "Lower your voice, cousin," I said, "here I am."

He scowled at me. William was a tall, well-built youth, splendidly dressed in a black velvet doublet, black calfskin gloves and boots, and a red mantle. A gold ring flashed in his right ear, and a golden pendant in the shape of a rearing lion, the arms of his house, hung from a silver necklace round his well-muscled throat.

This picture of noble elegance was marred by a streak of vomit on the mantle, and William's swollen, empurpled features. Never handsome at the best of times, after a surfeit of ale and wine he resembled an angry toad on the verge of bursting.

He had come alone, mounted on a beautiful, soft-mouthed chestnut destrier. I had seen him ride the beast before, in the lists at Steeping, and been filled with envy at the sight. He was a purebred war-horse, worth some three or even four hundred pounds. Any man of gentle birth would have been proud to own him.

My cousin was no gentleman, despite his noble birth. The horse's flanks were cruelly slashed by his spurs, and blood trickled down onto the cobbles.

William's eyes, full of drunken menace, struggled to focus on me. "You," he muttered thickly, "bastard. I want you out of Kingshook by sundown. Go. Vanish, like your father did."

I folded my arms. "If I refuse?" I asked, with a sweet smile.

His fingers closed about the hilt of his sword.

"Refuse," he snarled, "and I will come back with a troop of men-at-arms and a pack of hounds. We will flush you out, and hunt you like the vermin you are through Kingshook woods. I'll take your head back to Steeping on the end of my lance. My father's cook will boil away the flesh, so I may use it as a drinking vessel."

Barbaric stuff, and incredibly foolish. How old Sir Reginald, one of the shrewdest landholders in Sussex, managed to sire such an oaf is beyond me.

I treated William's threats with the respect they deserved, and laughed in his face.

That was a mistake. For a moment I thought he might suffer a seizure. He turned a livid shade of crimson, and bared his yellow teeth.

"Whoreson!" he grunted, and half-slid, half-tumbled off his horse. I moved to help him, but he was on his feet in an instant. Naked steel flashed in his hand.

Peter Busket and two of the grooms were on hand. None of them moved as William charged at me with murder in his eyes. They were only servants, of course, and didn't dare intervene in a private affair between gentlemen, even if I barely qualified as such.

The brief fight started in drink, and ended in blood. My cousin was strong as a bull, but slow. His ale-sodden state made him slower still, and I easily sidestepped his broadsword as it swept down to chop me in half.

"Enough!" I shouted. "Would you slay your own kin?"

He didn't seem to hear me. I retreated and drew my sword as he came on again, snorting like a wild boar.

Our blades met with a crunch of steel. He overbalanced, and I might have laid him open from shoulder to waist, but had no desire to kill. It would be murder, or at least his family would say so, and their word would count for more than any low-born witnesses.

My cousin was in poor condition for one so young and trained to arms, while I was fresh and light on my feet. For a time I skipped around him, and hoped he might see sense when his breath gave out.

He made one final effort. With a wordless roar, he hurled his sword like a javelin at my chest. I sprang aside, and in the next moment his fingers were at my throat. Wine-thick breath gusted over me as his knee slammed into my crotch. His free hand caught my wrist and squeezed it like a vice.

My grandfather's sword dropped to the ground. The hot pain in my groin made me gasp. Both his hands were at my throat now, thumbs pressed hard into my windpipe.

Sweet Christ, he was strong. He might have throttled me to death, if one of the grooms hadn't rushed forward and pressed the hilt of a dagger into my right hand.

I slid the knife into his side, under the ribs, through layers of velvet and linen and soft, greasy flesh.

His gooseberry eyes, mere inches from my own, widened. The irises contracted, and a high-pitched moan escaped his blubbery lips. His hands loosened on my neck. I stabbed him again, this time in the heart. The blade was good and sharp, and sank to the hilt in his chest.

William took a step backwards. And another. The knife was still stuck in his body. He reached out for me, his hands open, and a bead of bloody foam drooled from the corner of his mouth. With a sigh, he toppled over like a felled tree.

Horrified, I clapped my hands over my mouth. They were spotted with William's blood.

My kinsman's blood. My blood.

3.

I panicked. Even as William yielded up the ghost, I ran to seize the reins of his destrier. Fortunately the beast had little affection for his late master, and stood quiet as I climbed into the saddle.

"Money," I shouted at Peter, "enough money for three days, food and water, and my fur-trimmed cloak. Get them!"

He snapped his fingers at the grooms. One, Wilfred, ran inside the house. More servants peered out of the windows and the doorway, and wailed in alarm when they saw William's body.

"What shall we do with that?" Peter demanded in a hoarse voice. His finger shook as he pointed at my dead cousin.

"Lay him out in the hall," I replied, "when the High Sheriff and his men-at-arms come, as they will, tell them I slew William in fair fight. No blame will attach to you or the rest of the household."

Had I kept a clear head, I might have stayed and defended myself in court. Instead I reacted like a fool - and, let us speak plain, a coward - and thought only of escape.

Wilfred returned with a bag of silver pennies, my cloak and some bread and cheese hastily stuffed into a sack. I took the money and food, donned the cloak and turned the destrier's head to face south.

I was careful to handle him gently, mindful of the wounds on his flanks, and he responded. As I steered him onto the road that led south, towards Sundridge and the edge of the Weald, I heard a shout behind me.

It was Alan, the groom who had pressed a dagger in my hand at the crucial moment, and saved my life. He was a lad of maybe fifteen summers, tall and awkward, all pimples and knees and elbows.

While his mate fetched my supplies from the house, he had gone to the stables and saddled his rouncy. To my dismay, his spotty face was alive with excitement.

"John!" Alan cried as he tried to climb aboard the beast, hopping with one foot caught in the stirrup while she led him in a circle, "let me come with you. You promised!"

I cursed the boy's memory. Once, while maudlin in drink, I had promised we would one day ride off to the wars together.

"No," I said firmly, "they will outlaw me, boy. I would not bear your mother's curse to the gallows."

"My mother died two winters back," he replied smugly, finally managing to cock his leg over the saddle.

"We will go to France," he said, while Peter and three other servants carried my cousin's body inside the house, "the Sheriff can't follow our tracks across the Channel. A hard road lays ahead. You will need a friend."

He was a stubborn, brave youth, and I could not afford to waste time in argument. With a shrug, I turned my face back to the road and dug in my heels. The destrier surged into life under me, and I rode on without looking to see if Alan followed.

My plan, inasmuch as I had one, was to follow the road south, through the forest of the Weald, past Tonbridge and hence to some port, probably Hastings, where I could buy passage across the sea to Calais.

There I would think on my next move. I knew King Henry was planning his next French campaign, and would sail to Normandy before the autumn.

It was too dangerous to join his army at Southampton. Word of my outlawry might go before me, and I would arrive at the port only to be arrested and tried for murder. Far safer to travel to Calais via another route, and join the King when he landed on French soil. In the midst of a campaign, with a constant need for fresh soldiers, he was unlikely to enquire too deeply into the misdeeds of one poor man-at-arms.

Haste was vital, so I tore past the pretty little village of Sundridge at a hard gallop and approached the borders of the Weald. I gave the village itself a wide berth, and crossed the double stream of the Darent, a little to the north, where the land swells to a ridge of chalk hills.

Alan struggled to keep up. His rouncy wasn't fit to keep up with my destrier, and he was like to kill the beast under him before we reached Tonbridge.

With a muttered curse, I stopped just before the edge of the woods. My destrier snorted and pawed the ground impatiently, frustrated at being reined in just when he had hit his stride.

My admiration did not extend to Alan. "Only a fool refuses to heed a warning," I said, "turn back, while you can."

He shook his head. "No. I am your servant until death."

I might have forced him to leave, since I was armed and he carried no weapon. In truth, I was reluctant to be alone, especially with the darkness of the Weald stretching before me.

The shortest route to the coast led straight through the forest, which had covered the western part of Sussex since ancient times. I gave my reins a twitch and followed the highway where it led under the trees.

Alan continued to follow, and the hoofs of our horses clopped on the rough surface of the road. Save for their echo, and the jingle of harness, all was eerily silent.

I had always been frightened of the Weald. As a child I was discouraged from venturing into its shadowy depths by tales of monsters and bogeymen, as well as the very real threat of outlaws. It was also home to some of the finest archers and woodsmen in England, whose ancestors played a vital role in defending the land from the French. When Prince Louis, son of Philip Augustus, landed with an army to take the English crown for himself, his knights were shot down like deer as they blundered through the Weald. Not for the last time, the proud nobles of France were humbled by the English peasant and his bow.

The road passed by a little glade with a stream babbling through it. I dismounted and led my destrier down to the bank, so he might drink while I washed the cuts on his flanks.

"Curse William," I muttered as I dipped a corner of my cloak into the water and used it to sponge away the blood, "may he roast in the ovens of Hell for treating you so."

I felt little remorse for William's death. In life he was a monster who never showed me the slightest affection or even respect. He and his father made no secret of their contempt for my mother, whom they considered little better than a whore for her affair with Thomas Page.

I am blessed with keen senses. Something rustled in the trees beyond the stream, and I turned to shout a warning at Alan.

Too late. A red and black striped arrow whipped out of the forest like a giant wasp and hit him square in the chest.

The force of it jerked him off his feet. He sprawled in the dust, shot clean through the heart, and thrashed about horribly in his death-throes.

I froze in shock. One moment Alan was alive, and young, with the long road of his life spread before him. The next he was dead, snuffed out like a candle.

His horse whinnied in terror and bolted down the road. My destrier, trained to war as he was, remained calm. I stood by him, knee-deep in the stream, gaping foolishly at the second violent death I had witnessed in one morning.

The archer in the woods might have shot me down with ease, but I was saved by the appearance of nobility.

A rough, mocking voice rang out from the trees. "Step out of the water, if it pleases you, *my lord,* and throw that pretty sword onto the road. Leave the horse."

"Slowly, now," he added as waded back to the bank, "do as I say, or you'll get one of my stingers in your kidneys."

I climbed up the grassy verge onto the road, unclasped my sword-belt and let it fall. Then I raised my hands above my head.

Two men slunk out of the woods on the other side of the stream. Lean they were, like wolves, and their faces had a pinched, hollow-cheeked, hungry look. Bearded and sunburned, clad in faded green, each carried a yew bow as tall as themselves, and bore sheaves of painted arrows thrust into their belts.

"That's a decent bit of horseflesh," remarked the taller of them, leaning on his bow, "he'll fetch a good price at market. Not sure about the owner, though. What do you reckon he's worth, Will?"

"About six feet of English earth," grunted his companion, "since he's a tall lad."

He drew an arrow from his belt. Terrified, I blurted out the first words that entered my head.

"I killed a man!" I yelped, "I'm an outlaw, or will be. Just like you."

The archer paused. His arrow had a wickedly barbed point, and I sweated at the thought of it plunging into my flesh.

"Outlaws?" said the other woodsman, still in the quiet, amused tone, "who says we're outlaws, my lord? If I wasn't such a peaceful fellow, I might take that as an insult."

Silence followed. It can't have lasted more than a few heartbeats, yet seemed to stretch on forever. The tension broke when both men broke into peals of coarse laughter and started to cross the stream.

"Stay where you are, my lord," said the one called Will, who had notched an arrow to the string and levelled it at me, "you've made us laugh, which is something, but you're not safe yet. We killed your varlet, since he was a miserable-looking fellow of no account. You may prove more interesting. Or not."

I stood quiet and did nothing, trying not to look at poor Alan's body, while they inspected my sword and rifled my saddlebags for aught of value. The taller man gave a low whistle when he found the bag of silver pennies, and raised a hairy eyebrow at me.

"Stolen?" he asked.

"No," I replied with a shake of the head, "the money is mine. My name is John Page. I dwelled at Kingshook, until my cousin came and forced a quarrel between us. Even now he lies on a bench in Kingshook Hall with a dagger through his heart, while I am reduced to a hunted criminal, landless and friendless."

John Page. This was the first time I took my father's name, and did so instinctively. My mother would have despaired, but I was no gentleman, still less a Daubeney. I was the Wolf-Cub, the sell-sword's whelp, and would never pretend otherwise.

The outlaws - for that is what they were - seemed

impressed. "Murdered your cousin, eh?" said Will. He held my sword, and ran his palm lightly along the edge.

He made a few lazy cuts in the air. "This brand has seen service," he added, fingering the dint halfway up the blade, "you come from fighting stock, my lord."

The mock title was starting to irk me. "I am no lord," I said hotly, "my father was a peasant who rose to the captaincy of a Free Company. They called him the Wolf of Burgundy."

I had hoped the name might jog their memories. Instead they looked blank. "We are plain men," the tall one said gruffly, "with no interest in soldier's tales."

He stabbed a finger at me. "You're no soldier either, John Page. Just a petty fugitive and cut-throat, like us. Or is our company not good enough for you?"

I knew the right answer. To say otherwise was death.

"I'll gladly come along," I said, swallowing my hatred and disdain of these men, "if you will have me."

4.

I've always been something of a play-actor. Happily, the outlaws were convinced, and decided to take me to their master.

"You may have heard of our chief," remarked the tall one, who introduced himself as Long Hugh, "he was once the chaplain of Lindfield, before he tired of saving men and decided to rob them instead. Robert Stafford, he is named, though he prefers to call himself Frere Tuk."

It was my turn to look blank. I had heard of Friar Tuck, the jolly renegade priest of the Robin Hood ballads, but this Robert Stafford was unknown to me. The Weald was full of outlaws and outlaw captains, most of whom ended up as gallows-fodder.

Long Hugh laughed, and slapped me on the back with his hairy paw. "You must have led a sheltered life at Kingshook, lad," he grinned, "our master has made himself lord of the Weald, or the part of it that covers Sussex, and declared war on all foresters, verderers and wardens who would deny him his rights."

It sounded absurd, and this Stafford/Tuk was clearly a madman. The Weald, like every other forest in the land, belonged to King Henry, and he was not the sort to share power with deranged chaplains.

Henry, however, was in France. With the King out of the country, along with the best of his nobles and fighting men, England was a lawless place, where all manner of petty thieves, outlaws and draw-latches might hope to profit from the lack of royal authority.

The outlaws took me deep into the forest. They left Alan to rot on the road, and to my eternal shame I raised no protest. My own life depended entirely on their goodwill. One word out of place, and I had no doubt they would slit my throat and leave my body for the wolves.

I tried to make conversation with the outlaws. "Why does your master call himself Frere Tuk?" I asked innocently, "after the man in the ballads?"

"Yes, and because he rejects all earthly ranks and titles," replied Will, "a priest should be just that, and nothing more. A brother to every true man under the eyes of God."

He looked sidelong at me. "Now you come to a better

understanding of our master," he said, "and us."

I did, and my blood ran cold. It seemed, from the little they had told me, that Robert Stafford was a type of heretic, one who rejected the power and authority of the church. His followers, or at least Will and Long Hugh, shared his creed.

They were all dead men walking. As outlaws, who thieved and murdered for a living, the shadow of the gallows hung over them. As heretics to boot, they could be burned at the stake. I had fallen in with a dangerous fellowship, enemies of both secular and religious law.

For the present there was nothing to be done, save earn their trust and wait for the first opportunity to run.

They took me away from the road, following a path only their eyes could see. At times the woods opened out into little clearings, where I caught glimpses of the beautiful rolling hill country of the South Downs, and on occasion a distant glimmer of the sea.

It made my heart ache to look upon the distant blue water, which offered my only chance of survival. In a few short hours England had become a death-trap. I could almost hear the baying of the Sheriff's hounds, and feel the burn of the rope about my neck. My father had famously survived the gallows, though the scar stayed with him all his days. I doubted God or the Devil would allow his progeny to enjoy a similar miraculous escape.

My companions were cheerful, as men are when they have no fear of death or regard for law. They laughed and joked all the way, and swapped blood-curdling tales of the terrible crimes they had committed. Long Hugh, it seemed, had murdered his wife and her lover after returning from the fields one day to find them together in his bed.

"The old bitch did me a favour," he said, "she had a face like a pig's backside, and I was tired of getting drunk every night before I could bring himself to mount her. The blacksmith's lad she took for a bedmate was no prettier."

He grinned at me, and patted the hatchet at his belt. "Truth to tell, neither were a lovely sight after I gave them a few taps with this. I left them lying together in their own blood, and fled to the greenwood."

His dreadful tale, described with such callous relish, made me shudder. Worse was to come, for Long Hugh was but a child next to his companion. Will - William Bolle, was his full name, ex-vintner of Haslemere - boasted of no less than five murders. His first victim was a tax collector, who unwisely threatened Will with imprisonment and confiscation of goods if he failed to pay his arrears. Two were merchants who refused to hand over their money when ambushed in the forest by Stafford's outlaws, and the fourth a miller's daughter Will found washing clothes by a stream.

"I had her," he said, licking his lips at the memory, "and might have let her live, but she clawed me."

He tapped the thin white scars on his left cheek. "Almost took my damned eye out. Put me in a temper, she did, and fought like a wildcat. Messy business."

His fifth victim was, of course, my hapless groom. I swore a private oath to avenge Alan's death, the first of many oaths of vengeance I have taken.

I was sick with horror by the time we reached Stafford's

lair. The outlaws might claim to be no soldiers, but they had set up their headquarters in proper soldierly fashion. It lay deep in a wood, masked by natural walls of briar and thicket, with only one narrow path leading through the hedges.

A bird-call sounded from one of the thick cluster of trees as we started down the path in single file. Long Hugh cupped his hands around his mouth and returned it, a creditable impersonation of an owl, and beckoned at me to look up.

"There's a man in that beech yonder," he said, pointing at one of the trees towering over our heads, "who can put out a rabbit's eye at a hundred paces. He keeps watch for us."

"That's John Burnham," said Will, "the best archer in West Sussex. Took the prize at Chichester fair, three years in a row."

In which case, I wanted to say, he should be with the King's army in France, putting his skills to good use against French knights instead of fellow Englishmen. Instead I kept quiet, and trembled at the thought of the deadly shadow hidden among the swaying branches, far overhead, waiting for a target.

We followed the path until it reached a man-made ditch, six or seven feet deep, and spanned by a bridge made of half a dozen planks lashed together.

Two men guarded the opposite end of the bridge. They looked much the same as my companions, rangy, bearded villains with cold eyes. They hailed Will and Long Hugh, and stared at me with deep suspicion.

"What's this?" snarled one, nodding at me, "a hostage, or a rabbit for the pot?"

"Not enough meat on him," said the other with a smirk.

He whistled at the sight of my destrier. We had led the beast all the way through the forest, sometimes hacking a path for her where the woods grew too thick.

The outlaw picked at his filthy nails with a knife. "Fine horse," he added, "very fine. Should fetch a good price."

Will stroked the destrier's mane, a strangely tender gesture for such a man. "Should," he said curtly, "whether he will or not depends on Stafford."

The sentries at the bridge frowned, and Long Hugh shot his companion a look full of warning. There was a sudden tension in the air. In it I sensed my salvation.

We were allowed to pass over the rickety bridge, which bent and creaked ominously under the weight of my horse, and towards the little stockade, half-hidden by the trees, that lay beyond.

The stockade was roughly circular, and made of great logs cut into pointed stakes. There was another sentry on the gate, a black-bearded rogue who clacked his toothless gums at me as we passed.

A foul latrine stench wafted from inside. My companions laughed when I clapped a hand over my mouth and nose, and shoved me through the gateway.

Inside was a long-house, again made of logs and with a thatched roof, not unlike an ancient mead-hall. There were a few smaller outbuildings and tents scattered about, and maybe a dozen souls, all of them damned, lounged in the dirt and late autumn sunshine.

I noted three women among them. Pale, lank-haired slatterns, as lithe and nervous as the men. They looked at me with hostile eyes, and my heart thumped as Long Hugh seized my wrist and led me towards the long-house.

Will remained with my destrier. He guarded the animal jealously, glaring fiercely at any who so much as glanced at her.

A man appeared in the doorway. Long Hugh stopped dead at the sight of him, and gave a stiff little bow.

"Master," he said, "we found two horsemen on the road. This one is John Page, the Bastard of Kingshook, and says he wants to join us. We slew his companion, a serving-man of no account."

The one he called master stepped into the light. He looked like a humble clerk, thin and stooped and of medium height, with a mean, narrow face and puckered grey eyes. Unlike his followers, who wore the tough, practical clothing of those forced to live rough in the wild, he was clad in a dark brown clerical gown, and his only weapon was a bone-handled knife tucked into a red velvet scabbard. His age was indeterminate: anywhere between twenty-five and forty, with a few grey strands in his neatly brushed and curled brown hair.

He clasped his bony hands together and squinted at me. "I know of you, bastard," he said in a dry, oddly high-pitched voice, "you have taken your father's name, eh? That is good. No man should be ashamed of his origins."

"Take me, now," he added, plucking at the worn cloth of his sleeve, "I was once a poor chaplain, and destined to die as such. Then God sent an angel to whisper into my ear. He told me I was meant for greatness."

He spread his arms. "Look about you, John Page. This is

45

the seed of my kingdom on earth."

I stifled an urge to laugh. His kingdom, as he called it, stank of unwashed bodies, rotting meat and overflowing latrine pits. His subjects were a pack of thieves and murderers, driven out of society and forced to live like animals in this squalid encampment.

It mattered not. Robert Stafford was one of those men for whom reality is a mere trifling detail. Even at short acquaintance, I could sense the power in him, derived from an unshakeable belief in destiny.

He gently took my elbow and steered me away from Long Hugh. "You wish to swear fealty to me, eh?" he said, patting my hand, "I am glad. You are the first gentleman to acknowledge me as lord. Others will follow. One day I shall march on Westminster to claim Saint Edward's crown, with all the lords and commons of England behind me."

"You aim high, my lord," I replied courteously, "but England already has a King."

He raised a finger to silence me. "Henry Plantagenet will be dead inside six weeks," he said firmly, "the angel told me. God means to punish the House of Lancaster for usurping the crown. Henry will die of the bloody flux in France, leaving no heir, and his nobles will fall to squabbling among themselves. When they have all slaughtered each other, and England cries out for a godly master - then shall be my time."

I have lived long enough to see part of Stafford's prophecy come to pass, though his angel was sadly mistaken in the detail. King Henry did die of the flux, at Meaux, seven years after his triumph at Agincourt. He left an infant son, who grew to be a weakling, and even as I speak the nobles of England threaten to make war on each other. God help my native land in the days to come.

Stafford halted to gaze admiringly at my destrier.

"He's mine," said Will, shuffling closer to the beast, which ignored him and nuzzled at the grass.

"Master," he added hastily when Stafford gave him a cool stare. The former chaplain exerted a strange hold over his bestial followers, though he seemed a feeble creature in body. Any of them might have slit his throat with ease.

Stafford folded his arms in their heavy sleeves. "Yours, is he?" he remarked casually, "and what do you mean to do with him?"

Will cleared his throat. He looked fearful in the presence of his chief. "I have kin at Chichester," he replied, "respectable people, who live inside the law. They can sell the horse for me at Chichester market."

Stafford glanced at me. "How much is the animal worth?" he asked.

"At least three hundred pounds, my lord," I replied. A sigh rippled around the stockade. Three hundred pounds was more than any of them could reasonably hope to see in a lifetime.

"Enough to make you rich, Will," said Stafford, "you could leave Sussex, and start again in some other part of England, where no-one knows your face. Is that your plan? To break your oath, and abandon us?"

Will had some guts. "Any man may seek to better himself," he retorted, "is that not our creed? I was born low, the son of a vintner who sold bad wine. Why should I not take advantage of a stroke of good fortune, and seek to die a gentleman?"

His master tutted, and gave a sad little shake of the head. "You are dull of wit, Will. We stand or fall together, not for individual profit. Sell the horse at market, by all means, but the money from the sale will be shared among us. Better still, it can go into my strong-box, to be used as funds in the hard times to come."

A mutter of approval greeted this. Will's broken teeth flashed in a snarl. "Curse you, priest," he rasped. "You mean to rob me!"

Stafford didn't move a muscle as Will reached for his hatchet.

An arrow punched through his chest. Will jerked, and his mouth gaped wide in a silent scream.

I looked to the gate, where the arrow had come from. It was loosed by the toothless, black-bearded sentry, who exposed his filthy gums and raised his bow in salute.

Stafford nodded gravely at him. "My thanks, Stephen," he said. "Your timing was immaculate."

Silence reigned among the outlaws as Will choked out his last breath. I felt no pity for him, only terror at the nightmare I had stumbled into.

The indifference on the faces of the dying man's comrades, if I can call them that, only made it worse. A couple of them started to lay wagers on how long Will would last.

At last he was still, and Stafford ordered Long Hugh and another man to take his body into the forest. "Bury him deep," he said, "else the carrion-eaters will dig him up. He was our friend once. We owe him that much."

"What of the horse, my lord?" I asked cautiously, in the slight hope that Stafford would return him to me. He was a far nobler creature than any of the few spindly horses I could see in the stable beside the long-house, and would be invaluable when the time came to make my escape.

Stafford gave me a shrewd look. I think he had guessed my intention.

"The horse has caused me a deal of trouble," he said, "and the loss of one of my men. More than he is worth. An eye for an eye, John Page."

He rubbed his hands. "I grow weary of venison and rabbit meat. There is good eating on this knightly charger. We shall feast on him tonight. You can enjoy the finest cuts, as part of your welcome to the greenwood."

5.

Being forced to eat my own horse wasn't the end of my trials. Stafford needed to judge if I was worthy to join his little band of heretics. To that end he took me with him on their next raid, the day after the feast.

My guts were still boiling from the lumps of blackened and bloody horse-flesh I had made myself swallow, and the thick, vile-smelling ale that washed them down. Stafford, who also drank deep, was as fresh as a newborn lamb. He possessed extraordinary strength and stamina for such a weak-looking man, and always led by example. These traits, combined with his superior intellect and utter ruthlessness, made him a formidable chief. If he had chosen a different path in life, he might have become a great captain of routiers.

That morning we rode out under light rain and heavy, charcoal-grey dawn skies. We had a dozen horses between us, all stolen, and none in very good condition. The outlaws were a slovenly lot, and took no better care of their beasts than themselves.

"Remember," Stafford told us, "you know me as Robert Stafford, but in the wider world I am Frere Tuk. Let our enemies hear that name."

He still wore his monkish habit, hitched up to his bare calves. Over it he wore a brigandine, a sleeveless leather tunic lined with small oblong steel plates, and an iron cap on his head. His followers wore bits and pieces of armour, again no doubt stolen from their rightful owners: bowl helmets, round shields, brigandines and rusted mail hauberks.

I carried nothing save my sword, which Long Hugh had returned. Stafford let me keep my fur-lined cloak, an act of generosity that caused several of the outlaws to exchange dark looks. After the death of Will, none cared to protest.

We were a scarecrow crew, though little worse than some of the poorer mercenary companies I later knew in Germany and Italy. Stafford was every bit as savage as any of the captains I have encountered, and just as calculating. He saw himself as no mere wolfshead, concerned with plunder and survival and little else, but a king in waiting.

Stafford took us out of the encampment on foot, and along hidden paths in the deep forest beyond. When we reached the highway, he gave the order to mount.

The road was unfamiliar to me, and he insisted on absolute

silence. We rode at a canter, with him in the lead, taking no heed of the few startled farmers and drovers we met at such an early hour. They and their beasts scattered from our path, though one poor shepherd's lad, too slow to get out of the way, was ridden down and trampled.

The man who rode over him - it was Long Hugh - laughed out loud at the deed. I silently cursed him, and added it to the list of crimes I had sworn to avenge.

Stafford was taking us into the forested vale of Arundel. The Earl of Arundel, John FitzAlan, was locked in a violent dispute over his inheritance with the Duke of Norfolk, and as a consequence his lands were ill-guarded.

We came to a part of the forest where the earl kept a number of deer parks, enclosed by ditches and earthen banks and topped with wooden palisades. The red deer could be seen peacefully cropping the lush grass inside, and scattered at the noise of our approach.

"Have those fences down," ordered Stafford. Four of his men dismounted and set about smashing down the palisades with hammers and axes. The rest tethered their horses to nearby trees and strung their bows. These were proper war bows, capable of pinning a knight to the saddle through his layers of steel and leather, or bringing down a deer at two hundred yards.

The fence was broken, and our archers remounted and goaded their horses through the gaps. Stafford watched in mute approval as they spread out and rode after the deer-herds.

He kept me by his side. "You are of gentle blood," he said, with another familiar pat of my hand, "born to lead, not follow. I have it mind to make you an officer. A Joshua to my Moses, eh?"

I forced a smile to my lips. "You honour me, my lord," I replied.

He was very close, and carried only a bone-handled knife. I never saw him draw the knife, or handle any weapon in anger. Stafford relied on intellect and charisma to keep his rough followers in check. It was doubtful he even knew how to fight.

I, on the other hand, had been raised in a knightly family, and could think of a hundred ways to kill a man.

Perhaps shamefully, I resisted the urge. Stafford's followers were too near, and I had no confidence of outrunning them on my miserable nag.

The outlaws returned with three fat does slung over the saddles of their horses. Stafford applauded their success, and flipped a silver penny from his purse to John Burnham, the dead-eyed archer of Chichester, who had brought down the deer.

That was not the end of the day's work. Stafford knew the vale well, and led us into the earl's warrens and chases. Here we poached a great number of deer, hares, pheasants and partridges.

As night drew on, and shadows flitted among the gnarled boughs of the trees, Stafford changed his tactics.

Near the edge of the chase, not far from Arundel Castle itself, were some timber lodges for the earl's verderers and gamekeepers. Either these men weren't very alert, or had chosen to hide in cowardly fashion while we ravaged their master's lands.

It did them little good. Stafford waited until darkness had fallen, and then led us to the lodges.

"Leave the horses," he ordered, "I want absolute silence, my friends. The first one of you to flap a tongue will lose it."

The horses were tethered, and Stafford led us through the shadowy woods. He had good night vision, else we might have stumbled about in circles until daybreak.

His men had brought torches, wooden staves with the ends wrapped in rags soaked in sulphur and lime. Stafford waited until we were crouched in the undergrowth, some twenty yards from the thatched roofs of the rough timber huts, and raised his pale hand.

The outlaws worked swiftly with flint and tinder. Within moments the torches were alight. Then Long Hugh rose to his feet and uttered a shout that echoed like a war-horn through the night.

"Frere Tuk!" he bellowed, "the lord of the Weald is upon you! God for Frere Tuk!"

His comrades sprang out of hiding and charged. Stafford seized my wrist and dragged me in his wake.

Most of the lodges were in darkness, though lights flickered at a couple of windows. More lights flared as we approached, and a door banged open.

A man appeared in the doorway, still in his night-shirt, blinking and rubbing his face. One of the outlaws halted, notched one of the terrible striped arrows, and took aim at him.

I, who had seen enough innocents murdered in the past two days, pretended to stumble and fell against the outlaw's back.

He dropped the arrow and gave me a volley of abuse. I mouthed an apology and ran past him, hoping to save a few more lives.

The outlaws hurled their torches onto the thatch, or else broke the shutters on the windows and tossed the brands inside. Screams and yells of fear erupted as the flames took hold. Wild-eyed and dishevelled men spilled out of the lodges and fled in all directions.

"Let the hunt begin!" cried Stafford, "a silver penny per head!"

He lifted the hunting horn that hung from a strap on his shoulder, and sounded a long blast. His men ran down the fugitives, overpowering all they could catch and chasing the rest into the trees.

Most of the gamekeepers were killed, their throats cut as they were pinned and held down on the grass. Stafford moved among the wanton butchery and picked out a few to be spared for ransom.

This wholesale poaching and murder was the sum total of Stafford's strategy to conquer the Weald. He had no other plan that I could see, save to carry on breaking the law and waiting on further prophecies from his angel. The man was quite mad, and (so I thought) destined to end on the gallows or at the stake.

God reaches the faithful in many and various ways. I never expected to hear the truth drop from the lips of Robert Stafford, a man I secretly hated and feared in equal measure, but so I did.

The truth has stayed with me to this day. I have fought for it, betrayed my friends for it, and am prepared to burn for it.

Even now, so many years later, I would likely die for it if these writings fell into the wrong hands. Christian hands, O Sultan, my supposed brothers of the faith.

I am ready. God's truth is absolute, and flesh is but flesh after all.

6.

"The end of days," said Stafford, "it is coming, my friends. All things will change, and mankind emerge into a cleaner, fresher dawn."

We sat before him on the ground, cross-legged like so many schoolchildren, while he preached from the step of the long-house. His words were met with stifled murmurs and grunts of approval from his followers, who watched him with adoration in their eyes.

He spread his arms wide. "What is the Pope of Rome?" he cried.

"Antichrist!" the outlaws chanted in unison.

"Antichrist," he repeated, "false in all his workings. I tell you, my friends, he has no more power of God in him than any other man. Nor has he the power to make bishops, priests or any other holy order."

His voice rose. "All these grand titles, palaces, reliquaries, adornments and vestments the Pope and his acolytes adorn themselves with. All the wealth they seek to pile up on earth, as though they could use it as a stepladder to Paradise. All shall avail them nothing in the final reckoning. That man whom the people call Pope is naught but a false extortioner and deceiver!"

He paused, red-faced, while one of his acolytes handed him a cup of water. Not far off, I could hear the voices of the gamekeepers we had taken for ransom. They were held inside a pen, and turned to prayer to keep their spirits up.

Stafford had despatched a messenger to Arundel Castle with his ransom demands. The outraged constable responded by cutting off the messenger's left hand and sending him back with the hand in a box. This foolish act of cruelty all but sealed the fate of the prisoners, and their prayers were heavy with despair.

The mutilated outlaw lay on a sickbed inside the long-house, dosed with juice of the poppy. Gangrene had set into his wound, and a dreadful stench drifted from inside.

Stafford ignored these interruptions and carried on regardless. His heavy sleeves fell down, exposing stick-thin white arms, as he raised his hands to Heaven.

"Who is the true Pope?" he demanded, "who is most holy and most perfect?"

"Those who live on earth," the outlaws chorused. "Those who love freely."

They were well-versed, and I gained the impression Stafford had recited this same sermon many times before. He knew his students were rough and uneducated serfs, and that the only way of drumming ideas into their heads was through the power of repetition.

"Indeed," he said in a softer tone, "for those that are called priests, and serve Antichrist, are no priests at all, but lecherous and covetous men and deceivers of the people. Their false teachings and preachings are means by which they sustain their evil pride, their sloth and all their other vices. Even now the Pope's creatures in England make new laws and ordinances, to oppress and murder those who oppose the vicious living of so-called churchmen."

He smiled lovingly at a couple in the front row. They had just been married in a forest wedding. There were no vows spoken during the ceremony, if it can be called that, no prayers or hymns or liturgies, just a simple declaration of love and a feast afterwards.

"Those who love," he continued, "and wish to live as man and wife, have no need of solemn vows, or some shaven-headed fool to mutter Latin phrases over them. For love comes direct from God, pure and divine, and must not be polluted by the interference of false priests."

There was more in this vein. He spoke of the essential corruption of the church, and the duty of true priests to do no more than preach the scriptures and abide by their vows of poverty and humility.

After my initial shock at his blasphemies had passed, I found myself drawn to his words. From infancy I had been taught to respect the church, even though the naked greed and injustice of Christ's servants on earth were all around me.

As an example, my mother's late husband had been forced to pawn seven hides of land to Worth Abbey in order to raise enough money to buy horse and armour for his last campaign. The abbot showed no mercy to his widow, who could not redeem the pledge, and added those seven hides to the abbey's already vast estates.

Some might say the abbot only took what was owed. I say a true man of God has no business trading in land and goods, like some common huckster, and profiting from the death of good knights.

Stafford was obviously a hypocrite, who preached a doctrine of love while committing the foulest crimes. Even so, his message was still worth listening to, and he was by no means the only man in England preaching it.

He was a Lollard of sorts, though he never used the term, one of the breed of heretics who followed the teachings of John Wycliffe. The Lollards travelled about the country like wandering friars, teaching the essential purity of the Bible and demanding an end to the tyranny and corruption of the church.

I was still young and idealistic then, and drank in Stafford's heresies like honeyed ale. At the same time I quickly grew tired of his company, and of his band of ruffians, and bent all my thoughts towards escape.

For the time being I made a point of playing the good little *caporale,* obeying his every command with feigned enthusiasm. Thus, when King Henry's army sailed for Normandy, I was still trapped in the Weald, shooting rabbits and teaching clods how to use a sword.

"We must demonstrate our strength," Stafford told me in private, "and make the lords of Sussex tremble in their manors and castles. In time, when we have them in such a state of terror as to piss their drawers at the mere mention of Frere Tuk, they will renounce their allegiance to Henry Plantagenet and pledge loyalty to me."

In his own fractured mind Stafford undoubtedly saw

himself as the true King of England, not for his own glory, but to ensure England's salvation at the End of Days. He was certain the time was coming, and soon, when the heavens would open and showers of molten flame and ash pour forth, to cover the earth in fire and purge the sinful. To avoid God's wrath it was essential that a righteous man, uncorrupted by the lies of Antichrist, sat on the English throne.

It was hard to think of a more unlikely saviour than Stafford, or a less worthy person to sit on the throne. Still, I simpered and grovelled before him, encouraged his insane ambitions, and obediently rode off to poach game and terrorise the local verderers.

I was careful to befriend his two best men, Long Hugh and John Burnham. Both were fearsomely strong, quick to learn swordplay, and Burnham was one of the finest archers I ever knew. As summer faded, I carefully cultivated these two, and played on their natural greed and viciousness.

They were slightly more intelligent than the rest of Stafford's followers, and not content to follow him for much longer. I worked on them for weeks, breaking down their fear of the mad priest and dangling the promise of easy wealth before their eyes.

"Ride out with me on the next raid," I suggested to them one evening near the end of August, "just us three."

We sat around a supper fire, away from the others. I kept my voice low, and tried to sound brash and confident. All the while I was terrified lest my words were overheard and reported to Stafford. If the slightest hint of my plans reached his ears, he wouldn't hesitate to have me killed.

My companions were just as wary. "Where to?" murmured Long Hugh, staring down at his bowl of bean and venison stew.

"North-west," I replied, "out of Sussex, into Berkshire."

Their gnarled, weather-beaten faces creased into puzzled frowns. "There is something in Berkshire that belongs to me," I explained, "something of great personal value. You will profit as well. A rich manor. Chests of gold and silver taken from the French wars. More than enough for all three of us to roll in treasure for the rest of our lives."

I lied. My target was Steventon, the manor in Berkshire once owned by Sir Hugh Calveley, my father's murderer. Calveley was dead, and I had no idea how much, if any, of the great fortune he amassed in his many campaigns still remained at Steventon. He had left no heirs, only a Spanish wife who despised her husband and returned to her homeland while he was still alive.

The lie was necessary, and had the required effect. Long Hugh and John Burnham were born thieves.

"Done," they said.

7.

It was easy enough to persuade Stafford to let me go on another raid, though he expressed concern at how few men I wished to take.

"Hugh and Burnham are worth any ten of my lord Arundel's verderers," I said with forced confidence.

I pretended we were going to hunt the deer in the earl's parks, where the outlaws had enjoyed so much success in the past. My heart thumped in fear that he might see through the deception. Stafford liked to think he was a shrewd judge of men, though he never saw through my bluff exterior.

Stafford pondered awhile, frowning and stroking his pointed chin while I broke into a light sweat. "Very well," he said at last, "you know your business, John Page, more than any other man in my service. Come back with a brace of plump deer for our supper."

He solemnly muttered a blessing over me, made the sign of the cross, and shook my hand. His grip was like a wet fish, soft and oily, and made me want to wash.

We rode out on a raw autumn morning, with a strange heaviness in the air. I had no intention of returning, and so twisted in the saddle to take one final look at the stockade.

Stafford stood at the gate. I can still picture his thin, slightly stooped figure, one slender arm raised in a gesture of farewell. Smoke from the roof of the long-house curled lazily into the sky, and I could heard faint laughter and singing from inside.

That was the last time I saw him. He was never hanged, to the best of my knowledge, or burned at the stake. Many years after our brief association, I heard he was still haunting the forests of Sussex, leading the verderers a merry dance and waiting in confident expectation for the End of Days. He may be waiting still.

I vaguely knew the route to Steventon from maps of England held among my mother's papers at Kingshook. According to the Ballad of the Black Oak, one of the ballads sung by the troubadours of his life and death, Thomas Page was never buried, but left to hang in an iron cage until his bones fell to earth:

"The half-hanged man dwells not in Heaven,
His soul burns in the darkest deep,
In life he was fiercer than a lion,
A wolf among the sheep,
Alas! His shield was broke, his hauberk undone,
By one who sought him far and long.
Sir Hugh Calveley, the red dog of France,
Conqueror of many a foe,
Took his quarry by the slightest chance,
And slew him at the Black Oak,
The flesh of the wolf was left to rot,
No Christian grave for his bones,
He haunts there still, dishonoured and forgot,
His soul condemned to walk alone."

I wanted to see my father's bones, and look for his few possessions. Calveley would doubtless have taken his sword and ring, as well as the mysterious packet of letters Page carried with him. I thought they might be gathering dust in some coffer.

Long Hugh and Burnham knew little of my history, and I told them nothing of my true intentions as we rode north-west, following the King's highway beyond the borders of the Weald, into the pleasant green hill country I knew so well.

It was a dry autumn, and we made good speed along the roads. Once we had to dodge into the woods to avoid a troop of men-at-arms. Their steel bascinets and brigandines gleamed in the sun as they jogged along, perhaps towards the coast and a ship to take them to Normandy.

Otherwise we were unimpeded, and within two days had crossed into Berkshire. My memory of the route was at fault, so to avoid getting hopelessly lost we stopped a group of pilgrims and asked them the way to Steventon.

They were a motley band, as pilgrims usually are, tradesmen and labourers and widows and others, all united in their desire to reach the tomb of the holy blessed martyr at Canterbury. Few were armed, and they trembled with fear at the sight of us, grizzled and dirty from the forest as we were, and bristling with weapons.

"Steventon lies to the east, noble sir," said their leader, "follow the road past Farnborough, and you should reach the manor by noon."

"My thanks," I said courteously, "who holds it now, since the death of Sir Hugh Calveley?"

He didn't know, but one of his company, a hollow-cheeked clerk who looked in equal need of salvation and a good meal, piped up.

"The manor and rectory of Steventon, along with the advowson of the vicarage," he trilled, "were sold to Calveley by the abbey of Bec. Upon his death, leaving no heir, they were conveyed to the Bishop of Salisbury, who in turn conveyed them to His late Majesty King Richard the Second, who in turn conveyed them to the abbot and convent of Westminster."

I thanked the pilgrims and hurried on, before Long Hugh and Burnham could start casting greedy eyes at their purses. They needed little encouragement, those two, and I didn't want to get into a brawl on the highway.

The road led past a hamlet before we came to the larger village of Steventon, where we stopped at the inn to refresh our horses and sink a few cups of ale.

The innkeeper didn't look happy at our presence, and slapped down a jug of ale and a platter of bread and bacon at our table without a word. I nudged Long Hugh with my foot when he reached for his knife, and smiled at our host.

"Tell me, friend," I asked, "do you know the Ballad of the Black Oak?"

He sniffed, wiped his greasy hands on his stained apron, and narrowed his eyes at me. "I know it," he conceded, "and I know the oak as well. It lies not half a mile from here, a lone tree on the bare hillside."

I thought a small bribe might loosen his tongue. Fortunately, I had managed to retrieve part of the money I lost to the outlaws. Stafford shared the stolen silver among his followers, who promptly lost it to me in games of dice.

I took a shilling from my purse and laid it flat on the table. "Could you take us there?" I asked innocently.

"What for?" he demanded, his eyes wide as they stared at the coin. "It's a bad place. A man was murdered at the oak, as the ballad says. His spirit lingers on the hillside. Some have heard him weep at night."

"I know all that," I replied. "The dead man's name was Thomas Page. I am his son."

He crossed himself. "And you want to dig up his bones, is that it?" he exclaimed with a strange kind of fierceness, "take my advice, young man, and go home. The dead should be left to rest."

"Rest?" I said. "You just told me his soul haunts the place where he was murdered."

I produced another coin and laid it next to the first. "Two silver shillings," I added, "all yours, if you take us to the tree."

"Not I," he stammered after a moment's hesitation, "fifty shillings wouldn't get me to the Black Oak. But I know one who might take you there. His name's Wat. He's a charcoal burner. Spends much of his time in the forest. Darkness, and evil spirits that stalk the land at night, hold no fears for him."

I spread my hands. "He sounds a fine man. I look forward to meeting him. Soon."

The innkeeper nervously fiddled with the hem of his apron. "There's something else you should know. Wat saw your father die. He was in the woods, up near the hill, when Calveley and his rogues did Page in. Saw them cut his throat and hang up his body in that accursed cage. Some time later, Wat went back to the spot with a couple of lads from the village."

"Why did he go back?" I asked.

The other man looked sadly at me. "Why, sir, to cut the poor wretch down, and then to bury him."

8.

Wat turned out to be a sturdy old peasant, wrinkled and nut-brown from a lifetime spent in the open. The innkeeper sent a boy to fetch him from his hut in the woods, and we met him on the outskirts of the village, where the road started to narrow and wind up into the hills.

He looked me over without much interest when I introduced myself, and stuck out his gnarled hand, indelibly stained with the dust of his grubby trade.

"The boy said you had money," he snapped in a hoarse, cracked voice, "two shillings, maybe more."

I dug out the coins and dropped them in his hand. He closed his fingers and gave a brief nod.

"I'll take you to the oak," he said, "and show you where we buried your father. We'll need shovels."

Long Hugh shifted impatiently. "I'm weary of all this talk of ghosts and hanged men," he said, "where's this treasure you promised us, Page?"

"Patience," I said soothingly, "after we've finished at the tree, we'll move on to Steventon manor. Lots of plunder there. Enough to set you up for life. Plenty of drink and whores. You can both kill yourselves with pleasure."

He and Burnham grinned at the sound of that, and their good humour lasted as we toiled up into the forested hill country.

Wat led us in silence. There was a certain quiet dignity about him, and he moved through the woods with surprising speed and grace for his age. I struggled to keep up with his rangy, long-legged stride, and even my companions, both seasoned foresters, were tired and dripping with sweat when we came to a little clearing.

The clearing lay at the end of a track that was almost

vertical in places, and threatened to go on forever. Wat led me to the edge of the trees, while Long Hugh and Burnham unloaded the shovels. We had borrowed the tools from the innkeeper, as well as a tough little pony to carry them, at the cost of another two shillings.

"There," grunted the charcoal burner with a nod at the clearing, "over there lies your father."

I saw a giant, long-dead oak tree, its leafless branches spread like monstrous talons. The oak had been a king of the forest, once, before the sap ran dry and life faded from its raddled grey flesh, leaving a dead shell.

My jaw tightened when I spotted a length of chain dangling from one of the lower branches. The chain was stiff with rust, and ended in a curved hook. I needed no telling what it had been used for.

"Where is the cage?" I demanded.

"God knows," Wat replied with a shrug, "me and my mates left it on the hook after we buried your father's body. Someone else might have been up here since and taken it. Good iron is always useful."

I took a deep breath and stepped into the clearing. "Where did you put my father to rest?" I asked.

He pointed at the grass at the foot of the tree. "Just there. Under the cage."

"Could you not have taken him down to the churchyard in the village, and buried him like a Christian?"

Wat shook his grey head. "No, sir. Old Calveley was lord of Steventon, and would not have allowed it. All I could do was say a prayer when we were done."

"I'm no priest," he added with fear in his eyes as he glanced about the clearing, "hence your father's spirit still haunts these woods."

My companions were hard men, but looked pale as we carried our shovels to the tree.

Wat and his friends had buried my father deep. "To stop wolves digging up his remains," the old man explained as we hacked away at the soil.

It was growing dark by the time we found the earthly remains of Thomas Page. The hole we excavated was almost the height of Long Hugh, and he gave a shout when the edge of his shovel cracked against something hard.

We cast our tools aside and grubbed in the dirt, clawing at it with our bare hands. More bones gradually became visible, wrapped in the mildewed scraps of a woollen grey shroud.

Wat knelt and carefully peeled back the shroud to expose some greenish ribs. "We had no coffin," he muttered, "just an old cloak to wrap him in."

Overwhelmed with sadness and pity, I knelt beside my father's skull and stared into the empty eyes.

"What an end," I murmured, "to die here, in the wilderness, after he had known the glory of the world. Set upon by cowards and murderers, with none to help him."

I stared at my companions. "This man once led the Company of Wolves, and marched proudly under the banners of England, Castile and León. He deserved better."

The others said nothing. I traced my finger over the curve

of the skull, and noticed a tiny fracture on the back. Doubtless the result of a blow on the head, taken in combat.

I pondered his death. None of the ballads explained the reason for Page's feud with Hugh Calveley. The cause had died with them, leaving only a gruesome narrative. Many more years passed before I learned the root of it.

Wat started to clear away the dirt over the finger-bones of my father's right hand. "It's still here," he said excitedly, "the others wanted to sell it, but I wouldn't let them. Wasn't right, pillaging the dead."

He ripped something from one of the skeletal fingers and held it out to me. My heart skipped when I saw the object resting on his grimy palm: a silver ring decorated with a perfectly round black crystal.

I took the ring and held it up to the light. The crystal was inscribed with the image of a white raven, wings outspread.

"The Raven of Toledo," I breathed.

The Raven of Toledo was the nickname for my father's lover, a Spanish noblewoman of Badajoz. Her real name was Eleanor Menezes de Alonchel, and I knew of her from the ballads, in which the Wolf and the Raven fought and marched together for many years until they met their grisly demise at the hands of the Red Bull, alias Sir Hugh Calveley.

Unusually for a former routier, Calveley had not stripped my father's body of valuables after murdering him. Perhaps some grim sense of romance compelled him to leave the ring on Page's body.

I brushed away the spots of dirt and slipped it onto my finger. A perfect fit.

My eyes were moist. I irritably blinked the tears away, knowing it was fatal to show weakness before the likes of Long Hugh and John Burnham.

"Some treasure," grunted Burnham, "one poxy ring. You promised us more than this, Page."

Long Hugh fingered the hilt of his broad knife. "Aye," he said, "that you did. I didn't leave the Weald just to dig up some dusty old bones."

I faced them down. It sounds absurd, but I felt like a different man with Thomas Page's ring on my finger, as though part of his warlike soul dwelled inside the crystal.

"You'll get your plunder," I snarled at them in an aggressive tone I had never used before, "we'll go to Steventon, as I promised, and strip it to the bone."

"Remember one thing," I added forcefully, "I'm in charge. You do as I say, when I say it. Understand?"

Neither of them challenged my bluff. Long Hugh could have twisted my neck in one of his big hands, but wouldn't even meet my eye. They were cravens, fit for nothing save poaching and highway robbery.

Wat looked pensive. He had overheard us talking of the intended raid on Steventon. If we let him go, he might warn the High Sheriff or his officers before we attacked the place.

Had I been twenty years older, I would have cut the charcoal burner's throat without hesitation. I was still young then, and inclined to mercy.

"Here," I said, offering Wat the last of the silver from my purse, "take this. Let it buy your silence."

He snatched the money, gave us one last furtive look, and hobbled off into the trees. I noticed Burnham reach for one of the red-fletched arrows in his quiver.

"Don't," I growled, laying a hand on my sword.

"You're a fool," he muttered, "that old man will get us all hanged."

He said no more, and worked with Long Hugh in meek silence as we filled in the grave. I had abandoned the notion of giving my father a proper Christian burial. We lacked the time and the means to move his remains, and perhaps six feet of English earth was as good as a churchyard. At least I had his ring, which may have served to calm his restless spirit.

When all was done, and the Half-Hanged Man covered over again, we gladly quit that dreadful place.

I have never been back.

9.

Calveley's manor house at Steventon was old, perhaps as old as Kingshook, but with new red tiles on the roof and fresh plaster on the walls. My mother's house was a barn by comparison. The same wars that made Calveley rich had condemned her to live in penury, loaded down with debts she could not repay.

I first saw the place from the shelter of a little wood, where we halted to spy out the land. The house was built in a typical L-shape, with no outer wall, and surrounded by a deer park. There was good arable land in the distance, all brownfield at this time of year, and a few scattered farmsteads in the distance.

"Pity the poor monks," sneered Long Hugh, "forced to dwell in such a place. Look at those deer cropping the grass.

I'll wager the impoverished servants of Christ dine on venison pasties every night, washed down with a quart of French wine."

Burnham nodded in agreement. "Fat as butter," he said, "eating and drinking of the best, while preaching the virtues of temperance to the poor."

He spat on the ground, and lovingly stroked the fletches of his arrows. "You ever seen a monk dance, Hugh? You will after I've put a few of these in their lardy backsides."

"There won't be any monks in Steventon," I said, "the abbey of Westminster will have a steward in place, to run the manor and ensure it turns a profit."

They were a murderous pair, and looked sorely disappointed at being denied the opportunity to shoot a few monks.

"Look," I said, pointing at the house, "there is no gate or high wall to stop us. The steward and his servants shouldn't be a threat. This will be easy as stretching a rabbit's neck."

Steventon was ill-guarded. I saw a couple of grooms by the stables near the left wing of the house, rubbing down a white gelding. Some hens scratched about in the yard, and an old mongrel hound lay on its side beside the front door, enjoying the sun. Otherwise all was quiet.

The grooms put me in mind of Alan. My throat tightened, and a wave of anger coursed through me.

I had sworn an oath to avenge Alan's death. Today, if God was kind, that oath would be fulfilled.

We approached the house on foot. Burnham notched an arrow to his bow, and I trembled at the thought of one of those wickedly barbed shafts plunging into my back.

I had judged him well. Neither he nor Long Hugh would betray me until it was convenient. The robbery came first.

The house lay some three hundred yards from the wood where we left the horses. There was no cover in the space between, so the abbey servants had ample time to spot us. I saw the grooms shade their eyes to stare at us.

I held up my hands, palms outwards, to show we meant no harm. If possible, I meant to spill no innocent blood, and hoped to plunder the house without violence.

Burnham had other ideas. One of the grooms saw him draw to shoot, and turned to flee for the refuge of the stable.

He was too slow, and Burnham too good a shot. The striped arrow hit him square in the middle of the back. He went down with a shriek, limbs flailing.

"You cursed idiot!" I shouted, rounding on Burnham,

The anger rose inside me. I failed to control it, and reached for my sword.

He was quick. My blade was not even half-drawn before he had another arrow on the string.

Burnham took aim at my head. "You're too soft, Page," he hissed. "Did you think we came to play at pat-a-cake with them? Stand aside or I'll put this through your eye."

We were distracted by an outbreak of frantic, deep-throated barking. "They have loosed a mastiff!" cried Long Hugh.

I swung round, careless of Burnham and his arrow, and glimpsed a monstrous black shape galloping straight towards us. The kennels stood next to the stables, and a fair-haired youth had shot out of the house to knock the chain off the gate.

Burnham loosed at the mastiff. His hand must have shook, for the arrow flew well wide. Then the huge animal, all slavering yellow jaws and rolling eyes, was upon us.

I leaped aside and dragged out my sword as Burnham screamed. The mastiff had launched itself at his chest, knocked him to the ground and sunk its teeth into the meat of his shoulder.

Neither I nor Long Hugh made any effort to help him. Hugh sprinted towards the kennel, axe in hand, roaring curses at the boy who had released the dog.

I ran for the door, and almost reached it before two hard-faced churls with long staves burst from the shadows inside.

The first man's eyes widened when he saw me. I had no wish to kill, and swatted him to the ground with the flat of my blade.

His mate almost tripped over the unconscious body, and fell back as I sprang at him. He blocked a downward cut of my sword with his stave, so I got in close and punched him in the face with the hilt. His eyes crossed, blood spurted from his mouth and nose, and he slumped down against the wall.

I ran through the open doorway into the short corridor that lay beyond. It opened onto a long, narrow hall, sparsely furnished and with a vaulted wooden ceiling.

It was purely functional, with little in the way of comfort of decoration. No tapestries or friezes adorned the plastered walls, and the windows had wooden shutters and thin sheets of horn in place of glass. A fire burned low in a hooded grate at the northern end, where a kitchen maid sat crouched in terror, her filthy hands pressed to her mouth, surrounded by the pile of kindling she had just dropped.

I paused to take stock, breathing hard, and spied a man I took to be the steward cowering behind one of the benches. He was stout and bald, dressed like a priest of sorts in a white gown and black mantle. His broad face was ashen as he goggled at me, and I thought he might die of fright.

"Please," he moaned, dropping to his knees, "please don't hurt me or my servants. Take all you like. Just spare our lives."

I puffed out my cheeks and slid my sword back into its scabbard. "The abbot chose well in you," I said scornfully.

The wretch lacked the spirit to even meet my eye. "Show me to the strongroom," I ordered him, "or wherever the valuables are kept. Now!"

Bowing and drivelling, he led me down another passage to a black-timbered door, which he unlocked with the largest of the set of iron keys at his belt.

I put my boot to the door, which swung inward to reveal another vaulted chamber, windowless and empty save for three heavy chests shoved against one wall.

"Th-there's some silver plate and candlesticks in there," the steward babbled, pointing at one of the chests, "we only use it when guests come to dine. The r-rest of the time we m-make do with pewter."

"Your dining arrangements are of concern to me," I growled, "nor is your silver. What's in the others?"

He stared, probably thinking I was the most unusual of robbers. "The others? Nothing of m-much value. Junk, mostly."

"Let me see."

I stood over the steward as he threw back the heavy lids of the two smaller chests.

"Empty them," I told him. He knelt on the bare floor and lifted out piles of moth-eaten old clothes, stumps of candle, a pewter tankard or two, and other such worthless rubbish.

Near the bottom of the second chest I picked out a badge, much faded and discoloured with age. It was a livery badge, such as a retainer might wear on his coat, and displayed three black bull-calves against a white field with a red bar. I had a good grounding in heraldry, and recognised them as the arms of Sir Hugh Calveley.

There was something else, right at the bottom of the chest, a roll of black silk carefully folded and tucked into one corner. I tossed away the badge and reached inside for the fabric.

I unrolled the piece of silk. One edge was badly torn and showed half a wolf's head, embroidered onto the silk in red and gold thread. A golden eye stared balefully at me, undimmed by the passage of time and the indignity of being stuffed inside an old chest.

This could only be a scrap of my father's wolf banner, which he had carried into battle at the head of his Company of Wolves.

I clasped the silk to my chest. This was why I came to Steventon. Not to look for treasure, but to find some other remnant of Thomas Page. Something tangible.

How the banner came to be at Steventon is difficult to say. I knew Calveley had fought for the English at Najéra, where the Prince of Wales won a great victory over the forces of

Henry of Trastamara. My father fought on the losing side, and his Company of Wolves was destroyed in the rout. Maybe Calveley captured his banner at Najéra and kept it as a trophy of war.

It was too much to hope that Page's letters had survived. They were lost forever, most likely burned by Calveley. Still, the banner was something, another link to the father I never knew.

Long Hugh appeared in the doorway. The blade of his axe dripped red, and his face and hands were spattered with blood.

"I slew the mastiff," he grunted, "and that fool who loosed it. Burnham's done for, though. The dog ripped out his throat."

The steward squealed at the sight of Hugh, all gaunt and stinking of death as he was, and shrank into a corner.

"Burnham's dead, is he?" I said with a shrug, "no matter. All the more loot for us. There's some good stuff in the largest of these chests. Take as much as you like. I've got what I came for."

He gave me a quizzical look, and wasted no time sifting through the gold and silver.

"Fetch me something to carry all this," he barked at the steward, who scurried away, long robe flapping round his fat calves, and returned with a draw-string leather bag.

Hugh snatched the bag and stuffed it with plate and candlesticks. I left him to it and went back outside.

I was greeted by a scene of carnage. The two churls I had fought still lay unconscious, and would sleep for a good while yet.

The fair-haired boy who had released the mastiff lay in the dust beside the kennels, his head split open by Hugh's axe. Bright red blood pumped slowly from the terrible wound.

I looked for the mastiff, and saw it lying next to Burnham. Hugh's busy axe had shattered the animal's skull, though not before its teeth ripped out our comrade's throat.

I walked over to inspect the bodies. Burnham's body still quivered, and blood dripped from the teeth-marks in his neck. His eyes stared blankly at - what? The gates of Hell, most probably.

I picked up his bow and ran my fingers over the six feet of smooth English yew. It was a peasant's weapon, one I was raised to despise. Gentlemen of coat-armour fight hand-to-hand. The notion of killing our enemies at a distance is thought both cowardly and dishonourable.

Great Sultan, never underestimate the English talent for hypocrisy. Our kings have made good use of archers for generations, and relied on them to win great victories in France and Scotland. Fellows like John Burnham, rough, uneducated commoners, are obliged by law to practise archery at least once a week. Thus the yeomen of England are kept in a permanent state of readiness for war.

The war bow, as we call it, has a seventy-pound draw weight. All the long years of endless practice had left Burnham with a slightly deformed right shoulder. His right arm was slightly longer than the other, thanks to stretched sinews and tendons, and the fingers of his draw-hand were swollen and marked with calluses.

I squatted next to him. "A pity," I said, closing his eyes,

"you might have accompanied me to France."

Ambition struck me. I would resurrect the Company of Wolves, and lead them to fresh victories all over Christendom. Become a famous captain-general of routiers; carve my way to fame, honour and riches under the wolf banner, and lay to rest my father's ghost.

"Page! Stop daydreaming. We have to be gone from here before the hue and cry is raised."

The glorious images in my head dissolved at the sound of Long Hugh's voice. I took the dead man's dagger and the handful of pennies in his purse before standing to face Hugh.

He carried a sackful of stolen plate over his shoulder, and a smaller bag in his right hand.

"Money," he said with a grin, raising the bag, "I threatened to put out one of the steward's eyes if he didn't show me where he kept his secret funds. Turns out the little swine had a stash hidden under a false board in his bedchamber."

I grimaced with distaste. We had scared the steward half to death, murdered one of his servants, and committed assault and robbery into the bargain. Any man with a scrap of decency in him would have felt ashamed (I did, a little), but Long Hugh's conscience had died with his many victims.

We hurried back to the horses, and rode away from Steventon as fast as they could carry us.

"South," I said, "to the coast, and a ship to take us to France."

Long Hugh agreed, with good reason. He dared not return to the Weald, and Stafford's anger at the loss of Burnham.

Besides which, the hue and cry would soon be raised for our work at Steventon. Our lives now depended on speed and luck.

Southampton lay directly to the south. It would take us two; maybe three days to reach the port, assuming nothing befell us on the way. Fortunately we had Burnham's horse to use as a remount. It wasn't hard to guess at Hugh's thoughts. When his own horse was exhausted, he would murder me and take the spare. There is little honour among thieves.

We halted at dusk, sore and sweating from a long ride at breakneck pace. I dismounted and led my weary horse off the highway.

"We have to get some sleep," I said in response to Hugh's questioning look, "the High Sheriff may already be out hunting for us. Best we take refuge in the forest tonight."

Hugh saw the sense in that, and followed me under the shadowy branches. I had little notion of our whereabouts - somewhere between Newbury and Winchester, perhaps - only that the woods were deep and dark, and suitable for my purpose.

There were no convenient paths, and for an hour so we fought our way through webs of brambles and deep undergrowth, blundering over fallen boughs and at one point sinking knee-deep into a hidden bog. There were no sounds of pursuit, only the night sounds of the forest: an owl hooted, small creatures rustled among the leaves, and once we heard the distant howl of a wolf.

"Wolves," Hugh panted when the echoes of that dismal cry had faded away, "I've always hated them. One snatched my brother from his cradle when I was young. They would make a meal of us, if we let them."

I grinned in the dark. He had no idea of the truth of his words.

At last, when it became almost too dark to see any further, I called a halt. I had hoped to reach a clearing, but had to be content with a patch of sloping ground where the trees thinned out a little.

"This is a dismal place to rest," grumbled Hugh, "scarce room enough to stretch my bones on the ground. I need a good seven feet of earth to get comfortable."

"There's hardly any moon," I said. "You want us to blunder about in the darkness until dawn? Tether the horses, and let's have a bite to eat. We can't risk a fire."

I handed him my reins, and he turned away, still grumbling, to bind them to a nearby trunk.

I drew Burnham's dagger - a long, sharp sticker it was, perfect for the task - and stepped close to drive it into Hugh's massive back.

Some might call it a coward's trick, to knife a man from behind. I say my victim was a black-hearted rogue, a smear of blood and grease upon the world, and deserved a far worse death than the one I gave him.

He jerked violently when the blade sank into his kidneys, and threw back his head. I clapped my free hand over his mouth to stifle the yell, and gasped in pain as his teeth closed on my fingers.

Hugh was strong, and squirmed and wriggled like a dying fish as I yanked the blade free of his body. I was stronger still, for all his great height and reach, and dug my bleeding fingers into his eyes as I stabbed him again, this time under the breast-bone, to push the steel up into his heart.

It was a dirty, difficult kill, and worthy of such a man. "This is for Alan," I hissed into his ear as he died, "remember him? My companion your friend murdered on the road."

"Give my regards to Will in Hades," I added, and drew the edge of the knife across his throat. Then I shoved him onto his face in the grass, where he bled out his last.

The forest was silent, as though appalled, while I knelt and wiped the dagger clean.

Now I had two deaths on my account. The first, my cousin Sir William, was done in the heat of combat. The second was done in cold blood, and will count against me on the day of judgement.

Two deaths. How many more have I committed or brought about since? Hundreds, if not thousands. Not all of them in the line of a soldier's duty. I shudder to think of the bruises on my soul.

One must be practical. I also had three horses, a sackful of treasure, and a clear road to Southampton.

And France.

10.

The war in France drew me, as surely as it drew any landless, homeless, wifeless young Englishman with a price on his head. I reached Southampton with one horse under me, having virtually killed the other two in my haste and left them to founder on the road.

It was early August by now, and the King had long sailed to Normandy with an army of some twelve thousand men. They landed safely at the mouth of the River Touques, on the northern coast of the duchy.

There were still a fair number of troops in Southampton, and I encountered hundreds of soldiers along the road leading to the walled town. These were reinforcements, intended to cross the Channel in support of Henry's invasion. I recognised some of the banners of the lesser captains, knights and barons, and soon learned that most of the great English lords had already sailed with the King.

"They've all gone over," a master-bowman told me as I rode alongside his company, "Clarence and Gloucester, Salisbury, Warwick, Pembroke and the rest."

"Who is your captain?" I asked, looking over the long files, ten men deep, of fierce, bearded faces.

The archers marched in the rear of a long column of footmen, marshalled by under-officers who rode hither and thither, barking curt orders or rebukes at the sturdy rogues under their command. The spears and halberds of the infantry twinkled in the bright autumn sun, and every one of the bowmen wore a parti-coloured tunic, emblazoned with the red cross of Saint George and a device showing three black lions against a yellow field.

"My commander is Sir Thomas Carew," the master-bowman replied, "you will have heard of him?"

I shook my head, and he gave me a hard look. He was a wary, experienced fighting man, his face stern and lined in its mail coif.

"Sir Thomas is a Welsh knight," he said, "and did good service in the recent affrays at Harfleur and Agincourt. He is still at Southampton, awaiting reinforcements before he sails. You have not been to the wars, then?"

I replied that I had not, but was bound for the port, and wished to join the King's army in Normandy.

He gave me another long, searching look. "You have no master," he said slowly, "and ride alone. That's a good sword you carry, along with two daggers. No armour, and your horse is like to collapse before dusk. What's the device on that bit of fabric you wear?"

I had wrapped the wolf banner around my neck as a scarf. "A wolf's head," I answered proudly, "I hope to carry it on a standard one day, at the head of my own company."

He rubbed his bristly chin. I could see the smile playing around his lips. It must have been clear to any man with a degree of sense that I was a fugitive from justice, hoping to find safety and redemption across the sea.

"I wish you good fortune, lad," he said at last, "and advise you to ride hard for the port. Get on the first boat that will take you. Worry about the army when you reach Normandy, not before."

"One last bit of advice," he added when I made to ride away, "don't try and enlist under Sir Thomas' banner. Unlike many lords, he takes no thieves or draw-latches into his service, and will hang any man he suspects of being one."

I galloped on, and learned later that Sir Thomas Carew, knight of Pembrokeshire, had mustered a company of three hundred archers to serve the King in Normandy. Added to these were one hundred and fifty men-at-arms.

This was the first time I had seen an organised body of troops march to war, and despite my haste I took careful note of their array. Behind the archers strode two drummers and a pair of trumpeters, decked out in Carew's livery and playing in time to the march. After them came a long line of sumpter-horses loaded down with the necessary gear and baggage: tent-poles, cooking pans, horse-shoes, wedges, spurs, spare weapons, and anything else that might be of use on campaign.

The men-at-arms marched and rode three abreast. In marked contrast to the archers, they advanced in disciplined silence, each face grim and set inside its steel hood, as though they already beheld the French. Many had the tough, weathered look of veterans, and all fairly dripped with weaponry. Every man carried lance, sword and mace, a shield emblazoned with the Carew arms, and was encased in plate and mail.

They were led by a knight on a grey destrier at the head of the column, followed by a squire carrying an enormous square standard. The standard rippled in the slight breeze, and the black lions of Carew seemed to dance and bare their fangs as I cantered past.

To me, a plain country esquire who had spent almost all his life in West Sussex, Southampton was overwhelming. The sheer size of the place, its crenellated walls and turrets, and the mighty stone keep on the knoll overlooking the packed streets filled me with awe. From a ridge on the highway I was able to see over the walls and rooftops to the harbour, where a cluster of ships bobbed at anchor. The bulk of the fleet had already gone to Normandy, but there were still a fair number of cogs, awaiting supplies and reinforcements.

I screwed up my courage to join the steady stream of traffic that flowed through the gatehouse in the northern wall. None paid much heed to me, just another face among the throng of soldiers. Even so, I half-expected my name to be called out at any moment, and a dozen hands to lay hold of me.

There is wonderful anonymity in a crowd. The press of bodies near the gatehouse was so great I was obliged to dismount and lead my exhausted horse on foot, under the iron teeth of the portcullis.

Once through the arch, I found myself on a wide, cobbled street that ran the length of the town, all the way to the gatehouse at the southern end. To my right was the stark grey pile of the castle, and beyond it, to the south-east, lay the docks and the open sea.

The captain of archers had advised me to get aboard the first boat willing to take me. His advice seemed sound, but first I wanted to equip myself as a soldier. Appearance counts for much, and I wanted to avoid being taken for a fugitive again.

I still had the purse Long Hugh stole from the steward at Steventon. After much thought, I had reluctantly left the sack of plate next to his corpse in the forest. There was no way I could have sold or pawned them in Southampton without arousing suspicion. Perhaps some woodcutter found the sack, and spent the rest of his days in wealth and comfort.

The money, along with the sale of my horse to a trader who most likely turned the poor beast into dog food, was enough to equip me in reasonable fashion. From the many armourers and shops in the high street I bought a sallet, padded jack, plackart, gauntlets and greaves, so I was fit to serve in a company of men-at-arms. I had weapons enough already, and was able to afford a rouncy, a tough little chestnut gelding I named Odo, after the old Germanic word for riches or fortune. With luck, and the grace of God, he would carry me to the glory I sought.

I kept a little money to pay for food and my passage across the Channel. It was still midday by the time I had bought all my gear, and there seemed little point in searching for an inn to spend the night. Every moment on English soil increased the risk of capture.

With my new horse in tow, I fought my way through the bustle and stench of the narrow streets near the castle, until I found my way to the docks. There I saw Sir Thomas Carew's men boarding ferries to take them out to the troopships in the harbour, and wondered if I dared ask to join his company.

Natural caution warned me not to chance it. There was a gibbet set up in the middle of the high street, and the sight of the corpse - some pickpocket or other petty criminal, no doubt - slowly rotting inside the cage that hung from the cross-beam reminded me of my father's fate. My fate also, if I failed to step carefully.

In the end I found the captain of a fishing vessel willing to take some extra cargo on board in exchange for the last of my silver. He was a Cornishman, his accent almost incomprehensible to my ears, and like as not smuggling goods back and forth across the Channel.

"Stay above deck, even in bad weather," he warned me amiably, "and don't go prodding any loose timbers. Otherwise we'll heave you, horse and armour and all, into the deep. Got that, lad?"

By now I was used to the company of ruffians, and

obediently stayed on deck, though my horse proved skittish and had to be put in a stall below. The boat had a wide stern, with enough room in the fat-bottomed hull to store more than a few barrels of fish.

I wasn't the only soldier aboard. There were more troops in Southampton than the royal ships could bear, so other boats were pressed into service. My Cornish fisherman reluctantly agreed to take a troop of Lancashire archers. Their captain, Sir James Harrington, awaited them in Normandy. He in turn was under the command of the King's brother, the Duke of Gloucester.

All this I learned from the archers themselves. They were young and raw, nothing like the veterans I saw on the road outside Southampton, and eager to get stuck into the French. Like me, they were infected with the stupidity of youth, and thought of war as a great game, in which any man with a bit of courage could earn fame and fortune.

"Our duke has already led one raid," one of them told me excitedly, his beardless face flushed with enthusiasm and too much ale, "the French ran like rabbits before his banners. Soon the whole of Normandy will be in our grasp!"

"God knows," he answered carelessly when I asked him about Gloucester's objectives. "All I know is that we shall kill Frenchmen, and take their land for our own."

"It is ours by right," added another young bowman, "we once owned the whole of their country, not just Normandy. They are a race of thieves. God wants us to punish them."

Thanks to my noble education, my history was rather better than theirs, yet I couldn't quibble with the sentiment. The

Normans under William the Bastard stole the whole of England from its rightful owners, centuries ago. It seemed only fair that Englishmen should return the favour. An eye for an eye, as it says in holy writ.

We enjoyed a smooth passage across the Channel, the sun bright in a cloudless sky. My spirits rose as the English coastline receded behind us, and one of the archers played a lilting North Country tune on his pipe.

There were plenty of other ships at sea, cogs and galleys and merchant vessels, all heading in the same direction. The royal arms of England flew from their masts, and good-natured shouts and snatches of song drifted towards us over the crystal waters.

All was set fair for Normandy.

11.

"John Page," said the clerk, "esquire of Sussex. A man with no lord, no companions, no coat of arms...nothing, in fact, to prove or disprove his very existence."

"I'm here," I replied, "I stand before you. Isn't that enough?"

He smiled thinly, looked me up and down, and tugged thoughtfully at his lower lip.

The clerk looked ill, his skin like yellowed parchment, cheeks fallen in, eyes sunken and listless. Some illness had ravaged him and left a hollow, used-up ghost of a man.

"I don't suppose there's any chance of getting the truth out of you," he said with a sigh, "God knows you won't be the first man to run away to war for more pressing reasons than a desire to serve his country. You can use that sword, I take it?"

He nodded at the sword at my hip. We stood outside a white tent among a vast, sprawling forest of tents and pavilions near Touques, a large supply port on the northern coast of Normandy.

The King had landed his army here, unopposed by the French, and immediately set about securing his position. A second army of diggers and engineers laboured like ants to surround our camp with defensive ditches, watchtowers and a wall of stakes. Henry had also sent out raiding parties to probe the defences of Normandy and seize minor towns and castles.

"I can use it well enough," I said, patting the hilt, "I was raised as a knight's son in Sussex, and trained in the knightly arts."

The clerk raised an eyebrow at me. More was required.

"I'm bastard-born," I added shortly. "Hence I carry no device."

A light of understanding, even sympathy, dawned in the other man's eyes. "We live in a sad world," he remarked, "none of us can help how we came into it. To be judged on one's birth is a great injustice, or so I have always thought. When Adam delved and Eve span, as John Ball had it, who was then the gentleman?"

It seemed this little clerk was something of a rebel, as well as a philosopher. That sort of language would get him into trouble, if any of the nobles heard it. The revolt of the English commons, under the leadership of Wat Tyler and the rogue preacher John Ball, was still within living memory.

"Our company suffered some losses," he went on, "in the

attack on Honfleur. Stubborn place. So far it's the only town the French have managed to hold against us."

He squinted at me. "Good men are scarce to find. I doubt you're a particularly good man, John Page, but you have the look of a killer about you. That's good enough."

He scribbled down my name on the muster roll, a long stretch of parchment, already covered with a list of several hundred names. Mine was written near the bottom.

"There," he said happily, and blew on the ink until it was dry, "a moment ago you were merely John Page, bastard-born son of Sussex. Now you are John Page, bastard-born son of Sussex, and a man-at-arms contracted to serve under the command of Sir James Harrington for the length of the war."

As a man-at-arms in Harrington's service, I was given a jupon bearing his arms. These were Argent, as a herald might say, on a bend Sable three lozenges of the first, each charged with a saltire Gules. In plain English, they displayed a diagonal black band against a white field. The band was decorated with three white squares, painted with the red cross of Saint George.

I hated wearing another man's device, but the Daubeney arms were denied to me as a bastard, and I had not yet earned the right to wear my own. When the time came, I would wear the red wolf's head on my jupon.

Harrington's company was stationed near the King's own pavilion in the middle of the encampment, a sign of the trust and favour Henry placed in him. Sir James was a knight of Lancashire, and the Harringtons had been loyal supporters of the House of Lancaster for generations. As the son of a usurper, Henry wisely favoured those with a long history of service to his family.

At first Sir James' retainers treated me with suspicion. They were all Lancashire men, and wary of outsiders. I was careful to keep my mouth shut, speak only when spoken to, and try to cultivate an air of brooding mystery. The tattered scarf I insisted on wearing - a strange affectation for a common soldier, if not a knight - only added to their confusion.

Fortunately, they were also practical men, as northerners tend to be, and could see I was well-equipped for the campaign. As a rule, volunteers who turn up with their own horse and armour are always welcome, so long as they prove competent and don't hog the rations.

I spent my first evening in Harrington's company wrapped in silence, sat alone by the fire and listening to the others talk. Thanks to my time with the archers, I had grown reasonably used to their accents, and could understand much of what was said.

Most of the talk was on warlike matters, though a few maudlin souls insisted on whining of the homes and families they had left behind. I ignored the latter and listened carefully to the former.

"Easy pickings so far," remarked one man, a cold-eyed brute with skin like cold porridge, "the King knew his business when he chose this bit of coast for a landing. The Normans have no stomach for a fight."

One of his mates, who had a ginger beard pronged like a fork, nodded complacently. "Aye. None of our sorties have met with much resistance so far. That place - Doe veal, is it called? Curse these French names, I can't roll my tongue around them -

surrendered to Warwick yesterday."

"Deauville," another man corrected him, "I've got a mate in Warwick's company. He was there at the taking of the castle, and told me all about it. The Normans abandoned the place before our soldiers arrived, leaving a pack of women and children behind."

A few of the men leaned forward. One or two moistened their lips. "What happened when our lads stormed the castle?" asked cold-eyes, "did they get their hands on those French sluts, the lucky swines?"

The third speaker grinned. "No. Our captains remembered their orders. God bless King Harry, but he permits no rape or plunder. The women and their brats were allowed to go unmolested, with as much as they could carry."

That was worth hearing. I knew the king was said to be more than conventionally pious, though not to the extent of restraining his soldiers. Later I learned that he hanged men on the Agincourt campaign for robbing French churches, and once personally cut off the hand of an archer who notched an arrow without waiting for the order. He could be the hardest of men, could Harry, though many choose to forget it these days.

The soldiers round the fire looked uneasy, and exchanged dark looks. None spoke a word of criticism against the king's policy. Some, I think, because they worshipped him too much, while others were afraid to say anything that might be construed as treason.

I have served in many armies. This was the only one where a soldier's right to pillage the countryside, and abuse the enemy as he pleased, was totally denied him. Our warrior-king's discipline was iron, and I can remember very few instances of anyone being so foolish as to break his laws. Those who did got short shrift.

The next morning I saw the king himself for the first time. I was seated on the grass beside the remains of the fire, wolfing my breakfast porridge and bacon, when I saw a tall, striking figure emerge from the royal pavilion.

He was deep in conversation with a man I assumed to be my new captain, since he wore the Harrington arms on his jupon. Sir James Harrington was about forty, a veteran to his boots, burly and hard of face, seamed with lines and old scars.

Henry was a clear foot taller. Your Sacred Majesty may have seen the portraits of him: lean and somewhat ascetic, clean-shaven, with a long nose, full red lips, hooded brown eyes and a heavy jaw. His body was slim and athletic, of the sort that carries no fat. He moved with an almost feline grace, and radiated the presence of a king. Heads turned as soon as he strode out of the pavilion. Every man, from lord to esquire to the humblest archer, bowed before him.

In the silence, I overheard snatches of conversation between the King and Sir James.

"...not concerned with Honfleur, James," said Henry, "it is a fly-speck, and can wait until Caen has fallen."

"Agreed?" he added sharply when Sir James opened his mouth. The older man choked back his words, mustered a smile, and gave a brief nod of assent. The King was clearly in no mood for a debate.

Henry turned his face towards me. The breath caught in my throat when I saw the near-perfect symmetry of his features carried a blemish. There was a long white scar on his right cheek, an inch or so below the eyeball. This was the mark of the arrow that hit him in the face at Shrewsbury fight, where Hotspur died and Henry's father, old Bolingbroke, had the victory.

The scar gave him an almost sinister aspect. For a second his hazel eyes bored into mine, until I remembered to bow my head and drop to one knee.

"We march on Caen," Henry said as I grovelled in the dirt, "it must fall, and quickly, else the French think we dither."

He stalked away, followed by Sir James, six bodyguards and a rabble of priests. Henry always liked to have clergymen about him, even in the midst of a war.

I was revolted by the priests. They were hateful to me now, these shaven hypocrites, mumbling their Latin nonsense and dripping poison into the King's ear.

The House of Lancaster was enslaved to the church. Bolingbroke had agreed to allow the persecution and burning of Lollards, and Henry himself was fiercely pious. I recall one grim story of how, when he was Prince of Wales, he tried to persuade one John Badby, a tailor, to recant his so-called heresy, after the poor man had been condemned by the Archbishop of Canterbury to burn alive inside a barrel.

The prince was naturally inclined to be merciful. He even offered Badby a pension if he would recant, but the tailor, already singed from the flames, refused.

"Then you must burn," said Henry, "for the good of your soul."

Thus the dreadful sentence of execution was carried out.

The prince is said to have watched until the end, and shown not a hint of emotion as Badby cooked inside his barrel.

Left to himself, Henry might have been the best man to have ever sat on Saint Edward's chair and rule over the English. The pious teachings of holy mother church twisted him, I think, and corrupted the gentler side of his nature.

Even in the camp at Touques, mere days after I had joined the English army, seeds of doubt were planted in my mind. Could I, in all conscience, be content to serve under the banner of a man who roasted his subjects alive for daring to stand against the tyranny of the church?

The tailor in his barrel wasn't Henry's only victim. Some months after I arrived in Normandy, a rebel knight named Sir John Oldcastle was also hanged and burned in Smithfield, gallows and all. Oldcastle was admittedly a traitor who plotted the King's death, but the manner of his execution proved how in thrall to the priests Henry was.

For the time being I suppressed my doubts, and played the faithful soldier. In the middle of August, some two weeks after my escape from England, the army embarked to sail down the coast towards Caen.

Next to Rouen, the capital of the duchy, Caen was the largest and most important town in Normandy. It had suffered terribly during the reign of Henry's great-grandfather, King Edward, when the English stormed the place in a single day, slaughtering thousands of innocents and destroying much of the merchant's quarter. Caen had paid a heavy price for its stubborn resistance, and our troops were confident that the memory was still fresh in the minds of the citizens.

"If the Frenchies have any sense, they'll throw open the gates and offer to kiss our backsides," confidently declared Roger Floure, the Lancashire man-at-arms with the forked ginger beard, "like they have everywhere else."

"Except Honfleur," another soldier reminded him, "the buggers are still holding out there."

Roger spat on the grass. "Piss on Honfleur. Our lads must have been swine-drunk when they tried to scale the walls. There's not a Frenchie in this whole God-damned duchy that can stand against us in a fair fight."

There were good reasons for his confidence. Henry's strategy of invading a poorly-defended region of Normandy had paid off, and most of the enemy towns and castles had gone down before us like skittles. The exception was Honfleur, a port town on the southern estuary of the Seine, which had stubbornly resisted our efforts to storm it.

We marched in disciplined order, with the Duke of Clarence, Henry's second brother, in the van. Sir James' mounted men-at-arms, including myself, rode just behind the King's own retinue. Behind us the rest of the army marched in high spirits, buoyed by the run of easy victories.

An army on the move is a grand sight. I recall twisting in the saddle to gaze in admiration at the long lines of horse and foot, knights and men-at-arms in gleaming steel, bright pennons streaming in the breeze. Some of our archers were also mounted, and the bulk of these men, called hobelars, brought up the rear. They served as useful light cavalry, watching out for French outriders and guarding the baggage train that creaked along in the wake of the main force.

Henry had planned the assault on Caen to the last detail. While the bulk of his army marched on Dives-sur-Mer, a small town about halfway between Touques and Caen, he sent men ahead to block the mouth of the River Orne. This cut off the routes from Caen to Bayeux and Vire, while another detachment hastened to the south of the town and barred the roads to Rouen and Paris.

Caen was left isolated and surrounded on three sides. Before advancing to lay siege, Henry sent an advance guard of a thousand horsemen to work their way around the north of the town and block the road to the west.

His brother Clarence volunteered to lead them. Henry accepted, and prudently ordered Sir James Harrington to take a few men to accompany his brother. In other words, to ensure he did nothing rash.

This Clarence was every bit as brave as the King, but headstrong, over-ambitious, and thirsting for glory. He had missed Agincourt, thanks to being stricken with dysentery at Harfleur. The young duke's vain desire to outdo his elder sibling, and win an even greater battlefield victory over the French, was the great ambition of his life.

I was among the two hundred men-at-arms Sir James took to follow Clarence. We clattered down the highway towards the outskirts of Caen, a thousand men four abreast, pennons flying, and swung north-west to cross the Orne where our men had seized the crossing.

Plumes of black smoke became visible on the horizon as we neared the town. Clarence called a halt at the ford so he could talk to our sentries, and word swiftly passed down the line that the French had fired the suburbs outside the town.

"Clever," remarked the man to my left, "we won't be able to use the buildings as cover now. The French commander knows his business."

"Do we know who he is?" I asked. The men around me hesitated before replying - they were still leery of the outsider - before Roger Flour grudgingly answered.

"The Sieur de Montenay," he said, "some high-nose or other. Supposed to be a good soldier, even if he is French. God knows how many men he has inside the town. They'll be holed up in there like rats."

The oldest quarter of Caen lay to the north, and was guarded by a square white donjon on a hill, surrounded by a moat and stone fortifications. With typical recklessness, Clarence led us far too close to the outer ramparts, almost within bow-shot of the defenders.

If the duke hoped the garrison might sally out and give him a chance of glory, he was to be disappointed. They confined themselves to a few hopeful cannon-shots. I cringed as the missile streaked overhead (I had never been under fire before) and a few of our horses shied, but the aim of the French gunners was hopelessly off.

We worked our way around the northern part of the town, until the peaked towers of a large monastery came in view to the south-west. This was the Abbaye de Saint-Étienne. It lay just west of Caen, outside the walls, and was almost as impressive a building as the castle.

Clarence rode at a furious pace, and our formation had broken up to avoid the salvo of gunfire. Hence I was near the front, just a few paces back from the duke's standard bearer, when a monk galloped into view.

For a churchman, he rode uncommon well, his long black robes (he was a Benedictine) hitched up above the knee as he bent low over his horse's head, flailing the beast into greater efforts with his sandaled feet.

He was riding towards us from the monastery with a pack of French devils at his heels. The late afternoon sun glinted off their helms and spears as they rapidly gained on the fugitive.

I could have sworn that Clarence sobbed for joy. Without waiting to give orders, he unlooped the black iron mace from his saddle-bow and charged straight at the French, as though he was some lone knight-errant instead of a senior commander with a thousand men at his back.

Youth is a time of great folly. Instead of hanging back and awaiting the outcome, I clapped in my spurs and galloped after the duke. His household knights did the same, and a roar of sheer exhilaration burst from our throats as we bore down on the enemy.

My rouncy delighted in being unleashed, and the ground seemed to fall away beneath his hoofs. It was though we flew, man and beast together. The thunder of the horsemen around me rose like a storm in my head, mingled with the pounding of my blood. Some bellowed 'Saint George! God for Saint George!" while others made a strange droning noise in the back of their throats - animal sounds, fuelled by a savage desire to kill, to rend the enemy limb from limb.

The French saw the tide of armour and horseflesh rumbling towards them, and turned away to avoid the clash. I can't blame them for running away. They had no hope. Clarence and his knights were all clothed in steel and mounted on superb destriers, while the French were mere light horse. We would have ridden straight over them, and hundreds more of our comrades galloped in support.

Clarence swore in frustration as the French veered away and fled back to the safety of the monastery walls. They were too far to catch, but the monk still rode towards us.

"Someone ride on and meet that fool," shouted Clarence, "before his horse founders or he breaks his neck."

Seeking to impress, I started forward, along with a couple of the duke's knights. My light armour gave me an advantage in a race, and Odo easily outstripped their destriers over a short distance.

"Mon ami! Mon ami!" the monk hollered as I drew closer to him, letting go of the reins to wave frantically with both hands.

That was almost his undoing. His horse gave a sudden jerk, flung back her head, and a gobbet of slobber hit the monk full in the face. He screamed as though it was boiling oil and toppled sideways out of the saddle.

Somehow he managed to cling on, his long fingers buried in the horse's mane, until I rode up next to him and seized the hood of his cassock.

He switched his claw-like grip to my neck, burbling *"Mon camarade! Vous m'avez sauvé!"* over and again, while I tried to get his skittish horse under control.

The Benedictine was surprisingly strong, and stank of sweat and terror. His horse nearly bolted away from me, and would have done so had one of Clarence's knights not ridden up and caught her bridle.

My French was passable, though I hadn't used it since Father Stephen, the stern old chaplain employed by my mother as a tutor, forced me to construe verbs in the schoolroom at Kingshook until my brain rattled.

"Be calm," I said to him in his own language, "no harm will come to you."

He carried on gibbering, and clinging to my neck with his pale, moist hands until Clarence and Sir James arrived.

"Well?" the duke demanded, "why did this rascal fly from his own countrymen?"

"I can't get any sense out of him, my lord," I replied. Clarence made an impatient noise, trotted up to the monk and slapped him across the face.

Clarence wore steel gauntlets, and the blow almost knocked his victim into the dirt.

"Mercy!" whined the Benedictine, clutching his bruised jaw, "mercy, milord! I am your friend!"

"And I am a duke, you little turd," snarled Clarence, "you will address me as Your Grace, or lose your tongue."

The monk babbled apologies, until I felt quite sick at the sight and sound of him. He possessed not a flicker of pride, the snivelling wretch, and my opinion of churchmen plummeted even further.

It was left to Sir James to restore some dignity to the scene "How are you a friend to us?" asked the knight in a far gentler tone than Clarence.

The Benedictine swallowed and wiped a dribble of blood

from his lips before pouring out his tale.

"My abbé," he mumbled, "was ordered by the Mayor of Caen to remove all the treasures from our house, and let the mayor's servants take them into the town for safe keeping. This was to prevent your valiant soldiers from, ah, requisitioning them."

Clarence's thin face lost some of its sour look. "The Mayor sounds like a sensible man," he remarked, "and your abbé is an idiot. The treasures are still there, then?"

The Benedictine nodded. He was an ugly, sickly looking creature with bulbous eyes, no chin to speak of and a hooked nose. His severe tonsure made him uglier still.

"The Mayor sent soldiers to take what we would not give," he went on, staring dolefully at Clarence, "so the abbé ordered me to ride out and beg the English for aid. Those villains you saw pursuing me were the Mayor's men."

Clarence and Sir James exchanged glances. "From us?" exclaimed the duke, "your abbé is so concerned with his wealth he chose to turn traitor, and ask for help from his country's enemies?"

"Ah, milor-Your Grace" the monk stammered, "Caen is doomed. Everyone knows it, though the Sieur de Montenay has threatened to hang anyone who openly talks of surrender. Your King Henry is Alexander reborn, and we will get no relief from Rouen or Paris."

"Your King is also known to be a pious man," he went on, "most devout and reverent towards the church. It is well known he allows no looting or destruction of religious houses. My abbé hoped..."

103

Clarence finished the sentence for him. "Your abbé hoped His Majesty would look kindly on your monastery," he said wearily, "and allow your plate and gold ornaments to remain where they are."

He gave an acid smile. "My pious brother. How many fortunes will not be made in France, thanks to his scruples?"

Only a man of his status and royal blood could criticise the king without fear of reprisal. While the rest of us stayed quiet, he looked thoughtfully at the distant bulk of the monastery.

"So much for French valour," he murmured, "the rats are fleeing back to their nest."

I turned to look, and saw two score horsemen emerge from the gate of the outer wall. They were the hobelars we chased earlier, along with a few comrades. As we watched, they rode hastily back towards the gatehouse at the northern wall of the town, occasionally glancing over their shoulders to check for pursuit.

Clarence frowned at the monk. "How many soldiers did the Mayor send?" he asked.

"That was all, milord," the other replied.

Sir James moved forward. "The monastery can be fortified," he said, ever the practical fighting man, "and used as a headquarters. It's strong enough. A few score men in there, well supplied and equipped, could hold out against a thousand. We could also mount a few light cannon on the roof. There is a clear view to the town."

This was true enough. The monastery was well placed to control the road east of Caen, and there were no French troops guarding it.

Clarence agreed, and sent Sir James with a hundred men to seize and garrison the place, while he returned to our main camp east of the town.

"You," said Sir James, crooking his finger at me, "I don't know your face, though you wear my arms. Name?"

"John Page, my lord," I replied with a respectful duck of the head, "esquire of Kingshook in Sussex. I but recently joined your company."

He looked me up and down without much interest. To him I was just another soldier, one of the many thousands he had encountered in his long military career.

"I recall your name on the roll," he said, "one of seven replacements for the losses we suffered at Honfleur. If not for the King keeping me busy, I would have met you before now. You ride well."

"Thank you, my lord," I replied. *I'm even better at shooting the King's deer*, I thought guiltily, *or putting the fear of God into his foresters.*

He jabbed his finger at the Benedictine. "You got to this creature first," he said with a grin, "so you can escort him back to the monastery and inform his abbé of our intentions. Make it clear we have no interest in their gold."

I glanced in dismay at the monk, whose watery pop-eyes gazed back at me with pathetic adoration. He appeared to regard me as his saviour, even though I had only been trying to impress the duke.

"My name is Christopher," he said, placing a hand on his breast, "I owe you my life, sir knight."

I turned Odo's head towards the monastery gates. ""I'm not a knight," I growled, "and we owe each other nothing. Stay behind me and keep your mouth shut."

Thus, with my new and unwanted companion in tow, I joined the troop of horsemen despatched to secure the Abbaye de Saint-Étienne.

12.

Christopher must have sensed that mine was a soul in dire need of salvation. No matter how many times I rebuffed or slighted him, he continued to dote on me with a gentle Christian patience I found irritating almost beyond measure.

His abbé turned out to be a puffed-up toad of a man, concerned only with the fate of his precious vestments and trinkets. The monastery was rich, even by the standards of religious houses, and the glint of burnished gold and silver was everywhere in the vast, shadowy corridor of the nave.

While I explained to the abbé, in my slightly awkward schoolboy French, that we had no intention of robbing him, Sir James set about turning the house of God into a fortress.

This was easy enough. The central building was surrounded by a curtain wall, with a gatehouse and two stout towers, and he posted twenty of his men-at-arms on the battlements. We had no archers, though Clarence had promised to send three hundred hobelars to strengthen the garrison as soon as possible.

The remainder of his command was stationed inside the church. There we waited, listening to the gloomy plainchant of the monks and waiting for the French to attack at any moment.

They didn't come. The Sieur de Montenay was too prudent to waste lives attempting to retake the monastery, and kept all his men behind the walls of Caen.

His preparations for the siege could not be faulted. He had ordered the governors and bailiffs of the town to stuff Caen with provisions, and draw in all the livestock from the surrounding countryside. He managed to scrape together some five thousand troops for the garrison, well in advance of our arrival, and put another two thousand civilians under arms. Caen was also well-stocked with artillery, ballistas and catapults as well as guns.

No-one could accuse de Montenay of neglecting his duty, but his efforts were in vain. Unless the French sent reinforcements, Caen couldn't hope to hold out for long. King Henry had made a careful study of the defences, and in the next few days the jaws of his trap closed about them.

The main body of our army soon arrived before the walls. De Montenay ordered the suburbs to the north and east to be destroyed, which left much of the ground between our camp and the town burned and desolate. This had the unwanted effect of clearing the line of sight for our great guns. Henry had brought an impressive artillery train over from England, and soon Caen was surrounded with serpentines, culverins and bombards.

I was idle inside the monastery, with nothing better to do than listen to Christopher's prattling and watch our army dig in.

"You must confess your sins," he kept telling me, "and be shriven before the day of battle. Else you will suffer the torments of the damned."

Then his already damp eyes would fill with tears, and he would pluck mournfully at my sleeve. "What if, Heaven forfend, some chance blow struck you down? Your soul is fated burn, my friend."

Great Sultan, you may wonder why I didn't punch the greasy little runt. Firstly, he was a monk, and despite my growing contempt for the church some residual ingrained respect for men of the cloth still clung to me. Secondly, he meant no harm. Indeed, he was the first person since the death of my mother to care a whit for me.

Soon the bombardment started. Henry meant to shock Caen into a quick surrender, so he could turn his energies to the rest of the duchy. To that end he pounded the town with every piece of ordnance at his disposal. The storm of gunfire was relentless, and for some three or four days I, along with every other soul cooped up inside the Abbaye de Saint-Étienne, got little sleep.

To make things worse, the frightened monks insisted on keeping up their dreary prayers and plainchant all through the hours of darkness, beseeching Almighty God to have pity on them - only them, you understand, not the poor citizens of Caen who were the real targets of the bombardment.

Sir James might have ordered them to be quiet, but he was a devout man, and found comfort in the sound of their voices lifted in prayer. I recall sitting with my back against one of the mighty pillars in the nave, red-eyed and befuddled through lack of sleep. Sir James and a few of the more pious members of our company knelt before the altar in a row, their heads bent and hands crossed, helmets and swords laid aside on the flagstones.

The fat abbé moved among them, mumbling pompously in Latin and making the sign of the cross over each man, while behind him a pack of monks made the church hideous with their noise. I thought they looked like so many overweight crows in their black robes. The dismal chanting was echoed by the boom of artillery fire as the world outside dissolved in smoke and flame.

Brother Christopher once again demonstrated his knack for sniffing me out, no matter where I tried to hide. "Many of your comrades are being shriven," he said, nodding at the men who knelt before the altar, "the abbé has repeated the pater, the ave and the credo to them. In the name of Christ and His infinite mercy, will you not lay aside your blasphemous pride, and do the same?"

I looked up at him in surprise. There was unusual force in his voice, with none of the begging and wheedling tone that made him so contemptible.

"Very well," I replied, "will you do the honours? I don't relish the thought of that fat toad muttering over me."

Christopher's sallow cheeks flushed, and he wrung his hands. "Certainly," he said, after a nervous glance at his abbé, "if you wish it."

He seemed both confused and flattered at my request. In that moment I pitied him, and the way he crept through his miserable life, despised by all. I had noticed how even his fellow monks shunned his company.

"Come, then," I said briskly, kneeling upright before him and clasping my hands in prayer, "save me from the fire."

The damp heel of his hand trembled as he laid it gently against my brow, and let it rest there for longer than necessary.

Frowning, I looked up and met his eyes. There was a desperate yearning in them, craving and sadness and desolation, and for the first time I understood Brother Christopher's true nature.

Here was the reason he dogged my steps. I realised it, and slowly closed my hand over his.

"Some of us," I whispered, "must live in fear, and hide our true natures from the world. You cannot hide from God."

He tried to clasp my hand in both of his.

"No," I said, pulling away, "that's enough. You must not follow me any longer."

I stood up and walked away.

"You must be shriven!" he moaned.

I carried on walking. It was not in my power or nature to comfort him.

The next day Henry ordered another assault on Caen. He had already tried several against the western defences of the town. All had failed. The French garrison fought with bitter and unexpected courage, and the King was losing patience.

Now it was our turn to be hurled into the fray, though Sir James didn't confirm the order until dawn.

He sent his under-officers to summon the entire company to the inner precinct of the monastery, where we stood in ranks while he trotted up and down before us on his dappled grey charger.

My bowels quaked as he told us what lay ahead in a voice like a trumpet, loud and brazen and piercing.

"The French have stiff necks, lads," he cried, "we've given their walls a proper hammering, but still they refuse to yield the town. His Majesty has decided to teach these traitors a lesson."

To King Henry, the citizens of Caen were guilty of treason against their rightful monarch: he saw himself as the true King of France as well as England, thanks to the blood-claim he inherited from his forebears. It was to pursue his rights as he saw them, rather than the achievement of empty glory, that he invaded French soil.

"For the duration of the siege, the King has decided to repeal his own laws," Sir James boomed, "when Caen falls, as it must, our soldiers are free to pillage the town at will. The French will learn the price of defying their liege lord."

There was some shifting and whispering in the ranks. Sir James waited patiently for it to die down, his harsh features softened into a smile. He had seen plenty of towns given over to the sack in his time, and knew how soldiers relished the opportunity to run wild.

We marched out on foot, with Sir James at our head. Doubtless the monks weren't sorry to see us go, though we had held to our promise and left their wealth and ornaments untouched.

I was in the rear rank, and turned my head to get one final look at the monastery. For a brief second I thought a pale face peered sadly at me from one of the high windows. Then it was gone.

God knows what became of Brother Christopher. I hope he left the brethren, and found some kind of happiness. It seems doubtful. He lacked the strength of will, and was one of the millions of lost souls who prefer to choose security over fulfilment.

Our company tramped over the fields towards the eastern

wall of Caen. The battlements rose before us, grey and gaunt, buttressed by five strong towers. To the south lay the River Odon, which effectively cut the town in half, dividing it between the old quarter and the new, called the Ile Saint Jean.

The halves were joined in the middle by an island, upon which stood a gatehouse that connected the northern and southern ramparts. Our guns had concentrated on the gatehouse, which stood exposed to their fire, and punched ragged holes in the masonry of the upper wall.

Still, the French flag flew bravely from the battlements, and the towers of the eastern wall that enclosed the old quarter. The Earl of Warwick, encamped on the southern bank of the Odon, had spent the best part of two weeks pounding the defences, and the stonework bore the marks of the endless hail of shot his guns had spat at Caen. The French did their best to repair the damage, feverishly propping up the sagging walls with heaps of soil and rubble.

While our artillery wreaked havoc above ground, our sappers dug beneath to undermine the foundations of the defences. The French used an ingenious method to detect the mines: they balanced vases full of water on the walls, and if the water began to ripple, knew our moles were at work directly under them. They dug counter-mines to meet ours, and vicious combats were fought in the stifling heat and darkness under the earth.

We made siege ladders, and a number of wooden towers on rollers. These were three storeys high, with slits in the walls of the lower platform for crossbowmen to shoot through. Meanwhile storming parties waited on the upper levels for the bridge to be unfastened and dropped down onto the battlements.

I quailed at the thought of charging across the narrow plank bridge, high, high above the ground. At the far end a cluster of French pikes would wait for me, with the option of a sheer drop to my left and right.

Thankfully our men were sent to the ladders, which lay ready for us in neat rows on the grass. There was no moat around the wall of the old quarter, only a shallow ditch, hastily dug from the looks of it.

The sun beat down mercilessly as we filed onto the field in disciplined silence. Drums, fifes and trumpets announced the arrival of more English troops, company after company of archers and men-at-arms, marching under the banners of Lord Maltravers, Sir John de Grey, Sir John Cornwall, the Earls of Huntingdon and Salisbury, and others that have slipped my aged memory.

My belly still griped with fear and hunger. We had eaten no breakfast, but that was soon remedied as servants and pot-boys passed among our ranks, ladling out bowls of steaming porridge. There was wine also, half a pint per man, coarse stuff, yet strong and hot enough to make my head spin.

"Drink deep, lads," cried Sir James, "it will stiffen your courage, and dull the pain of French spears."

Henry would not send men into action with empty stomachs. Nor did he want us to be too sober. Even the bravest man appreciates a stiff dose of alcohol before risking his skin.

I tailed on to the end of a ladder. They were some thirty feet long, tall enough to reach the battlements of Caen, and required four men apiece to carry.

A heavy silence rolled across the field. It lasted only seconds before the war-yells rose and the trumpets screeched, but I remember it as a blessed interlude before the storm. I had time to mutter a quick prayer and touch the scarf about my neck for luck.

"Forward," shouted the officers and marshals, "in the name of God, King Harry and Saint George!"

We started to jog forward. A few paces on, and we came within range of the archers and crossbowmen on the walls. There were a few arquebusiers among them, and a hail of arrows and darts flew about our heads, sprinkled with lead bullets.

Our own archers, protected by wooden mantlets and pavises, tried to cover the advance of the men-at-arms. They drew and shot as fast as they were able, trying to shoot the French marksmen off the walls or force them to keep their heads down.

It was my first time in action, real action. I don't remember being frightened. My heart beat so fast it threatened to burst through my chest, and sheer excitement drowned the natural instinct for survival.

My companions quickened their step. Someone screamed behind me, a high-pitched squeal of pain that cut through the massed roar of our troops as they swarmed towards the walls.

I kept my head down against the storm of missiles. My bascinet had no visor, and one stray glance upwards might have proved fatal. My breath came in short gasps as we stumbled over the rough ground. The ladder seemed to get heavier. More shrieks of pain exploded around me. The French had a number of small cannon mounted on the towers, as well as catapults and springalds, and the boom of gunfire added to the chaos.

The man in front of me fell, swatted to the ground by a well-aimed shot from a springald. An iron-tipped bolt the length of a javelin had skewered him, pierced the breast of his padded jack and thrust clean through his spine.

"On!" shouted the sergeant at our head, "just a few paces more, lads!"

We stumbled forward and reached the foot of the wall. The three of us put our shoulders to the ladder and heaved it up against the rough stonework.

"Who's the first man to the top?" cried the sergeant, and gave me a hideous wink. Then his entire head vanished under a torrent of steaming oil poured from above.

His shriek, as the oil seared and melted his flesh, was inhuman. I staggered back in horror, throwing up my gauntleted hands for protection as drops of the stuff splashed my armour.

"Goddam!" I heard a woman's voice yell, *"goddam!"*

Goddam. This was the first time I heard it, the popular French curse for all Englishmen. Foolishly, I looked up and spied a woman in a red shawl on the parapet directly over our heads. She had a mane of greasy black curls, and shook her grimy fist at us in triumph. It was she, and another woman, who had upturned the pannier of oil onto my comrade's head.

"I'll murder those sluts," growled one of my comrades. He drew his falchion, sprang onto the ladder and clambered upwards with furious haste, careless of the stones and arrows that rained down about him.

115

I hesitated. The initial rush of excitement had passed, and I am not ashamed to admit my courage faltered. In front of me, not two yards away, the dying sergeant writhed horribly. His screams had faded away, replaced by pathetic whimpers as he clawed at the mottled ruin of his face.

There was nothing I could do for him, save the mercy of a quick death. I drew the longer of my daggers, knelt beside him and rammed the blade into the side of his neck, then yanked it outwards, splitting his throat.

He gave one last shudder, his eyes bulging, and went still. His was the third death on my account, and the most blameless.

"A Harrington! A Harrington! Saint George!"

Fresh bodies stampeded past me and hurled themselves up the ladder. I crawled out of their path and pressed my back against the masonry of the wall, thinking I might be safe there for a time.

Sir James and his son Richard were nearby, urging on their men. My captain's face was red and swollen with angry blood as he brandished his sword, clearly desperate to carve a few French skulls.

He was a bold man, no doubt of that. Too bold. With a final oath, he ripped his standard from the hands of the young esquire who held it and hurled himself at one of the ladders. His son, just as burly though not quite so rash, tried to drag him back.

"Damn you, boy!" I heard Sir James shout, shoving Richard away with his free hand, "when did you know me to hide in battle? Shall I stand and watch while our fellows are slaughtered?"

The rickety ladder trembled as he clambered up the rungs. Sword in one hand, he used the other to climb, with the pole of the standard balanced across his shoulders.

His example lit fresh fires inside his men, myself included. Renewed cries of "Saint George!" burst around me as I pushed away from the wall and ran to the ladder.

The cries suddenly faded, and something glanced off my helmet. I looked down and saw it was Sir James' sword.

His body followed, toppling backwards off the lower reaches of the ladder into the arms of his son and three men-at-arms. Like me, he had no visor, and a crossbow bolt had impaled his right eye.

Fate chose this moment, as so often in my life, to grant me an opportunity. Sir James' standard dropped from his slackened fingers and fluttered to the ground. By rights his son should have snatched it up, but Richard stood paralysed, his face drained of blood as he stared at his dead father.

Instinct, rather than courage or a vain desire to play the hero, drove me to grab the standard and carry it up the ladder.

Sheer idiocy, considering what I had just witnessed. When I was halfway up, and come to no harm, I risked a glance at the battlements.

The woman in the shawl and her companion had vanished, replaced by a French crossbowman, perhaps the one who had shot Sir James. He was busy fumbling another bolt into the groove, and only saw me when I was almost at the top.

He had no time to reload, and raised his crossbow above his head to use as a club. Two grey-feathered arrows slammed into his chest and neck and pitched him off the walkway.

Cheers sounded below, and my ladder bounced and shuddered under the weight of more bodies.

I scrambled up the last few rungs and heaved myself over the parapet, to find the French in retreat. They quit the walls and fled into the town as our men surged over the walls.

By great good fortune, I was one of the first Englishmen over the wall. I made the most of it, brandishing Sir James' standard and roaring "Saint George! God for King Harry and Saint George!" until my throat was raw.

The defences were overrun, and Caen lay wide open for the sack.

13.

I handed over the standard to Sir James' esquire and made my way down into the streets. The crash of church bells sounded through the town, warning the citizens of the coming storm.

My first thought was to find a place to hide until the worst was over. It sounds ironic, from one who later grew rich in the Italian wars, but at that time I had no interest in robbing defenceless citizens and plundering their houses. Many of our men, from the highest noble to the lowliest archer, went to France for exactly that purpose. I, on the other hand, was more concerned with making my reputation than a fortune.

There was a church to my left, and directly in front of me a wide street that cut through the old quarter. Before I could see any more a rough hand shoved me headlong into a pile of refuse.

"Mind where you stand, soldier!" shouted an English voice. I turned over, groaning and spattered with dirt, just as a file of archers charged past. They were eager as hounds at the kill, eyes aflame with bloodlust, falchions and hatchets ready to hand.

While I picked myself up, they set about breaking into the nearest house. The residents had locked and barred the door on the inside and closed the shutters on the windows. Two of the archers started hacking at the shutters, while their comrades beat and hammered on the door.

"Open up, Frenchies!" they howled, "open up if you value your lives!"

The people inside were dead, whatever they did. The archers would dash the heads of their children against the walls, butcher the menfolk and rape the women before slitting their throats. I have witnessed the same atrocities repeated countless times, all over Christendom and beyond. The wrath of the soldier is a terrible thing, and can only be slaked by blood and gold.

I staggered further up the street in search of refuge. Our troops were swarming through the old quarter now, and met with little resistance as the survivors of the garrison retreated to the castle. The noise was deafening: church bells mixed with the shrieks of women and children, trumpets blasting a host of conflicting orders, the deep-throated roars and curses of our men as they set about their murderous work.

A few of the braver citizens had thrown up a makeshift barricade at a crossroads near the far end of the street. It was a pathetic, ramshackle heap of upturned furniture and bits of rubbish, behind which maybe a score of men and women huddled, urged on by a fat burgher with a heavy silver chain about his neck.

I found a side-alley and watched from the shadows while Sir Richard Harrington led his knights against the barricade. The death of his father had driven the young man into a frenzy, and he paid no heed to the arrows bouncing off his armour as he smashed the fragile heap of timber to bits with his pole-axe. I winced as the burgher stepped forward to block his path and jabbed clumsily at Sir Richard's helm with a rusted spear.

The pole-axe is a difficult weapon, and requires a strong man with years of training to wield it effectively. Sir Richard swung his with furious skill, as though it weighed no more than a reed. He dashed aside the trembling spear and drove the spike on the butt of his weapon into the burgher's foot. Even as the hapless Frenchman opened his mouth to scream, the axe whirled in a lethal arc and swapped off his head.

His body stood upright for a few seconds, blood fountaining from the neatly carved stump of its neck. Sir Richard's men tore aside the remainder of the barrier, bellowing 'Saint George!' as they laid into the citizens. More blood splashed over the cobbles, and the few survivors fled like hares.

Later, when all was over, I managed to piece together the events of the final assault on Caen. While I witnessed the pillage of the old quarter, King Henry led an attack on the gatehouse that linked the defences of the town, while his brother Clarence attempted to storm the western wall. This triple-pronged assault should have been enough to overrun the town, but victory was delayed when word reached Henry of a surprise attack on our camp. He charged back to deal with the threat, only to find it was a false alarm, possibly spread by French agents.

In the midst of all the slaughter and confusion, I wandered down my alleyway to find it opened out on a square, occupied by a cluster of large public buildings. They were enclosed by a high wall, and a battle raged before the gates, where the people inside struggled to resist a mob of archers.

I saw two of the archers attempting to rape a woman, without much success. She had her back against the wall and a bloody dagger in her hand, wet to the hilt with the blood of a third archer, who lay groaning with his hands cupped around his groin. The other two kept their distance, snarling in rage and frustration, too cowed to venture within range of the dagger.

"Goddam!" she kept yelling at them, along with a stream of French obscenities, "Goddam!"

I recognised her as the woman in the red shawl, who had tipped the oil over the head of my luckless sergeant.

"What is the knight's oath?"

The stern voice of Father Stephen, my childhood tutor, drifted down the years. I still remember him, a tall, spare figure in a black gown and hat, always ready to strike me across the knuckles with his birch if I proved slow in my answers.

"To ever be a good knight and true," I would squeak timidly in response.

"Yes?" he snapped, "and the rest? Spit it out, boy, we have been over them enough times!"

"To fear God and maintain his Church...to protect my liege lord in valour and faith...to defend the weak and helpless...to respect and defend the honour of women..."

To respect and defend the honour of women. I wager not a single knight in Henry's army lived up to this particular vow, or any of the others, during the sack of Caen. Only one penniless bastard esquire, inspired more by lingering fears of his old tutor than aught else, stepped forward to redeem the honour of English chivalry.

I was not born to play Sir Galahad, and almost made a mess of it. "That's enough, lads," I shouted, raising my voice to be heard above the sound of battle, "she wants none of you."

Both men turned to stare at me. Their faces were thin, dirty and brutish, with mossy growths of beard clinging to their unwashed necks and chins.

The nearest spat at my feet. "Piss off and find your own meat," he growled, and turned back to his quarry.

"Watch out," cried his mate as I stepped closer, sword ready.

I hesitated. As yet the blade was clean, and I had no desire to dirty it in English blood.

The archers had no such scruples. They came at me like a pair of wild dogs, stabbing with their falchions. I guarded myself as best I could, praying fervently none of our nobles or officers were on hand to witness the brawl.

If not for the Frenchwoman, they might have finished me. Instead of taking the opportunity to bolt, she sprang at the closer of her would-be rapists.

The point of her dagger skewered the artery in the side of his neck. Blood poured from his mouth as he crumpled to his knees.

"Help!" yelped his mate, who was now trapped between me and her, "this English traitor and his whore mean to butcher me!"

Perhaps my first instinct is flight, for I allowed the Frenchwoman to grab my wrist and lead me away at a dead run.

"This way," she gasped in heavily accented English as we darted down an alley.

The half-hearted sounds of pursuit swiftly faded behind us. Swept along by fears of reprisal, I followed her down the street. It ended next to the curtain wall. To our right was a gatehouse, and beyond that the swell of the hillock with the white citadel on its summit. The French flag still flew from one of the turrets, and light glinted off the rows of helmeted heads on the battlements.

I thought she meant to take me out of Caen via some hidden postern gate. Instead she turned left, past a group of archers busily sorting through a heap of goods they had dragged out of a house, and down some steep stone steps to a narrow alley.

It was dark and cool here. The buildings were close-packed, and the bright August sun almost blotted out by the sharply pointed roofs above our heads.

Another flight of steps, flanked by an iron rail, led down to a arched doorway. My companion tried to pull me towards the stair.

"Wait," I snapped, wrenching my hand away, "where are you taking me?"

The Frenchwoman rolled her eyes. She was about thirty,

striking rather than pretty, with a strong-boned, angular face and olive skin that hinted at mongrel blood. The plain blue robe under her shawl was belted tightly at the waist, revealing a slender, muscular figure. She had sheathed her dagger, which I noticed had an ivory hilt.

"Safety," she replied in French, "safety for us both. Will you come, or shall I leave you here to explain matters to your friends?"

My instincts screamed at me not to follow her down the stair. For once I ignored them. There was something beguiling about her, and the lure of adventure and the unknown overrode my natural caution.

She produced a small iron key from a pouch at her belt, twisted it sharply in the well-oiled lock on the black door, and led me inside.

The room beyond was lost in shadow. I pulled the door closed behind me and waited in the cool darkness while she moved about, hunting for candles. There were flagstones under my feet, and the small of cheap tallow, stale wine and unwashed clothes hung heavy in the air.

I listened to the torment of Caen. The occasional boom of gunfire still echoed in the distance - King Henry had turned his cannon on the castle to intimidate the garrison into surrender - all but drowned by the voices of our soldiers as they ran amok in the streets. The people of Caen were paying a heavy price for their resistance, just as their forebears did in King Edward's day.

My companion lit two candles and placed them on the sill under the locked shutters of the single window. The weak light cast the details of the room in silhouette. I made out a single table and three-legged stool, a narrow bed shoved against the far wall, a battered wardrobe, and an iron bucket in the corner. Bits of laundry hung from a rope across the low ceiling, and there was a platter of black bread and gnawed cheese on the table.

"There," she said with a mock curtsey, "my humble home. What do you make of it?"

She had switched to English again, possibly to keep me off-balance. I looked around the room, trying not to clap a hand over my nose against the smell, and cudgelled my wits for something to say.

"Snug," was all I could manage. She gave an unladylike snort and moved past me to turn the key in the lock.

That done, she slipped the key back into its pouch and crossed to the wardrobe. There she knelt and sang softly under her breath as she rummaged inside a drawer.

"*Dieu Merci*," she said happily, producing a dusty bottle, "I knew there was one left."

She also produced a couple of small tin cups. For a moment I thought this extraordinary woman might uncork the bottle with her teeth, but there was an opener on the table.

A stream of wine, red as blood, filled both cups to the brim. "Here," she said, offering me one, "drink. It will take the edge off your fear."

I took the cup and drained it it one swallow. The wine was thin and tart, with a bitter aftertaste. Cheap muck, doubtless bought from some backstreet wine-shop.

"I'm not afraid," I said sullenly, wiping my lips. She gave another crude little snort and refilled her cup.

"Yes you are," she said, winking, "I can see it in your eyes. You tremble like a leaf in the wind. Don't be ashamed. I'm afraid as well. We all are. Even your King, who carries all before him, trembles under the eye of God."

"I am Catherine," she added, "you saved my life earlier, or at any rate my virtue. What remains of it."

She grinned, displaying strong if uneven teeth. There was a gap in the middle of the top row, which added to her strange charm.

"I'm John Page," I replied curtly, "there is no need to thank me. I acted on the spur of the moment."

"I am also God's own fool," I added with a sigh, "why did I run? None of our captains would have blamed me for trying to defend a woman. Even a Frenchwoman."

Catherine set down her cup and watched me for a long moment. Her expression was unreadable. I tensed, half-expecting her to set about me with her dagger. The blade was still wet with the blood of one of her attackers.

She stepped forward and took my hand. *"Je suis une pute,"* she said gently, "and whores have no honour to defend."

Catherine offered me her body as payment for my rescue act. I was too much in need of comfort to refuse. She was attractive enough under the grime, and I hadn't lain with anyone since tumbling one of the kitchen maids at Kingshook. That was back in the spring, though it felt like a lifetime ago.

We made love on her bed while death ruled the town above

us, and afterwards lay naked together, listening to the English army celebrate its victory. The initial wave of slaughter, rape and larceny had ebbed, due in no small part to the vast stores of wine our soldiers found in the cellars of the houses they pillaged, and now the streets rang with drunken merriment.

Catherine walked her long, brown fingers through the hairs on my chest. "Poor fools," she said, "how many will live through the winter, do you suppose?"

"Perhaps a third of our men will die," I replied, "slain by dysentery rather than French blades. Dysentery is the bane of any army."

"The Devil shall take their souls," she said, "for all your people are of the Devil, and forged in his kilns. Your King Harry is of Angevin stock, *non*? Everyone knows the Angevins are descended from a witch named Melusine. She gave Count Fulk of Anjou four children. Two were carried down to Hell when the witch returned to her master. The other two remained on earth, and became the ancestors of the Devil's Brood."

I smiled. My nurse had taught me the same story as a child, though mother disapproved of it. The cruelty and vile temper of the Angevin kings that had ruled England, and their Plantagenet descendants, made it easy to see where the story came from.

"The Devil won't take Harry," I said, "he spends too much time at prayer."

"Half the time on his knees," Catherine murmured, her breath moist against my neck, "the other half on horseback, tormenting my people. Killing our menfolk, levelling our castles, destroying our towns and cities. For what? So he can make himself King of France?"

There was anger in her voice. "When he is done, there will be nothing of France to rule. Just bones and ashes. Will God approve of that, do you think?"

"France is rich," I said, running my hand through her mop of greasy curls, "and huge. Our army could tramp from one end of the country to the other and back again, until their beards reached their ankles, and still only tap a fraction of her wealth."

"Rich?" she exclaimed, *"pardieu!* Am I rich? Are the people of France rich? Open your eyes, John Page!"

I looked around the squalid little garret. It was the kind of rat-hole a common whore might be expected to live in. Even so, part of me was beginning to suspect Catherine was no common woman.

"I am a poor man," I said, deciding to test her, "yet I possess a treasure beyond price."

Her liquid brown eyes widened, and it amused me to see them fill with hunger. "A treasure beyond price? What treasure? Show me."

I leaned over the side of the bed and searched among the pile of discarded clothes and armour. At last I found my purse, and took out my father's ring: the ring would not fit over the steel fingers of my gauntlet, so when I was armed I kept it in the purse for safe keeping.

"Here," I said, holding the ring up to the dim light, "this belonged to my father. He was a great soldier in his time. Captain-General Thomas Page of the Company of Wolves."

Catherine puffed out her cheeks. "Wolves," she sneered,

"France is full of wolves. English, French and those beasts of Burgundy, forever tearing at each other for scraps of land."

The ring briefly held her interest. I got the impression she grew bored easily, and the light in her eyes faded when she realised it was only of personal value.

"So your father was a soldier," she said, turning onto her back, "and you wish to be like him. Which means you will rob and kill all your days, until you are killed yourself in some battle or other, or die of camp fever. Perhaps, if you are lucky, you will live long and grow fat off misery and bloodshed, and end your days as a famous *chevalier* in a castle stolen from its rightful owner."

While she talked, I quietly placed the ring back in its pouch and unsheathed my dagger.

I could move fast in those days. My free hand seized a fistful of her curls, and the edge of my blade pressed against her throat.

"You're right," I hissed, "I am a killer. So are you. Earlier you slew a comrade of mine, though I had to finish him off. You and some other harpy emptied a pannier of hot oil onto his head."

She betrayed no sign of fear. "Yours is not the first blade to be held against my throat," she replied in a conversational tone, "I have lain with many men here. Some were reluctant to pay for my services."

"What of it?"

"Nothing. I ask you merely to consider the life I have led, that's all."

It would have been easy, so very easy, to snuff out her life. What would that make me? I was already a murderer.

Murderer. Horse-thief. Draw-latch. Poacher. Outlaw. All these terms I could bear, yet woman-killer was not one I cared to add to the list.

I slowly released my grip and climbed off the bed. She rubbed her throat, where my blade had left a red weal. A little more pressure, and it would have drawn blood.

She watched in silence as I dressed. Again, I sensed no fear in her, only a kind of detached interest.

"We shall see each other again, John Page," she said when I had tightened the last buckle, "I am sure of it."

I held out my hand. "Give me the key," I ordered, "and stay on the bed until I am gone."

She gave one of her coarse laughs. "*Pardieu!* Do you fear me so much, then, that you will not turn your back on me?"

"I've seen what you can do with a knife."

She rummaged through her clothes, found the key, and threw it at me. I caught it and paused a moment. What would happen if I returned to the army? Would I be punished for desertion, and assaulting fellow Englishmen?

I brushed aside my doubts. It was time I learned to brazen things out, instead of running away from danger like a startled deer.

Without another word I tossed the key back to Catherine and stepped outside.

14.

I had lain inside her garret longer than I thought. The first rays of the morning sun were already breaking over the distant hills, and shone a wan light on the ruin of Caen.

I retraced my steps back to the centre of the town, hoping to find Sir Richard Harrington. He was said to be an honest, even-tempered character, much in the mould of his late father, and would not have forgotten the man who carried his standard onto the walls. With luck, I might end up being fêted as a hero.

My path took me past all the horrors of the sack. Heaps of drunken soldiery, snoring off their excesses, lay strewn about like so many corpses. There were also a fair number of true corpses, citizens who had died trying to defend their property and loved ones.

I picked my way through piles of stolen furniture and furnishings, emptied barrels of ale and broken pots and tankards, soiled and ripped clothing, curtains and tapestries, bits and pieces of jewellery: it seemed as though every shop and house in Caen had been ransacked, and the private possessions of every citizen dragged out and scattered about the streets.

I followed the street leading to the gatehouse that divided the old quarter from the new. The gatehouse had been stormed (by King Henry in person, I later found, at the head of his royal bodyguard) and the Plantagenet arms flew from its turrets.

There were four halberdiers on the gates, the first sober men I had encountered since leaving Catherine. They wore royal livery, and glared at me suspiciously.

"I'm English," I said, tapping the badge on my surcoat, "of Sir Richard Harrington's company."

"Got lost, did you?" remarked one, to the sniggers of his comrades, "your captain is lodged yonder, next to the King, in the street they call Les Jacobins."

His pronunciation was terrible, and I had to ask him to describe the route. I followed his directions and walked down the main street beyond the gatehouse for a short distance, before turning right into a wide avenue dominated by a church .

The avenue was lined by rows of large stone houses with tiled and gabled roofs and half-timbered upper storeys. They belonged to the wealthier of Caen's citizens, and had been requisitioned by King Henry and his nobles. I recognised several of the banners and tabards hanging over the doorways, including the quartered red and white arms of the Earl of Salisbury, the five-leafed golden flower of Sir Robert de Umfraville, and finally, hanging from a pole over the largest of the houses, the lilies and lions of the King of England.

It was a chill morning, and a group of soldiers stood warming themselves over a brazier set up in the middle of the avenue. Otherwise all was quiet. The hour was yet early, and most of the nobles were still abed.

I sauntered over to the soldiers, trying to appear confident. A couple of them wore the Harrington arms, and raised their hands in greeting.

"Page," cried one whom I recognised as Robert Caunfield, a tough, foul-mouthed veteran of the Welsh war, "not dead, then? We thought some Frenchie had stuck his dagger up your bum-hole."

All sentiment, he was. "Blame excess of French wine for

my disappearance," I lied, accepting the drink he offered me from his flask, "I woke with a sore head in some alleyway or other inside the old quarter. God knows how I ended up there."

"Probably after some skirt," Caunfield grunted, "you were lucky not to get your throat cut. More than one of our lads died that way last night."

As I drank, I caught a whiff of burning, and turned my head to see a gauze of smoke hanging over the town centre. A few wisps of charred sheepskin tumbled lazily through the air.

"King Harry ordered all the town records to be piled up in the street and burned," explained Caunfield in response to my questioning look, "the Mayor and the burghers begged him not to, but Harry had that look on his face."

"Like my wife when she catches me raiding the larder," remarked another man, to a ripple of laughter.

"Made a pretty fire, they did," said Caunfield, "all those old ledgers and chests and heaps of parchment. Lit up the night sky. Harry's way of wiping out the past, I suppose."

So it was. Henry punished the citizens of Caen by destroying the evidence of their past. He knew that history is malleable, little more then marks on parchment, and aimed to wipe out the history of Caen as a French town. It was English now, part of the reborn Plantagenet empire.

There was something else in the air, a foul slaughterhouse reek that made my eyes water.

"What in God's name is that?" I demanded, clapping a hand over my mouth.

"Dead Frenchies," one of my companions said carelessly,

"all piled up in the town square. Men, women and infants. About two thousand, I reckon. When the fighting was done, King Harry had them herded into the town square and put to the sword."

I stared at him. "Why? Why kill so many innocents? To what end?"

The other man shrugged. "Harry offered terms of surrender. They were rejected. The Frenchies had to be taught a lesson. Now all the other towns in Normandy will think twice before thumbing their noses at us."

He was right. The deliberate, organised slaughter of two thousand citizens at Caen, regardless of age or sex, was intended to act as both punishment and warning. Henry's heralds had issued a summons to surrender before the final assault, and the citizens had chosen to fight rather than submit. They could have expected no mercy, and received none.

These are easy words to write. Decades of soldiering have hardened me, and I have seen enough atrocities to know how commonplace they are in war. At the time, I was still a raw youth, and the massacre of Caen shook me.

I had heard rumours of King Henry's cruelty, such as his cold-blooded slaughter of French prisoners at Agincourt, but now the stench of dead children confirmed it.

"Harry has an iron stomach for such work," said Caunfield, "we were up to our knees in blood, and I thought the killing would never end, until at last he gave the order to stop. They say he stumbled over a headless woman with a live babe suckling at the teat. That was enough to bring him to his senses."

My shock and disgust must have been plain, for Caunfield abruptly changed the subject. "Sir Richard will be pleased to know you're alive," he went on, with a sly grin, "he saw you carry his father's standard up the ladder. Everyone did. We were very impressed."

"Quite the hero," said Nicholas Russe, another of Harrington's company, exchanging winks with his fellows. "They'll be singing ballads of you next."

I laughed along with their gentle mockery, though my laughter stemmed more from relief than amusement. It seemed my little exploit had been noticed after all. There was no mention, Christ be thanked, of my brawl with the archers. Or Catherine.

Caunfield jerked his thumb at the nearest house. "Come and have a bit of breakfast," he said, "there's fresh bread, or ought to be. Otherwise I'll take my belt to the cook's arse. The villain speaks no decent English, though he understands blows and kicks well enough."

I followed him inside to the kitchen and tried to quell my suspicions. Caunfield had never exchanged more than a few words with me before. His sudden friendliness disturbed me.

For an hour or so I sat and chewed warm bread and listened to his lies about the feats of arms he had performed in Wales.

"I served at Pilleth, soon after the rebellion broke out," he said, "you've heard of that battle?"

I made the mistake of saying I had not, which inspired him to describe the fight in detail. It seemed that the Welsh rebels thoroughly chased our soldiers up hill and down dale, all except the noble exception of Robert Caunfield, who fought like a lion

135

while his comrades ran for their lives.

He used bits of wheaten bread to show the movements of the armies, with himself as the largest crumb in the middle.

"I fought Glendower hand-to-hand," he boasted, "he was a strong swordsman, but I had the measure of him. I might have ended the rebellion, there and then, if my sword had not broken on his helm."

Caunfield was a poor liar, as well as a bore and a bully, and I started to entertain cynical thoughts about the truth of his performance on the battlefield, or even if he had been there at all. Eventually the sun came to my rescue. Fresh golden daylight streamed through the bars of the latticed window and recalled him to his duty.

"Let us find Sir Richard," he said, rising from the table, "he mourns his father, yet doesn't neglect business. Come."

I followed him down the street to a small chapel with a tall spire. Two guardsmen in Harrington livery stood by the entrance. They exchanged grave nods with Caunfield as we crossed the threshold.

The nave was cool and dark, dappled by coloured light filtered through the tinted panes of the stained-glass window behind the altar.

Beside the altar was a wooden bier, surrounded by a golden blaze. The blaze came from the tall candelabras placed at each corner of the bier, upon which rested the body of Sir James Harrington. He still wore the armour he had died in, washed clean of blood and dirt.

Sir James' visor was open, and the crossbow bolt that slew him had been removed. His eyeball went with it, and the empty socket stared blankly up at the vaulted roof of the chapel.

A white-robed confessor stood next to the bier. His head was bowed, and he muttered low prayers. Otherwise the chapel was empty, though I fancied I caught an unusual odour: not of decay, but something fresh, like the smell of new hay or spring flowers.

They say that when Christian saints die, the chambers they die in are filled with such an odour. Sir James Harrington was no saint, but a good knight and loyal servant to the House of Lancaster. Perhaps my mind was affected by the holy stillness of the church, and caused me to imagine the smell.

Caunfield beckoned me to follow him through a door inside a partition to the left of the nave. Inside was a little closed-off chamber, with a gilt crucifix hanging on the wall.

We found Sir Richard Harrington alone at prayer. He knelt in full armour on the bare stone, hands clasped, eyes fixed on the crucifix.

"Your pardon, my lord," said Caunfield, "but you wished to be informed the moment John Page was found, dead or alive."

Sir Richard stood up to face us. His broad, homely features were ghastly pale, and his eyes bloodshot from tears and lack of sleep.

"I did," he said shortly, "thank you, Robert. Duty comes before grief."

He wiped his eyes with the back of his gauntlet, and blinked wearily at me. "I thought you were dead, Page," he said, "lost in the chaos of the sack. God saw fit to preserve you."

"He preserved me, too, to atone for my humiliation," he added before I could speak, "when my father's standard fell from his hands, it was not I who heeded the call of honour, and carried it into the fray. No, I stood there like a stuffed dummy, while a mere esquire did my duty for me."

He prodded me in the chest with his steel finger. "You were the first man up the ladders, Page. The troops saw you wave my standard from the battlements. It gave them fresh heart, and ripped the guts out of the French. If not for you, the assault on the eastern wall might have failed."

I knew none of this. As I have said, my decision to snatch up the fallen banner and carry it up the ladder was born of pure instinct. That single act of unthinking courage - or madness - gave birth to a reputation I scarcely deserved.

"Don't think me envious," said Sir Richard, "for envy is a sin, and unworthy of a belted knight. No, I would gladly praise and reward you for the deed."

His face clouded, and I braced myself for the worst. Had word of my crimes in England drifted across the Channel? I cursed my folly in not assuming a false name when I joined the army. John Page, bastard esquire of Kingshook, must have been on the lips of every sheriff and bailiff from Steventon to the Cinque Ports.

My fears proved groundless. "The tale of your exploit spread quickly, as such tales so," Sir Richard went on, "and reached the ears of the Duke of Clarence. His Grace wishes to see you."

The rest of that day was like a glorious dream. I believe I floated in the wake of Sir Richard as he took me to the duke's lodgings, which were suitably magnificent. Clarence always stood on his prestige, and held court inside the largest of the grand public buildings inside the Ile Saint Jean.

Sir Richard took six men-at-arms, including Caunfield, and we shouldered our way through a large square crowded with townsfolk and soldiers. The wealthy burghers of Caen had largely avoided the horrors of the previous night, since they were rich enough to hide behind stout walls and hired guards. Now they had emerged, like so many greedy parasites, to feed off their new rulers.

The crowds were thickest around the tall iron doors of Clarence's house. Here a score of archers stood guard, and threatened to beat any who came too near with their staves.

The archers let us through into a large hall filled to bursting with people. My eyes watered at the blizzard of coat-armour. At first I thought every Englishman fit to bear arms was packed inside, though there can't have been more than twenty or thirty, including servants and esquires.

These were the men of Clarence's retinue, still rolling drunk from the night's celebrations. The hall was lit on one side by four arched and mullioned windows. Opposite was a huge fireplace, inside which the best part of a tree burned merrily. Braces of fat capons roasted on a number of spits laid over the fire, as well as an entire hog. Servants in Plantagenet livery moved among the hungry throng at the tables, doling out slabs of charred meat balanced on flat knives.

On the further side of the hall was a door guarded by four halberdiers. Sir Richard pushed his way through the diners, exchanging offhand jests with those he knew, and spoke quietly to one of the guards. The guard nodded, vanished through the door, and re-appeared moments later to beckon at us.

"His Grace is still at breakfast," Sir Richard said to me as we filed through, "but happy to receive us. Take care to speak only when spoken to, and don't look him in the eye."

We entered the inner chamber. Though small, it was as splendidly furnished and decorated as the duke's servants could make it. Rich tapestries were draped over the bare white walls, depicting the battles of Joshua and Gideon and the fall of Jericho. The ancient hosts of the Israelites and Midianites were all clad in modern plate and mail, and rode knightly chargers, an artistic conceit that has always baffled me.

At one side of the room there was a high perch. Two gerfalcons sat upon it, still and silent in their velvet hoods. Beside them stood their keeper, who fed them tidbits of raw chicken from a platter.

The duke sat alone at table. He was dressed plainly, in a dark grey jupon with black sleeves, and spooned meat broth into his mouth from a wooden bowl. A young page stood behind his chair, ready to refill his master's goblet with wine from a silver ewer.

Sir Richard and I bowed, while he put down his spoon and dabbed his mouth with a napkin. This was the first time I had met the duke in private. He looked much like the king, if slightly fleshier, with the prominent nose and heavy jaw characteristic of their family.

He was about thirty, still young enough to carve a name for himself in the annals of history, but old enough to feel the weight of time pressing on his shoulders. Thus far he had achieved little of note, and I believe he and all his brothers lived under the crushing shadow of their father, Henry of Bolingbroke.

By the age of twenty-five, Bolingbroke had already led a successful rebellion against his King, fought on Crusade against the pagans of Lithuania, and won a glittering reputation as one of the best military captains and tournament fighters in Christendom.

King Henry's victory at Agincourt had somewhat lifted the burden from his shoulders. His third brother Humphrey of Gloucester fought at that battle and shared in some of the glory. The youngest - and in my opinion, the best of the whole brood - John of Bedford, had won a sea-battle against the French before the walls of Harfleur.

The list of Clarence's military honours, by sad contrast, was thin to the point of non-existence. His mediocrity and lack of achievement chafed at him, gnawed at him like a sickness, and eventually led him to catastrophe. How we are all dominated by our fathers!

Clarence rubbed his thin hands in a businesslike fashion and nodded amiably at us.

"Sir Richard," he said, "I see from the pallor of your skin, and the dimness in your eye, that you have been at vigil all night. Words cannot express the sorrow in my heart for your father. He was the best of knights, and the most loyal of men."

"My thanks, Your Grace," the other man replied heavily, "I have brought the esquire John Page, as Your Grace requested. We thought him lost during the final assault on the town, but he appeared this morning, hale and sound."

Clarence lounged in his chair, one long arm draped over the

back. Like his eldest brother, he had the common touch, and could be charming when he wished.

"Ah, the man who held aloft the standard on the eastern wall," he said with an agreeable smile, "that was a noble feat. You are valiant, Master Page. Valiant men should be honoured. And rewarded."

He pushed back his chair. I remembered not to meet his eye, and bowed my head as he rose gracefully and strode towards me.

"You signed an indenture to serve in the company of Sir James Harrington," he said, "Sir James is dead, and your term of service passes to his heir."

"Sir Richard," he added, turning to my companion, "my brother Humphrey is your commander, is he not?"

"Indeed, Your Grace," came the reply.

"Humphrey shall raise no objection if I poach one of his men-at-arms. I want John Page to serve in my retinue. Give him to me."

I swallowed, and looked from one to the other. Clarence's smooth-shaven features were impassive, the face of a man born to supreme wealth and power, who could gain almost anything if he desired it. His request was typically arrogant and high-handed. God only knew how his brother, the equally proud Humphrey of Gloucester, would react when he heard of it.

Your Majesty may marvel at how I, a free-born Englishman and a Christian, was passed around between masters like some bonded serf. It wasn't my place to object, only obey, and seek to profit.

Sir Richard was not one to deny the duke's wishes. "Take him, Your Grace," he replied, with another elegant bow.

Thus I entered - or rather, was given over to - the service of the Duke of Clarence, and my life thrown onto a new and unexpected course.

15.

The garrison of Caen, holed up inside the citadel and subjected to a relentless artillery barrage, soon surrendered and opened their gates. Now the town was his, Henry could afford to show his merciful side. With carefully calculated generosity, he allowed the common soldiers and their families to march away with honour. They took their goods with them, and two thousand crowns in gold.

Their commanders, including the Sieur de Montenay, were too valuable to set free. These men were sent to captivity in England and held in honourable confinement until their ransoms were paid.

Henry ordered the Plantagenet banner raised over the keep, and with that his conquest of the town was complete. Now he could turn his mind to the rest of Normandy.

Much of the northern half of the duchy was in English hands, and the next few months were spent in capturing one town after another. My new lord, Clarence, was despatched east, to march through the Pays d'Auge. At the same time Gloucester moved west into the Cotentin, and the Earl of Warwick swept through the south. King Henry marched on Falaise, birthplace of his ancestor, William the Bastard. Henry always appreciated the value of symbols, and knew that seizing the Conqueror's birthplace would strike a terrible blow to

Norman morale.

Enemy resistance crumbled in the face of our simultaneous advance. Most of the major towns in Normandy, including Bayeux, Argentan and Alencon, offered terms rather than risk the same fate as Caen. Save for a few pockets of resistance, almost the entire duchy had fallen into our hands before Christmas.

Clarence's division marched east. I vividly remember that march through peaceful countryside, drowsing in the late autumn heat. The farmland is superb in that part of Normandy, and we fed on ripe apples from the orchards, as well as milk and rich cheeses stolen or bought from the local peasants. Clarence was less merciful to the natives than his brother, though he kept his troops on a fairly tight rein.

"It pays to pay," I heard him remark to his officers, "we mean to rule these people, after all, so there is little sense in spoiling the countryside too much. If we destroy the harvests in the fields, the peasants will starve, and the land go to ruin."

The duke took little notice of me during the march. I was little more than a useful piece of meat, to be hurled into a breach or up a scaling ladder, and thus win more glory for English arms - and, by extension, more glory for Clarence. He had spoken to me in a friendly fashion, once, in Caen, but the gulf between us was vast and unbridgeable. Dukes of royal blood do not consort with bastard-born esquires unless strictly necessary.

Only at the town of Louviers, where the citizens had repaired and enlarged the fortifications, was Clarence obliged to lay siege for any length of time. The town held out stubbornly for three weeks, and refused to surrender even after our cannon had blown massive holes in the walls. Bored and irritated by their defiance, Clarence sent in the pick of his men-at-arms to take the place by storm.

I took no part in the assault, thanks to a bout of dysentery caused by gorging on too much rich cheese, over-ripe apples and strong French wine. My view of the final battle was interrupted by frequent dashes to the latrine pits, though I saw enough to realise the French were making a fight of it. They had thrown up barricades behind the shattered walls, and our men were required to clear them out, street by street, in an entire day and night of vicious struggle.

Clarence, who had counted on an easy victory, flew into a rage when he saw our casualties being fetched back to camp on stretchers, or carried by their comrades. When the town was finally taken after a tremendous battle in the marketplace, he ordered two hundred of the leading citizens brought before him.

They were made to appear before the duke in just their nightshirts, with halters around their necks. This was how Clarence's famous ancestor, King Edward, had treated the burghers of Calais. The duke was aware of the legend, and deliberately aped it to remind all present of his noble descent.

The burghers were a pathetic crowd of knock-kneed old men, many with white beards trailing down past their waists, roped together and driven like cattle. It was difficult to believe these ancients had given our soldiers so much trouble. Many bore the scars of battle: one had lost an arm in the fight, and had to be carried on a litter. Delirious through loss of blood, he raved like a madman, beating his chest with his remaining hand and screaming at the top of his lungs.

"Beg," cried the duke, trotting his destrier back and forth in front of the prisoners, "get on your knees and beg for your lives, you traitors, and I may show mercy."

He went red in the face, working himself into a passion. "Yes, traitors, who defied your rightful liege lord and raised arms against his soldiers! By rights I should hang every one of you, and leave you for the crows to pick!"

The burghers could see Clarence was in earnest. They knelt in the dust and wept for their lives, groaning and weeping and imploring him to think of their families and loved ones.

Clarence basked in their terror. He loved to play the stern-faced conqueror, and in his mind probably compared himself to Caesar, scowling at the beaten Gauls after the fall of Alesia.

To do him credit, he shed no more blood at Louviers. The burghers were permitted to ransom themselves - for a hefty sum of fifteen thousand écus, if I remember rightly - and an English garrison was installed in the town.

The armies of winter advanced with frightening speed, and turned the idyllic summer country of Normandy into a frozen hell. We marched west, struggling along roads half-buried under layers of snow and ice, to join the King at Falaise.

Our column was frequently attacked by bands of Norman partisans, like so many Robin Hoods hidden in the white forest. They leaped out to pick us off with their bows and slings, and melted back into the wild before we could give chase. Clarence's knights managed to catch a few, and hanged them from the trees as a warning, but it did little to dissuade their comrades. If anything the attacks grew more savage and persistent, until Clarence was forced to post a strong mounted guard to patrol our flanks on the march.

The partisans reminded me of Robert Stafford and his band of outlaws. I started to wonder sadly if I would ever return to the quiet woods and fields of Sussex. It was unlikely, since naught save a gallows waited for me at home. Many years were to pass before I beheld the time-weathered old house at Kingshook again, and stood quiet vigil beside my mother's tomb.

We found the King's division mired before the walls of Falaise, where the citizens had chosen to follow the example of Caen and Louviers, and reject our demands for surrender. It turned out that many of the soldiers of Caen, whom Henry released after the town fell, found their way to Falaise and stiffened the ranks of the garrison. Thus the King's mercy rebounded on him, and I believe hardened him even further. The French, it was clear, would not be conquered with kindness.

The army spent a miserable Christmas camped outside Falaise. We were at least well-supplied, and suffered none of the evils of starvation and dysentery that had carried off so many of our troops at Harfleur.

I often saw the King, a slender figure in burnished silvery armour adorned with the royal arms, a golden circlet upon his helm, ride out to inspect the defences of Falaise. Secure in God's protection, he was careless of his safety and often ventured within bow-shot of the defenders. The arrows and bullets they aimed at him all fell wide of the mark, which can only have reinforced his belief that the invasion of France was a holy mission.

"My brother sees himself as the agent of Christ," Clarence

remarked one night.

He had invited his favourite knights and men-at-arms, myself included, to dinner. We sat huddled together for warmth, even as the guns roared outside and the canvas of his pavilion creaked and sagged under the ghastly howl of the wind. It was a dire night in late December, the day after the Feast of Saint Stephen, and the snow had been swept away by an entire week of rain and gales.

Clarence took a long swallow of ruby-red wine. He was quite drunk, and the steady flow of wine had loosened his tongue. "The Lord's strong right arm," he murmured, "sent to chastise the perfidious French, who have turned away from God and wallow in the pit of sinfulness."

The duke grinned at us. "He talks like that, you know. Conversation with Henry is like being subjected to an endless sermon. He was always the same. Even when we were children Humphrey used to call him the Little Priest."

His words met with silence. The little group of fawners and flatterers who usually applauded the duke's every word, and laughed uproariously at his feeble jests, were careful not to respond. Any criticism of the King veered dangerously close to treason, and unlike Clarence none of us enjoyed the protection of royal blood.

The duke, who hated silence, barked at his minstrels to play. While they filled the pavilion with a solemn air, I finished off the last of my venison and listened to the rain hammering outside. The King had ordered shelters to be erected over our guns, so they could fire in the wet. I knew his tactics by now, and that the barrage of gunstones would continue until morning. Then the storming parties would go in.

My brief bout of dysentery had passed, and I couldn't plead sickness this time to excuse me from being sent to the breach. What little sleep I got after the meal was haunted by images of unspeakable agony: steel-clad demons thrust dirty blades into my flesh, and laughed as they twisted them in my bowels. Childish nightmares of hellfire, reinforced by the murals I had seen every Sunday on the walls of the little church in Kingshook, mingled with every soldier's terror of death.

I crawled out of my damp tent at dawn, cold and exhausted, to arm and swallow a bite of bread and cheese. My head pounded from too much wine, and my hands shook as they fumbled with the strap of my helm.

For once God took pity on poor soldiers. A cheer rippled through the camp as a flag of truce was raised over the gatehouse of the town. After some shouted negotiations with men on the rampart, Henry permitted a group of envoys to ride out and meet him to discuss terms.

His relentless cannonade had broken the spirit of the citizens. Not so the garrison, which continued to hold out in the castle. Many of those inside were soldiers from Caen, who could not expect to be shown mercy a second time. They held out with desperate valour for another six weeks.

I was no longer at Falaise to witness their final surrender, and the execution of the men of Caen. Henry left a portion of his force to besiege the castle, while the rest marched away to begin the long-planned siege of Rouen.

So far I had experienced some of the trials and hardships of war, but nothing prepared me for Rouen. Twenty-four weeks of siege, one of the worst sieges any Christian ever endured.

That horror lay ahead of me as our victorious army advanced through the grey winter landscape of Normandy in high spirits, led by an all-conquering monarch whose life was already passing into legend.

On we marched. To Rouen, and Hell on earth.

16.

"A more solemn siege was never set,

Since Jerusalem and Troy were got."

These lines appear at the beginning of my one serious attempt at poetry. The poem itself, titled (appropriately enough) The Siege of Rouen, has enjoyed some small fame, and I occasionally hear it quoted even to this day.

Not, I suspect, for its literary qualities. I wrote it during the long months of siege, scribbled on bits of parchment by the light of candles and campfires. "All in rough and not in rhyme," as I admit in the final verse.

Englishmen like to remember the poem because it captures a glorious moment in time, now long past and never to be redeemed. Our hero-king was still alive, our victories were endless, and our enemies, the accursed French, fled from us like whipped dogs. The catastrophe of Agincourt was still fresh in their minds, and even their bravest captains refused to face King Henry in the field. To them he had become an ogre, merciless and unstoppable, a bloody-handed slaughterer intent on wiping out the entire French race.

Look closer, and you will see the poem is no false celebration of glory. I was careful to flatter the king and his nobles - part of the reason I wrote it was to gain their approval - but it doesn't shy away from the evils of that siege.

"There men might see great pity,

Children of two years or three.

Go about to beg for their bread,

Their mothers and fathers were dead.

Under the rain they stood,

And lay crying for food.

And some starved to death,

And others ceased to breathe.

Some crooked in the knees,

And others lean as any trees..."

There. It is mere doggerel, really, though I did my best to capture the misery and suffering of the wretched citizens, turned out of the city by their own people when food ran too short to feed them. Henry would not let them pass through his siege lines, so they were condemned to starve in the ditch below the walls.

I will speak more of that later. Henry's reputation has suffered greatly for his supposed cruelty at Rouen, and I wish to provide an antidote to a few of the more poisonous lies. He was neither the stainless hero that our people make him out to be, nor the cold-hearted monster the French remember him as.

Our army arrived on the eastern fringes of the city near the end of July, some ten months after I slew my cousin and fled Kingshook. By this time the whole of the duchy, save Rouen, was in English hands. We had fought no pitched battles, since the Normans preferred to hide behind strong walls and the Dauphin sent no troops to aid them. He was too busy fighting - or rather, running away from - his hated rival John the Fearless, Duke of Burgundy, to deal with us.

I had thought Southampton and Caen impressive, yet both were mere hamlets compared to the size and grandeur of the ancient capital of Normandy. My first glimpse of the city walls was obscured by clouds of smoke, since the citizens had copied the Sieur de Montenay's strategy at Caen and razed the suburbs outside the walls to deny us supplies.

Gradually, as our vanguard advanced down the highway that led from Rouen to Paris, the smoke started to clear. I counted twelve strong towers, besides those that flanked the city gate. The broad waters of the Seine lay to the south, and the curtain wall stretched away over green fields and pastures to the north.

The cheerful singing of our soldiers died away at the sight of the city's monstrous defences. At the foot of the wall there was a ditch, deep and wide, and stuffed full of caltrops. Every one of the towers was mounted with cannon, small bombards and serpentines and even a few old ribaults, multi-barreled guns mounted on wooden platforms.

There were other engines mounted on the ramparts, ballistas and onagers and trebuchets, and the battlements were crammed with troops. The bright summer sun flashed off their helmets and rows of lances and spear-heads, an endless fence of metal teeth.

I toyed with the ring on my finger, as was my habit in times of worry, and wondered at my father's thoughts when he first beheld the walls of La Charité-sur-Loire.

The capture of La Charité, a walled town on an island in the Loire south of Paris, was the first and perhaps the greatest of my father's victories. He was just a common soldier then, and led several thousand English and Gascon routiers to victory in a single night.

As I looked over the mighty walls of Rouen, rising like a white tide before me, it seemed unlikely I would repeat the feat. I pictured myself being sent forward to scale the walls, through a storm of bullets, arrows and gunstones, boiling pitch, burning straw and hails of rocks, only to die under the crush of bodies in that dreadful ditch.

I should have known the king could not afford to waste the lives of his soldiers. His army had whittled away, thanks to the need for garrisons to hold the towns he had won, and now he had only some seven or eight thousand men left to besiege Rouen.

The French equalled or even outnumbered us. Their garrison was divided among seven captains, including two hell-hounds named Gaunt Jakys and The Bastard of Thian. Both these men were fond of peeling the skins from captured soldiers and hanging their raw, bleeding bodies, still alive, over the walls.

Each French captain had at least a thousand men under his command, though I deliberately exaggerated the figures in my poem:

"And every one of these captains had,

Five thousand men and more at hand..."

The purpose of my exaggeration was to make the enemy appear stronger than they were, and thus celebrate our achievement in defeating them.

Or rather, King Henry's achievement. I wrote the poem
both to win royal favour, and as a way of passing the time.
While the summer months died away into a cold and dank
autumn, we sat outside the walls and did - nothing. Henry
would risk no assaults, and seemed reluctant to turn his guns
against the town.

Many of his soldiers were baffled by this sudden inertia.
"Harry was keen enough to blow holes in Caen and Falaise,"
grunted Robert Caunfield around the supper fire one night,
"why does he tarry now?"

"And Cherbourg," agreed another man-at-arms, who served
in the Duke of Gloucester's retinue, "the walls of Rouen are
bigger and stronger, I grant you, but they wouldn't stand up for
long against our guns. We should batter the whoresons into
surrender."

I was confident enough by now to make my own voice
heard. "The King wants Rouen for himself," I said, "he wants
to rule the duchy from here. If he fires on the city, he will
damage his own property, and have to pay for the repairs."

"True," agreed Caunfield, "and we all know Harry doesn't
like to open his purse-strings. Got that from his father. Old
Bolingbroke was ever tight with money, and short of it too."

There was some truth in all this. The King was reluctant to
damage a city he regarded as his own, and meant to use as the
capital of Normandy. If the defences were seriously damaged,
Rouen might also be vulnerable to a French counter-attack.

There was another consideration. He wanted to test the will
of the French to fight, to defend their own. By sitting outside

Rouen for months on end, doing little to storm the walls or bombard the place into surrender, he dared his enemies to come on and face him in open battle.

The Dauphin, whom I regarded as a weak and helpless creature, surprised us all. As the weeks passed rumours started to pass through the camp that the French were raising a large army to relieve Rouen.

At first I dismissed them as mere gossip. Bored soldiers love to try and frighten each other with tall tales of the enemy, and the dreadful threats that lurk just over the horizon.

Still the rumours persisted. At the end of October, a full year after my flight from England, they could no longer be denied. The Dauphin had raised the *oriflamme* and issued an *arriére-ban* or general muster, summoning all his loyal vassals to hurl the accursed *Goddams* out of Normandy.

Through the whole of that month and into a vile, rain-soaked December we waited for French banners to appear on the skyline. The King ordered his knights and men-at-arms to sleep in their armour, and every day drew his army up in companies with our backs to the city walls. If the French had attacked, they would have found us ready for them, day or night.

Ready in body, perhaps, but not in mind. In spite of all our bravado and boasting, I believe few of us relished the notion of fighting another Agincourt. Even the most devoted of Henry's admirers would have to admit that God smiled on him that day, and might not be so generous twice.

The tension broke when a messenger galloped into camp and was escorted to the royal pavilion. I glimpsed him, bareheaded and sweating from his furious ride, slide from his horse and kneel before the king.

Moments later the Duke of Gloucester, standing immediately to Henry's left, uttered a cry of joy and threw his hat into the air. A babble of voices rose, all at once, and a drum started to pound.

"What did he say?" I shouted, my words drowned in the sudden rush of noise.

Roger Floure, he of the forked beard and utter contempt for all Frenchies, seized me in a bone-crushing hug and slapped me on the back.

"The silly little Dauphin" (he pronounced it Daw-fin) "has lost his nerve!" he bawled into my ear, "marched his army up to Beauvais, and then turned around and marched away again! The spineless turd has run away! No battle! There will be no battle!"

He was wrong in that regard, poor fellow. Inside a few days he would be dead, his skull crushed by a pick-axe, while I choked and gasped for breath in the dark beneath the earth.

17.

The King had won his battle of wills against the Dauphin, but the citizens of Rouen proved harder to break. Inspired or intimidated by their hard-nosed captains, they put up fierce resistance.

Henry did all he could to starve and isolate the city. He set up camps at all the roads that to Rouen, cutting off any hope of relief by land. As at Caen, where we had seized the Abbaye de Saint-Étienne, he ordered Clarence to garrison the abbey at Mont-St-Katherine and mount cannon on the roof. The town of

156

Pont de l'Arche, upstream from Rouen, was taken to prevent the French sending supplies by river. As an extra precaution Henry had chains thrown across the river, barring access to boats.

He deployed bands of Irishmen to patrol the nearest villages and sniff out French partisans. These bloodthirsty savages, armed with darts and javelins and great knives, were free to forage the land as they pleased, and slit the throat of any Frenchman (or woman) they found bearing arms. Their chief was the Earl of Kilmaine, a shaggy-bearded savage who wore furs and skins over his mail, more like the captain of a band of starving routiers than a high-born nobleman.

Kilmaine's wild Irishmen did their work well, and there was no interruption to the vital flow of food and other supplies sent to us from England via Harfleur.

Meanwhile the people of Rouen began to starve. By mid-December the poorer citizens were said to be reduced to eating horseflesh, and then rats, dogs and cats after the horses ran out. Supplies of bread ran dangerously low, and food prices increased so rapidly the poor could not afford to eat, but had to beg or steal to stay alive.

"Meat and drink and other victuals,

In the city began to fail.

The bread was full-nigh gone,

And of flesh, save horse-saddle, they had none..."

I scrawled these lines while sat cross-legged on the frosted ground before my tent. A chaplain had given me some parchment and writing materials in exchange for a few pennies, and I had just eaten a good breakfast of salted bacon and rye bread, washed down with ale brewed in England.

Like many of our men, I was getting fat. We had done little for months on end save dice, drink, eat and argue, with some occasional excitement provided by sorties from the city. The French weren't content to sit on their backsides and starve, and every so often a band of mounted soldiers would erupt out of the gates, to wreak as much havoc as possible before they withdrew.

It was after one such sortie, in which the French slew a number of the Duke of Gloucester's men, that Henry showed a glimpse of impatience. Still reluctant to fire on the city, he ordered teams of workmen and engineers to undermine part of the western wall.

The miners worked under the shelter of timber mantlets, draped with animal hide to guard against them being set alight by fire arrows. My lord Clarence had his camp outside the western wall, and I watched with detached interest as a series of tunnels were gouged out of the earth with pick and shovel.

My detachment didn't last long. No less a knight than Sir John Cornwall, the most famous tourney fighter in England, volunteered to take a band of men-at-arms into the tunnels to guard the miners as they dug.

Their aim was to reach the foundations of the wall. These would be propped with timber struts, which were then set alight, causing the masonry to come crashing down. The French could see the mines being dug under the city, and dug counter-mines to break into our tunnels. Vicious combats were fought in the awful heat and darkness. I didn't envy Cornwall, or the men he chose to take with him.

I should have realised that Clarence would never allow himself to be outdone by a mere knight. As soon as word reached him of Cornwall's intention, he ordered his marshals to pick out a score of men to go down the mines.

The duke would not go himself, of course: princes of the blood royal do not grub about in the dark, brawling with French miners. Instead he appointed one of his veteran knights, Sir Maurice Bruyn, to lead the party.

Bruyn's esquire was quick to find me, curse him. "Master John Page," the lad said with a bow, "my lord Sir Maurice requests that you attend him at once."

"What for, puppy?" I demanded, though I knew the answer already.

He dodged the blow I aimed at his head. "Why, so you might accompany him to the mines. My lord says that he cannot possibly do without such a famous champion as the hero of Caen and the poet of Rouen at his side."

With much reluctance, I belted on my sword and followed the esquire to Sir Maurice's pavilion.

The hero of Caen and the poet of Rouen. This was flattery, in a way. The glory of my little exploit at Caen still lingered, and lines from my poem circulated about the camp. I was keen to recite them, even in the face of jeers and laughter from my comrades. A little mockery is nothing compared to the fruits of popular fame.

I found Sir Maurice outside his pavilion, among a group of men-at-arms. Robert Caunfield was there, and Roger Floure, as well as others I had come to know.

They all looked as sick as I felt, even Sir Maurice, though

he did his best to hide it. He gave me a curt nod, and tightened his mouth in a forced grin.

"Our very own Chaucer has deigned to join us," he cried jovially, "I'm afraid we must ask you to conduct yourself like a soldier for a change, Page, instead of a clerk. Remind me, how many Frenchmen have you killed so far?"

"None, my lord," I replied. I knew the grizzled knight's temper, and that he despised those who allowed him to bully them.

"None," he spat, "and more likely to get killed yourself, until you find some proper gear. The shame of it, to see an esquire in the retinue of the king's own brother, armed with naught save a padded jack and a soup-bowl on his head!"

There was some truth in that. Every man present save myself was covered in steel. I favoured freedom of movement over protection, and still wore the light bascinet and half-armour I had bought in Southampton.

One of my fears was to slip into a waterlogged ditch and drown, dragged under by weight of metal, or to suffocate in the heat of the press, unable to draw in enough breath through the tiny air-holes bored into my helm. In those days I preferred not to wear full armour, thought it cost me a few scars I might have otherwise avoided.

We went on foot to the section of wall being undermined. It was at the north-west of the city, where the moat fed by the Seine ran out. To the north and south were two strongly defended gatehouses, and further south lay the pile of the castle. The silver lilies of France flew from the high towers and ramparts, mocking us with their defiance.

Our workmen had opened three tunnels, spaced some twenty yards apart. They were at a safe distance from the walls, out of range of all save cannon. The French gunners tried their luck, and there was the occasional flash of orange flame on the battlements, followed by the whine of a gunstone as it passed far overhead.

A heap of French ammunition lay next to the mouth of the central tunnel. "These were the closest," explained the overseer who met us, a strongly built peasant in a filthy smock, his face and hands covered in dirt from the mines, "see that ball on the top? It came near to taking my head off."

"Where is Sir John Cornwall?" asked Sir Maurice. I noticed him glance nervously at the nearest tunnel, and a bead of sweat form on his lined brow. He was the bravest of men above ground, but I could almost taste his fear at venturing into that black hole.

"He went underground some time ago, my lord," the overseer replied, "maybe an hour gone. There is hard fighting in the mines. The French are knocking holes in our tunnels faster than we can seal them up, and we haven't even got close to the foundations yet."

We waited in nervous silence while the overseer rounded up his workers. I counted about forty of them, dirty, gaunt-faced men carrying picks and shovels and hammers, their clothes rank with dirt. They paid us no heed and filed by threes into the mouth of the right-hand tunnel.

Sir Maurice led us after them. I lagged close to the rear, and had to duck my head when I passed under the low entrance. The lintel was supported by timber props, cut from the forests near Rouen.

The passage inside sloped downwards, and was gloomily lit by rows of iron lanterns, hung from nails driven into wooden struts that supported the packed earth of the walls.

At first there was little room to move, and a sense of panic infected me as we delved into the bowels of the earth. My chest tightened, and I fancied I heard the echo of voices trapped in the deep.

Much to my relief, the passage started to widen. Ahead, over the steel helms of my comrades, I glimpsed the miners at work in a huge cavern, hacking away at the vertical rock face. The tunnel was some three hundred yards long, by my reckoning, which meant another fifty or sixty yards had to be dug out before they reached the foundations of the outer wall.

Sir Maurice held up his mace as the signal to halt. Our men stood in two rows, with our backs to the walls, while the miners cursed and panted and laboured away at their muscle-tearing task. The heat was intense, and a few of them stripped to the waist, or went naked save for their breech-clouts.

Not so the wretched soldiers, condemned to stand and suffer in our layers of metal and leather, while the sweat rolled down our flesh in waves.

I caught Caunfield's eye. The old boaster had turned ghastly pale, and I was tempted to ask if he wished himself back in the Welsh hills, trading blows with Owen Glendower.

The jest was strangled by the dryness in my throat. I took the flask from my belt and swallowed a long draught of ale.

As I drank, the noises in the dark grew louder. I made out the sound of scraping; the tap-tapping of hammers against solid rock; the distant echo of voices.

My heart skipped a beat. French voices, and not so distant either.

Sir Maurice heard them too. "Beware!" he shouted, "the enemy are near! Form line, form line!"

Even as we tried to shuffle into ranks, a few of the workmen downed tools and ran straight through us, yelling in panic. One of them, a huge oaf with a beard like a spade, knocked me down. We got tangled up together, limbs thrashing, and his naked foot kicked me in the chest.

All around me was noise and chaos and bodies struggling in the hellfire glow of the lanterns. I screamed as the left side of my face burst with pain. Some fool had dropped his sword in the confusion, and the edge of the blade scorched across my cheek.

The pain blossomed and dissolved. The babble of voices melted away. For a brief time I floated in a void, unable to move or see or hear.

My sight was the first to return. Some incredible force had lifted me off the ground and hurled me against a wall. I lay stunned on the floor, my head ringing like the inside of a belfry, my mouth rank with the salt tang of blood.

I blinked away the purple blotches flashing before my eyes. More bodies had poured into the tunnel, and a battle was raging. Men hacked and clawed at each other like wild beasts in the dark. I heard shouts of 'Saint Denis!" and 'Diex Aye!" among the cries for Saint George.

The air was full of dust and blood and foul black smoke, and the uneven floor covered in scattered heaps of earth and shattered rock. I gaped in horror at the massive hole in the far wall, through which French soldiers, men-at-arms and billmen and archers, poured in a ceaseless tide.

You may trust the French to do something unexpected. Despite the risk of collapsing the mine, they had set a charge of gunpowder to blow a hole into our tunnel. Too much powder was used, and the almighty blast ripped through the tunnel like a thunderclap, hurling bodies right and left and almost bringing the roof down on our heads.

Coughing out the blood in my mouth - I had bitten my tongue - I groped for my dagger and looked for the nearest Frenchman to kill. Swords were useless in this kind of close-quarter fighting, with the enemy mere inches from one's face, unless you used the hilt as a club.

A man in a dark blue jupon rose before me. He wore a badge embroidered with the lilies of France on his breast, and was about to drive a spear into the exposed back of one of our workmen.

I was still on my knees, and dived headlong at him, stabbing at his crotch. My aim was off, and the blade merely pinked his thigh as my shoulder crashed against his hip, throwing him to the ground.

He tried to push me away, but I was stronger and heavier, and managed to pin his arms with my knees. My knife flashed down, pierced the soft jelly of his left eye and sank into his brain.

Only then, with my gauntlet soaked in his blood, did I realise how young and thin he was. The pathetic wisp of blonde moustache over his top lip failed to conceal his age. No more than twelve, maybe. I had slain a child.

A gigantic shape loomed before me. Two men-at-arms were smashed aside by a black mace, and a demon stepped forth.

The demon was an enormous French knight, well over six feet tall, his face hidden under a pig-faced bascinet. His costly plate armour was painted black, save for an escutcheon displaying a red griffon with spreading wings inscribed on his breastplate. He wielded a mace in his right hand, and an axe with a half-moon blade in his left. Both dripped with blood and brains.

My limbs froze at the sight of this terrible apparition. He might have slain me, for I was incapable of defending myself, if a couple of brave fools hadn't hurled themselves at him.

One of them was Robert Caunfield. I have called him a vain braggart, and so he was, but none could deny his courage.

Little good it did him. The French knight fought with brutal skill, and his axe took off Caunfield's sword-arm below the elbow. My comrade's shriek of agony almost burst my eardrums. Hot blood gushed from the stump of his arm, even as the Frenchman carved a deep gash into the other fool's belly.

More English soldiers closed around the black knight, screaming for revenge. He effortlessly battered them aside, crushing skulls and cleaving limbs, while triumphant shouts of *'SAINT DENIS!'* echoed down the length of the mine.

Our men started to break. The knight of the red griffon was unstoppable, and the French outnumbered us at least two to one. I was carried along in the flood of bodies streaming back down the passage. Soldiers and workmen shoved and trampled each other to get past, yelling in fear, cursing each other, all their pride and courage melted away.

I tripped over a discarded helm and fell flat on my face. Pain flooded through my ribs as some whoreson ran over me. I tried to crawl towards the mouth of the tunnel, a mere glimmer of light maybe fifty yards ahead of me. The pain was excruciating, and I had to use my knife to drag myself forward, almost weeping at the fire in my side.

A trumpet screeched through the vault. Through a mist of tears, I glimpsed bright colours, silver and blue and gold, and a sword flamed in the darkness. Fresh war-cries tore through my head.

"Saint George! God for England and Saint George!"

I had just enough strength and sense left to roll against the wall. A tall, slender figure in burnished steel leaped past me, the lilies and lions on his surcoat whirling before my eyes.

"The King! The King! Rally to the King!"

I have said that princes of the blood royal do not, as a rule, risk their persons in the mines. Yet here was one who did - King Harry of England, the victor of Agincourt, who ever led from the front, above ground or below it.

Close on his heels were Sir Robert Umfraville, a stone-faced Border knight who had slain more Scots than the plague, and the screeching, hairy ruffian that was the Earl of Kilmaine. Behind them charged a horde of wild Irish knife-men and royal bodyguards in white jupons emblazoned with the red cross of Saint George.

Henry closed with the knight of the griffon, who waddled in pursuit of the English fugitives. While the Irishmen and the royal guard ploughed into the rest of the French, the King and the black knight exchanged an eye-blurring flurry of blows.

From my vantage point, it soon became clear that the Frenchman was outmatched. Despite his weight of steel, Harry moved with the grace of a dancer on a marble floor, elegantly avoiding or turning aside his foe's bloodied axe and mace.

The duel was over in seconds. Henry ducked under a laboured attempt to cut him in half and thrust his dagger under a joint in the black knight's armour, where the right arm met the shoulder.

His blade sank deep into the other man's armpit. Disabled, the knight could only parry desperately with the axe in his left hand. Henry caught the underside of the half-moon blade on his hilt and gave a sudden twist, forcing his foe to drop the axe. For the *coup de grâce*, he rammed the point of his sword into the narrow slit of the knight's visor.

With a final shudder and a groan, the giant warrior slowly keeled over, like a felled tree, and landed with a deafening crash of ironmongery. The French, seeing their talisman slain, uttered a cry of dismay and started to fall back, hotly pursued by our reinforcements.

Shrieks of joy and pain echoed through the mine as the wild Irish slew with gleeful abandon, dragging French soldiers to the ground and stabbing them to death where they lay.

"Curse their eagerness," shouted the King, "sound the recall, in Heaven's name, before the roof comes down!"

Now the immediate danger had passed, I noticed how the ground shuddered. I glanced up, and some dust from the ceiling landed on my face.

The shock of the blast had sent a tremor through the earth.

Coupled with the noise and violence of the fighting, the mine would soon collapse and bury us all under tons of rock.

Gasping at the agony in my side, I used the wall to help me stand. While Henry and his officers bawled at their men to run, I limped towards the entrance, picking my way over fallen bodies, abandoned tools and bits of war-gear.

"Retreat!" the cry echoed and re-echoed behind me. I risked a glance over my shoulder, and saw the Irish being dragged off their prey like hounds from a kill. In their mindless rage, some turned on their officers, even as more dust fell from the ceiling and the lanterns swayed alarmingly.

There were men just inside the entrance to the mine, helping our wounded to get out. One of them, the overseer I met earlier, gave me his brawny shoulder to lean on and half-carried, half-dragged me outside.

He laid me carefully against a heap of rubble, where I sat and coughed the filth out of my lungs. I was drenched in a film of blood and sweat and dirt. My heart rattled like a drum. The pain in my ribs throbbed in time to my heartbeat until I felt dizzy with shock and nausea.

Yet I was fortunate. I had come out of that evil vault alive and reasonably whole, which could not be said for many of my comrades.

The earthly remains of Roger Floure were carried past me on a stretcher, his head a mangled ruin, the broken end of a pick still buried in his scalp. Save for his forked ends of his russet beard, now slick with blood, I would not have recognised him.

Henry was among the last to emerge from the mine. His

fine silver armour was spattered with dirt, and he carried a wounded miner over his shoulder.

"Water," he snapped. His companion, Sir Robert Umfraville, carried none, so I took the leather flask from my belt and offered it to him.

Henry took the flask with a curt nod of thanks, and knelt to put the nozzle to the miner's bruised and swollen lips. The man was insensible, but the water revived him. As he coughed and spluttered, Henry dropped the flask on his lap and straightened up.

"God's teeth," he said, grimacing at the long line of wounded and bedraggled men being helped out of the tunnel, "what folly was this? I swore never to gamble with the lives of my men, and yet I have done just that. Christ forgive me."

"At least the mine has held firm," remarked Sir Robert in his thick border accent, "once the hole is sealed up, work can resume."

Henry wiped a smear of dirt from his scarred cheek. "No," he said firmly, "I was a fool to try and undermine the walls. We have few enough men, without risking their lives in such a perilous venture. The mines shall be filled in."

Sir Maurice Bruyne appeared, supported by two esquires. I had lost sight of him in the fight. Blood trickled between the joints of his leg-armour, and he was clearly sore wounded.

"What cheer, Sir Maurice?" asked the King, "I blame myself for the wounds you earned today. My own physician shall attend to them."

"My thanks, sire," the veteran knight gasped, "though I am already in Your Majesty's debt. But for your timely intervention, we would all have perished."

Henry shrugged that off. "I thought to inspect the mines," he said, "and ended by slaying a French knight. He was a valiant man. I wish I had asked his name."

This was how our nobles - true nobility, high-born lords of ancient stock, not bastard country esquires like myself - spoke of war. It was a game to them, hedged about with the laws of chivalry, in which one politely asked a man's name and lineage before driving a sword into his head.

Sir Maurice turned to me when the King strode off to talk with Kilmaine. "Still alive, then, Page," he said, "I see you took a knock or two. Will you write a few verses of this day's work?"

"Unlikely, my lord," I replied, "fighting in the dark, like so many blind rats, is not for me. I would rather forget it."

He sniffed. "All part of a soldier's duty. Perhaps you are not suited to the military life."

He limped away and left me to chew on his words. Was I really cut out to be a warrior? The savage brawl in the mine, and the violent death of so many comrades, shook my resolve.

For a year I had cheated death. How much longer could I hope to evade his scythe? I needed a respite from war, and to get out of harm's way without sacrificing my reputation.

God took pity on me, for once, and offered a way out.

18.

"Poor men, women and children who had nothing to live on, also priests, women, young women, bourgeois and elderly who were in need and who had nothing else or no other way to help

them."

This was how a French chronicler described the poor citizens of Rouen, driven out of the city by their own people to starve in the ditch between the walls and our siege lines.

The chronicler did not lie. With my own eyes I witnessed them herded out of the gates at spear-point, many hundreds of helpless starving wretches, considered useless mouths by the garrison and thus expelled to live or die, as God or King Henry willed.

This happened near the end of December, the coldest and bleakest part of the year. Our army was slowly throttling the city to death, and Henry was prepared to sit and wait until every living thing inside had expired. He would have Rouen for his own, even if it meant turning the place into a mass grave.

Men become prey to sentiment as they get older. My eyes cloud with tears when I remember the suffering of the people in the ditch. Even now I can hear some dim echo of the babies, wailing as they cried for their mother's milk. I saw them, suckling in vain at the teats of their dead mothers, who had perished of sheer hunger and exhaustion. A few infants were born inside that nightmare pit, and hoisted in baskets over the city walls for baptism, before being sent back down to die.

Stripped of their humanity by the madness of hunger, the starving fed on the dead to keep themselves alive for a few more hours. Women prostituted themselves for a few scraps of food, and rutted with any man who would have them, careless of who watched.

There were plenty of hard cases in our army who pretended to care naught for the suffering of French peasants. Even their hearts must have bled a little at the sight of so much relentless misery. There were also a fair number of decent men, with wives and children back home in England, who could not bear to look upon the horrors being perpetrated in the ditch. More than one of our nobles and captains went down on their knees before the king, and begged him to allow the citizens to pass through our lines, or at least feed them.

I have heard it said that Henry callously refused all such pleas, and sent no aid to the people in the ditch. This story became accepted as truth over the years, and even now his name is a curse in Normandy - not for all the men he slaughtered in battle, or the towns and cities he conquered, but for what passed at Rouen.

The story is a lie. True, Henry would not let the citizens pass, and gave them no official help. I think he saw their expulsion as a deliberate ploy on the part of the French, to force him into showing the weakness of compassion. If he had bowed to the pressure, all would have seen that the would-be conqueror of France was not the man of iron he pretended to be.

Henry was not tricked so easily. He let it be known, through word passed via his officers, that any man who wished to might take food to the citizens in the ditch, without being punished for it. Thus he squared his conscience and rebuffed the efforts of the French to discredit him.

Not that he regarded the suffering of the citizens as his responsibility. "Who put them in the ditch?" he demanded of a French envoy, "not I. It is none of my affair if your people choose to abuse each other."

In my poem I was careful to praise the king's great charity and mercy:

"Henry hath now more compassion,

Than doth the entire French nation,

That God who is full of might,

Grant him grace to win his rights..."

The Siege of Rouen now ran to some fourteen hundred lines, jotted down on a great heap of parchment leaves I kept stuffed in a satchel in my tent. The common soldiers cared little for my verses, but they were popular among the nobles, who warmed to my shameless flattery and exaggeration of their deeds.

As the poem grew more famous, until I heard whispers that the king himself was fond of it, so my desire to quit the army increased. I was sick of the dreary, never-ending siege, and feared I would run mad if exposed for much longer to the vice and cruelty and squalor of that terrible ditch.

Desertion was too risky. The king treated deserters the same way as looters, and strung up their bodies for the crows. I had my precious reputation to think of, and no desire to return to the life of a fugitive, hunted by English and French alike.

Salvation arrived one chill January eve. The night was crystal-clear, and I lay stretched out on my bedroll and gazed at the stars. They twinkled like so many tiny lanterns, scattered across the velvet arch of the sky.

My mind was once again being drawn to heretical thoughts. The church taught that God ruled the heavens and the stars, just as He ruled us. Some believed that the pattern of the stars could be used to predict the future, though the church generally disapproved of this astrology or 'magic science', as it was known. My old tutor in Kingshook, Father Stephen, had dabbled in this practice, and once told me that Jewish scholars equated the twelve astrological signs with the twelve tribes of Israel.

What if, I wondered, there were other civilisations, somewhere out there in the broad universe, where faith in God was unknown? Where the sacrifice of Christ meant nothing? What if it was only mankind, stranded on our little planet, just one star among countless billions, who held to the truth of the scriptures? After all, mankind had written them.

What if man had invented God?

"Page."

A stern voice jolted me out of these dangerous musings. I sat up and reached for my dagger.

"My apologies," said the newcomer, "I didn't mean to startle you."

He was little more than a tall silhouette in the light of my supper fire. I glimpsed the red and gold of Plantagenet livery under his dark woollen cloak. The light also sparkled off the gold rings on his fingers, and the jewelled hilt of his sword.

"Come," he said, his face still hidden in darkness, "the king wants you."

I wordlessly got up and followed him, through the neat rows of tents, torches and banners and pavilions and hanging shields, the alert sentries and groups of men yawning about their campfires.

To the east rose the vast shadow of the city wall, a permanent and unbreakable landmark, speckled with lights near the summit. The quiet waters of the Seine flowed past to the south, and in all other directions stretched the rich, undisturbed fields and forests of Normandy.

My guide picked his way through the camp with the ease and silence of a ghost. I stumbled after him, rubbing the sleep from my eyes, and almost tripped over the guy-ropes of Sir Robert Umfraville's pavilion.

Sir Robert's esquire, who slept outside like a faithful hound, leaped up and shook his fist at me. I ignored him and followed my mysterious companion towards the royal pavilion.

This miniature palace of silk and canvas dwarfed the lesser pavilions that surrounded it. Twelve men-at-arms, all wearing the cross of Saint George, guarded the entrance, and the interior was lit by the rosy glow of braziers.

There was nothing unusual in King Henry receiving visitors after dark. Like Caligula, he only needed a few hours of sleep, and frequently worked long into the night. I often saw his nobles, pale and heavy-eyed after being forced to attend a royal council that lasted into the small hours.

My guide exchanged salutes with the guards, and beckoned at me to follow him inside. Gulping down my nerves, I ducked through the flap.

The interior was warm and stuffy, and blazed with light. I stood blinking foolishly, trying to get my bearings, until someone touched me on the arm.

"Kneel," whispered the stern voice. Panic swept through me as I remembered I was in the royal presence, and dropped to one knee.

I kept my eyes fixed on the ground, which was covered in thick carpets displaying images of Jerusalem and Damascus and Constantinople, among others: all the great cities of Outremer and the Near East, worked in gold and silver thread. It was the great ambition of Henry's life, after he had finished the necessary business of conquering France, to lead the united armies of Christendom in a Crusade to liberate Jerusalem from the infidel, once and forever. Alas, the pictures on the carpets were as close as he ever got to Jerusalem and the Holy Land.

The air was not only over-warm, but heavy with the odour of incense. There was a square of meadowsweet laid between the carpets, which gave off a pleasant smell when crushed underfoot. It made for a pleasant change from the stench of horse dung and unwashed bodies and gunpowder that permeated the camp.

"Rise, John Page," said the King. Sweat trickled down my back as I slowly got to my feet and lifted my eyes to meet his.

Henry was seated on a high-backed couch, padded with red silk cushions. He wore a long, loose robe of some rich dark stuff, and sipped wine from a slender golden cup. Steam rose gently from the brim. Our warrior-king, it seems, was a martyr to the cold.

His armour, freshly oiled and polished, hung from a rack in the corner. I had never seen him out of his metal shell before. Without it he looked much smaller, almost delicate. I was shocked at how thin he was, and the tightness of the milk-white skin stretched across the fine bones of his face.

The only other soul present was my guide. He was unknown to me, a slim youth with buttery yellow hair and mild blue eyes. Doubtless some knight or esquire of the royal household.

The king set down his cup on a little silver table and laced his slender fingers together. "I saw you at the mines," he said, his hazel eyes bright as they raked me over, "are you recovered from your wounds?"

"Yes, sire," I replied truthfully. The pain in my ribs still irked me, and the livid black bruise would take weeks to fade, but there was no break or fracture.

"Can you ride?"

I tried not to wince. Riding would be sheer torture, especially over rough ground, though I dared not say as much. The king hadn't summoned me to enquire after my health. He had thought of some use for me, and I lacked the courage to admit weakness to that cold, severe, priest-like countenance.

"Yes, sire," I repeated.

Henry raised his left hand in a languid gesture of dismissal. The fair-haired youth bowed and ghosted out of the pavilion.

The king was silent for an uncomfortably long time. Henry studied me with cool, practical detachment, as he would any kind of weapon.

"My brother Clarence has agreed to lend me your services," he said finally, "you are no ordinary man-at-arms, Page. I have read your verse. Gower and Chaucer might have scorned them, but I detect a certain wit."

I ducked my head in recognition of the almost-compliment. "You honour me, sire," I said, risking a smile.

A sense of outrage swelled inside my breast. I had been passed about among the royal brothers, from Gloucester to Clarence to the King, as though I was some chattel, with no say in my fate.

I was almost tempted to remind this royal icicle that I was a free-born Englishman of noble blood, at least on the maternal side. A loyal servant, not a slave.

"It is foolish to waste a man of unusual talents," Henry went on before I could muster the courage to speak, "I have to make use of all the tools at my disposal. You were recommended to me."

"Recommended, sire?" I said, "by whom?"

He snapped his fingers. A female figure detached itself from the darkness at the rear of the pavilion and strode into the light.

For a moment I forgot to breathe. The woman was Catherine, the French whore I lay with in Caen. She still wore her red shawl, though now her mass of curls was bound up in a linen coif, and she wore a dark blue woollen gown in place of a ragged smock.

She said nothing, though her blue eyes twinkled at me. There were gold studs in her ears, and more gold adorned her wrists and fingers. Her long knife, which she had used to slay the archer who tried to rape her, rested snugly inside a sheath lined with dark red velvet.

"I believe you two have met," said Henry, "Lady de Santaella was good enough to spare me the details."

There was a dry undertone to his voice. He took another prim sip at his wine, and for one terrible moment I thought he winked at me.

"Majesty," I stuttered, "this woman is an enemy. With my

own eyes I saw her kill two of our soldiers at Caen."

Henry's full lips twitched. "An enemy? If so, then you stand guilty of fraternising, Page. You need not describe her sins. I know them well enough. The deaths she caused were regrettable, though at least one was fully deserved. Had I caught the men who attempted to ravish her, I would have hanged them."

"My lady had a role to play," he added, "she played it well, and brought me useful information concerning the citizens of Caen. Their virtues and vices. Who could be bought, and who could not. Things of that nature."

I stared at Catherine. "You're a spy," I hissed, "why didn't you tell me?"

She glanced at Henry for permission to speak, who granted it with a nod. "For that same reason," she replied, "spies who reveal their true names to strangers cannot expect to live long."

The heavy French accent had gone from her voice, replaced by something more exotic. Spanish, I thought, or maybe Portugese.

"But you're perfectly willing to bed them," I threw back with pointless malice. She merely grinned, and raised her delicately plucked eyebrows at me.

I was angry at being fooled, and yet intrigued. Henry had called her Lady de Santaella, which suggested noble blood. I could well believe it. She carried herself with the proud insolence of the high-born, and there were traces of refined breeding in her dark, angular features.

"Catherine the whore is just one of my guises," she said, "my true name is Constanza de Santaella."

"Lady Constanza is the daughter of a Castilian knight," said Henry, "and widow to another. Her late husband, Ruy Garciá de Santaella, was a loyal friend to the English crown. His father fought for my ancestor, Prince Edward, at the Battle of Najéra. Before I first sailed for France, two years ago, Ruy came to England to offer his sword to our cause."

Henry crossed himself. "He was a bold and valiant knight, and it was my good fortune to know him. Dysentery took him at Harfleur, as it did so many of our brave fellows."

"Lady de Santaella hates the French, every bit as much as her late husband. Other men of her family also served Prince Edward, and she has lost a number of kinsmen to French swords."

He talked of Constanza as though she wasn't there, and the effect of his words was obvious. Her eyes sparkled with anger, and she gripped the hilt of her dagger until the knuckles turned white.

"My lady has proved a most useful agent," the king went on, "as well as a consummate actress. Now she is to be despatched on another mission."

"The Duke of Burgundy currently holds Paris. I am in frequent contact with him. You, Page, shall escort my lady to Paris with a message for the duke."

Henry gave no explanation of why he wished to contact Burgundy, though I could guess. He needed powerful allies if his conquest of France was to succeed, and the military and financial aid of John the Fearless would be invaluable.

Thus far the duke had played a double game. He made public promises to break the siege of Rouen, without ever sending any troops, and secretly indulged in correspondence with the English. The course of the war depended on which side he eventually chose to throw his weight behind.

Henry glanced at Constanza for the first time, and then back at me. "I have never known my lady to ask for help before. She was, however, most insistent in this case. You are to accompany her to Paris."

Constanza smiled warmly at me. "My bodyguard," she said, "escort and companion. The roads to the capital are unsafe, thanks to the war, and the forests rife with bandits and partisans."

"You protected me once, John Page," she added, "now I ask you to do so again."

"My lady asks," Henry said curtly, "I command."

I had no choice but to accept. Whatever I made of Constanza's request, a direct order from the King could not be ignored.

Thus I left Rouen one raw, foggy winter's morning in the company of this enigmatic Castilian noblewoman, who had chosen to give up a life of wealth and comfort to spy for the English.

We rode side by side on the highway that led directly to Paris. For a long time silence reigned between us, broken only by the regular drumming of hoofs on the frosted road. My ribs twinged a little whenever I passed over a bump in the road, but the pain was more bearable than I feared.

My rouncy, Odo, was in good fettle. He had done little save eat, doze and wander about a paddock through the long months of siege, and was glad for the chance to stretch his limbs.

Constanza rode a glossy black courser, all sleek sinew and muscle, easily capable of outdistancing most horses if she gave the beast his head.

We met with a troop of hobelars. They were English, in the service of the Earl of Warwick, and happy to let us pass after I explained our purpose. One or two cast lustful looks at Constanza, whose form was not quite hidden under a thick woollen cloak. She rode athwart the saddle, like a man, and wore tight black hose that showed off the graceful slenderness of her legs.

Fortunately the officer had his men well in hand. "Keep your eyes to the front, lads," he snarled, "or lose them."

We rode on unmolested, and my mood started to lift. With every mile we left Rouen further behind. If God was kind, I wouldn't have to return until the city had surrendered. Perhaps not at all.

Not a word passed between myself and Constanza until we skirted the walls of Louviers, a few miles south-east of the suburbs of Rouen. The town was in English hands, and the lions and lilies flew proudly from the gatehouse.

Constanza finally broke the silence. "The road between Rouen and Louviers was safe enough," she said, "thanks to English patrols. From now on we have to be more cautious."

Another sixty miles or so lay between us and Paris. Constanza, who knew the route intimately, described the towns we would pass on the way.

"We are in contested territory now. English and French troops fight for possession of the land. We may encounter bands of soldiers from either side, though there are also brigands aplenty, many of them peasants who have lost their homes to the war."

"We must ride fast, and not spare our horses until Vernon. There is an English garrison there. I know a hostel inside the town where we can stay for the night."

"A hostel, or a brothel?" I sneered, unable to help myself.

"You are still young, John Page," she replied stiffly, "and the young are prone to make assumptions. You know little of me, who I am, and what I have done. Do not insult me again."

We were on a lonely stretch of highway, crowded by deep forest. The trees and undergrowth should have been cut back from the verge, to the length of a bow-shot, but all trace of law and order had fallen away in this part of France.

"I know your true name," I retorted, "and something of your history. I also know you played the whore in Caen."

She gave me a pitying look. "You should listen when your King speaks. Henry described me as a consummate actress, and so I am. Yes, for a time I assumed the guise of Catherine, a penniless French prostitute. It was just a mask, nothing more. I entertained no men in my little garret."

"Save one," I reminded her.

Another awkward silence fell. Constanza toyed with her bridle, and ran her fingers through the courser's mane.

"Come," she said, turning away, "it's another twenty miles to Vernon."

We had ridden another mile or so when the turrets of a castle rose over the trees ahead.

"That is the keep of Gaillon," she cried above the pounding

of her courser's hoofs, "where the Archbishop of Rouen has his residence. The town is still in French hands. We should give it a wide berth. I know a side-road."

She rode on a few more yards, and then a dreadful shriek erupted from the trees. Her horse threw back his head and neighed in fright, even as dark shapes leaped out of the forest.

My rouncy, a more even-tempered beast than her courser, was not so easily alarmed. I clapped in my spurs and urged him into a flat gallop.

There was no time to be frightened. Maybe thirty seconds passed between our talk and the flight of the arrow that pierced Odo's belly.

He screamed and jerked sharply to the right. The reins tore from my hands. A gout of hot blood hit me in the face. A violent shudder ran through the animal's body as another arrow slammed into his neck.

Blinded, I wiped away the gore with one hand and clawed at my sword with the other. Dirty hands seized my bridle.

I lashed wildly at the first man I saw, a grim-faced brute in a leather jerkin. He ducked, and my blade skimmed over his head.

"*Saint Denis!*" the cry echoed through the woods, "*Saint Denis et le Dauphin!*"

Constanza's courser leaped clear of the brigands that surrounded it, howling and trying to drag her down. She was a superb rider, and avoided the arrows and javelins that rained about her. Then she was gone, vanished around a bend in the road.

I was engulfed. Steel fingers ripped at my sword and tore me from the saddle. Odo's terrified screams were cut short by a knife.

I struggled and cursed in vain as they held me down on the road. A host of snarling, bearded faces glared down at me, and the tip of a sawn-off lance was pressed against my throat.

The wail of a trumpet echoed through the forest. My captors retreated, save for the man with the lance, and gave me a clear view of the knightly figure that clanked out of the trees.

Unlike the others, who wore little armour, he was clad in full plate. I noted patches of rust on the steel, and his soiled jupon showed a black crow against a blue field. He was burly, of medium height, lost somewhere in middle age. His face was clean-shaven, battered by life and war, and there were grey strands in his tight cap of reddish curls.

He barked a command at the ruffian with the lance, who bowed and withdrew. I gingerly rubbed my throat, where the sharp steel had almost punctured the skin.

"I am Sir Roland de Rougemont," said the newcomer in soft-spoken English with a lilting accent, "state your name and degree."

I had to lie, or at least exaggerate my status. If Sir Roland thought I was a rich nobleman, he might keep me alive for ransom. Otherwise I was worthless to him, and might end up as food for worms.

"Sir John Page," I replied, "Baron of Kingshook."

Sir Roland looked down at me for a moment. "I suspected you were English," he said, "who was that virago who rode with you?"

"My wife," I lied, "we were on our way to Vernon, where she has family."

The feeble lie made him grimace. "Ah, *monsieur*," he replied, shaking his head in disappointment, "a knight and his lady, travelling on these roads in time of war, with no retinue to guard them? I cannot believe it."

"I think you are a spy, *mon ami*. Please, do not insult us both with clumsy protests and denials."

I kept my tongue behind my teeth. For all his soft-spoken ways, this Sir Roland was clearly a hard man: his followers, as villainous a pack of cut-throats as ever I saw, cringed in his presence.

"Tell me, Sir John," he said, "do you know the romances of King Arthur?"

I blinked. It was hardly the first question I expected. "Ah...yes, of course. Very well."

"*Bon.* Then you will know the tale of Sir Carados and Sir Turquine?"

Still baffled, I replied that I did, and his ravaged features split into a wide grin.

"Excellent. Then you will be pleased to meet my lord, Sir Turquine."

19.

Sir Roland gave no further explanation, and had his ruffians host me aboard a spare horse. I wasn't allowed to ride upright, but slung over the saddle like a pile of laundry, my wrists and ankles bound tight enough to stop the flow of blood.

In case I insisted on light conversation, they also stuffed a

186

gag into my mouth. It was a foul rag, and judging from the
stench and taste had been used to rub down the horse. I retched,
which made them howl with laughter.

When my guts had eased a little, I tried to stay calm and
count heads. The brigands were were all on foot, save for Sir
Roland, who rode at the head of the little procession on a
dappled white destrier. There was twelve of them, including
their captain, and we followed a well-beaten track through the
forest, wide enough in places for two abreast.

I noticed that none of the footmen wore Sir Roland's livery,
or any badge at all. This Sir Turquine, whatever his real name,
made a strange lord.

Many years had passed since I was first digested the
legends and romances of King Arthur, in the nursery at
Kingshook. Every Christian boy of gentle birth is force-fed
them from early childhood. They are supposed to act as his first
grounding in chivalry, before the real business of learning the
knightly arts begins.

Arthur was the shining example of kingship, while the
tragic love of Sir Lancelot and Queen Guinevere warned
against the dangers of courtly love, and how even the greatest
knight could be brought down by a woman. The treacherous Sir
Mordred, meanwhile, was the greatest villain who ever
breathed, and the evil mirror-image of Sir Galahad. In my long
experience, there are far more Mordreds than Galahads in this
world, and always will be.

I ransacked my memory to recall the tale of Sir Turquine
and Sir Carados. These two were lesser characters, brothers and
robber-knights from Wales who stood for everything the Round
Table was against: they looted, pillaged and murdered at will,

187

ravished maidens, slaughtered peasants, and generally behaved like fiends in human shape.

In the tale they acted as foils for Lancelot to test his mettle against. First he slew Carados in single combat, and later chanced to encounter Turquine. The two fought for hours, so well-matched that neither could gain the advantage, until both were exhausted and the grass was speckled with their blood.

At last Turquine called a halt and raised his visor to speak. "Thou art the greatest knight I have ever crossed swords with," he said, "I hold in the dismallest dungeon of my castle five score and eight knights, all of the Round Table, whom I have bested in fair fight and taken as prisoners. Tell my thy name, and I swear on my troth as a knight to release them all."

"Except," he added with a fierce glare, "you be one man, Sir Lancelot of the Lake. He slew my brother Carados. I have vowed to slay him in revenge, or join Carados in death."

"I am that man," Lancelot answered. So the fight continued, with even greater heat than before, until Lancelot finally got the better of Turquine and cut off his head.

My thoughts dwelled on Turquine's hapless prisoners. After he defeated them in combat, he was in the habit of carrying them back to his castle, stripping them naked and throwing them into his deepest, darkest dungeon. Once or twice a day, depending on his mood, he liked to have the prisoners brought forth into the light, so he could beat them with thorns until their backs ran with blood.

My bowels were dissolving in terror by the time we arrived within sight of a drum tower, peering over the leafless trees. It was painted dark red, and a black pennon fluttered from the battlements. On the pennon I made out the image of a salmon worked in silver thread. The salmon's scales glistened like water by moonlight as the wind rippled the silk.

Sir Roland twisted in the saddle to address me. "Behold your new home, Sir John," he said, "the Chateau Rougemont-sur-Seine, seat of my cousin, the Baron de Rougemont. The local people have another name for it. *La Tour Sombre*."

La Tour Sombre, or The Dark Tower. I could believe it was well-named, and almost fouled myself at the thought of the evil that awaited me inside those red walls.

The path through the woods opened onto a vast clearing. In the middle the ground rose to a small mound, some fifteen feet high.

My new home, as Sir Roland called it, crested the mound. It was more a fortified manor house than a castle, with a single tall tower surrounded by a roughly circular curtain wall. The tiled roof and double chimneys of a hall rose above the battlements.

The clearing was eerily silent as our party made its way to the gate. There was a deep ditch at the foot of the wall, filled with sharp stakes. A sentry on the tower had spotted our approach, and shouted for the drawbridge to be lowered.

To my fearful mind the drawbridge was a tongue, and the gateway a maw. The thick iron spikes of the portcullis were teeth. I whimpered with fear at the image of being fed into the maw and crushed up inside the castle's guts, until there was naught left of me save bones and gristle.

A bell started to toll ominously as I was carried over the drawbridge and into the ward. The interior was a shambles of sagging, lean-to buildings, and everywhere the smell of damp and decay.

I saw a vat of pig's blood under the thatched roof of the smithy. The blood had congealed, and gave off a stench that threatened to make me sick again.

A group of soldiers, if they could be called that, stood clustered about something inside. I saw a flash of steel, a spurt of red, and one of them tossed something into the vat.

"You, there," shouted Sir Roland, "leave off your sport, and go and inform the Baron of our return."

The soldiers turned at the sound of his voice. "At once, *milord*," said one of them. He and his fellows bowed and hurried away towards the arched doorway of the hall.

Now they were gone, I was able to see the body that hung upside-down from the beams of the smithy. It was a man, or the remnant of one. His arms dangled limply as he swung gently back and forth from a stout rope tied about his ankles.

Mercifully, he was in shadow, so my eyes were spared the awful things that had been done to him. My imagination filled in the details as blood drip-dripped off his body onto the cobbles below. He occasionally gave a shudder, so he was still alive.

Sir Roland tore the gag from my mouth. "Pleasant, *oui*?" he hissed, with a nod at the body, "take heed, Sir John. That man was once an English knight like you. He showed a regrettable lack of courtesy to the Braon, and had to be punished for it."

His yellow teeth bared in a grin. "I should think he regrets his lack of manners now, eh?"

He nodded at two of his men, who lifted me off the saddle, none too gently, and cut my bonds. I gasped in pain as the blood flowed back into my wrists and ankles.

Sir Roland's grin vanished as footsteps sounded from inside the hall. "My cousin stirs. Tread carefully, Sir John, and mind what you say."

I had noticed the doorway was unusually tall and wide. The arch was some twelve feet from the ground, and wide enough for four men to pass through at once.

A monstrous shape appeared in the archway. At first I thought my eyes betrayed me, or else I had run mad.

Six brawny serving men marched out, carrying a stiff-backed wooden chair on their shoulders. The figure seated on the chair was birthed in nightmares.

I beheld a squat, misshapen body, mercifully hidden under a white gown or cassock, its face covered by a white silken mask and a pointed hood.

Little of the body inside was visible, save for a pair of heavily bandaged hands. The fingernails were black, and the flesh of his fingers, what could be seen of them, was reddish and swollen.

The Baron de Rougemont was a leper, obliged to hide his decaying body under white robes. I had seen lepers before in England, wandering in sad little groups through the countryside. They carried bells to warn of their approach, so the healthy might run away in time to avoid infection.

I had always regarded lepers as the most unfortunate of God's creatures, to be pitied rather than feared. Any sense of pity for the Comte dissolved as eyes full of malice glared at me through holes cut in the silken mask.

"Set me down," he rasped in French. His servants gratefully laid the chair on the cobbles.

"What's this, cousin?" demanded the Baron, "another chicken for the pot?"

His words were mangled by hideous noises, gasps and whistles and wheezes. My skin crept as I imagined the corruption under the robes, a man eaten away by disease, rotting like putrid meat left out in the sun.

"Another Englishman," replied Sir Roland, "he calls himself Sir John Page of...of..."

He snapped his fingers at me. "Kingshook," I said promptly.

"That's it," he went on, "some barbaric Saxon name. We caught him on the road to Vernon. A woman rode with him, but she got away."

The Baron lifted one bandaged hand to bat away a fly trying to crawl under his mask. "Spies," he coughed, "filthy spies. And yet this one calls himself a knight. What degraded creatures these English are. Animals."

He struggled in vain to sit upright in his chair. I got the impression he had been a big, powerful man once, before the terrible affliction of leprosy struck him down. Now he was a shapeless mass of decay, reliant on servants to carry him about. They would also have to bathe and undress him, as well as clean up his mess. I could only hope that wages were high at La Tour Sombre.

The Baron stabbed a bandaged hand at me. "You," he grunted, "English dog. What was your mission to Vernon?"

I remembered the body in the smithy, and decided to tell the truth. "King Henry despatched us to Paris, my lord," I answered respectfully, "with a message for the Duke of Burgundy. I am ignorant of the contents of the message. My companion carried it on her person, and did not reveal the contents to me. I was merely there to act as her bodyguard."

The Baron mumbled something I failed to hear. Irritated, he beckoned me closer. Sir Roland gave me a shove, and I stumbled forwards, almost within touching distance of the monster in the chair.

"I was right to call you a dog," he hissed, "the woman was the messenger, and you her faithful hound. Tell me, hound, have you noticed my retainers wear no badge?"

I replied nervously that I had. "Soon there shall be none to wear it," he added, "none to carry my pennon into battle . The direct line of my family shall perish with me. Hence the lack of badges. Why display the arms of a dying house?"

He placed his hand flat against his chest. "God saw fit to curse me with the leper's mark before I could father any sons. My only living kin is Sir Roland there. His crow banner shall fly over this castle after I am gone."

"Not for a long time, cousin," said Sir Roland, "you shall live many more years yet."

The Baron made an obscene noise, halfway between a laugh and a death-rattle. "Listen to him!" he gasped, "seeking to toady and flatter me, even as he prays for my death. Will you trouble to bury me with honour, cousin, in the ancestral vault, or simply throw my diseased body into the nearest waste-pit?"

Sir Roland smiled away the bitter words. He was evidently

used to such insults, and bore with them in the certain knowledge that his kinsman had only a short time to live.

"Before my soul escapes this vile prison," said the Baron, "I have vowed to die as I lived, and spend my last days in faithful service to His Majesty, King Charles."

He meant King Charles VI of France, once known as the Beloved for his enlightened rule, better-known by this time as Charles the Mad. The blood of the Valois, the ruling family of France, was tainted with madness. As a young man Charles suddenly fell victim to the family curse while out hunting, and murdered four of his knights with a sword before he was restrained.

Since then he had resided in Paris, more a prisoner than a king, shuttled about like a trophy between various factions. Bouts of relative sanity alternated with long stretches of howling madness. It was said that during these episodes Charles thought he was made of glass, and insisted on being strapped down to a table in case he fell over and shattered.

His son, the Dauphin, claimed to rule France in his father's name, and so far had made a remarkably bad job it.

"I have captured fourteen English knights and men-at-arms," wheezed the Baron, "and hold them all for ransom in my dungeons. I will use the money paid for their release to raise an army of mercenaries. Sir Roland shall lead this new army for me against King Henry, and all the traitors that plague France, until the realm is swept clean of enemies."

His feeble voice quivered with passion. "That shall be my last act in this world, my last gift to my country. Men shall remember me, not as a foul and contemptible leper, but as the saviour of a kingdom."

Small ransom would he get from my family, I thought. My uncle, Sir Reginald Ulverton, was more likely to pay the Baron to have me killed.

The Baron suddenly grew tired. "Take this dog to his kennel," he whispered, sagging in his chair, "and put him with the others. I shall have a little sport with them in the morning, after I have rested. Rest, rest, rest..."

Three of his retainers seized hold of my arms and dragged me away to prison.

20.

The dungeon was a cramped vault under the tower at the bottom of a winding stair. Ghostly snatches of song and muted conversation drifted up the stairwell as I was prodded down the steps.

"Give me an excuse, *goddam*," spat the guard who held the tip of his spear against my spine, "any excuse to stick this into your liver."

I was careful to give him none. We passed the occasional lantern, mounted on brackets, and the tawny light cast grotesque shadows against the wall.

The singing gradually became louder. I could have wept as I recognised it as *The Dream of the Rood,* an age-old English hymn:

"Then the young hero did disrobe - that was God Almighty,

195

Strong and resolute, on the wretched gallows he did ascend.

Bold and courageous as many observed,

For mankind's past he would amend.

Tremble did I as the hero embraced me,

But yet I dared not bend,

And fall to the earth's surface, therefore I stood firm.

A cross I became; lifted up with the mighty King.

The Heavenly Master; but yet I dared not bend.

With dark nails they pierced me,

On me the scars are visible,

The open and malicious wounds.

For him I dared not, so none did I injure..."

The Dream of the Rood is a song of hope and consolation, meant to lift hearts even in the darkest of hours, and remind men of their faith in the Almighty. The voice that sang it was English, high and tuneful, though wavering. Every so often other voices chimed in.

I reached the foot of the stair, which ended in an evil-looking black portal, nailed and timbered and cross-barred, with a small iron grille at head height. The hopeless singing echoed from the interior, mingled with the scrape and rustle of chains.

"Stand still, *goddam*," ordered the guard. One of his comrades moved to the door with a bunch of iron keys, while the third stayed behind on the stair. He levelled his crossbow at the doorway.

The man with the keys hammered his fist against the timbers."Be silent in there!" he roared, "and prepare to greet another of your Devil-sent countrymen!"

The singing died away as he threw up the heavy bar and turned the keys, not without some effort, in the rusted lock. After a brief struggle he got the door open and thrust it inward with his boot.

Determined to maintain some dignity, I stepped inside without waiting to be pushed. The heavy door crashed shut behind me, and I was immediately shrouded in darkness.

I could hear and smell the other prisoners. My eyes watered at the reek. It got into my nose and throat, and made me gag.

"Welcome to the palace of the damned, my friend," said a soft voice with a slight West Country burr, somewhere to my left.

I slowly turned around. The only light in the dungeon came from the lantern outside, pouring through the narrow grille on the door. I blinked, and waited for my eyes to adjust.

"My name is Sir John Page," I said, deciding to stick to my falsehoods, "baron of Kingshook in Sussex. The leper said he had taken fourteen prisoners, all Englishmen. Did he lie?"

There was a rustle of chains, and some mirthless laughter. "There are fifteen of us now," said a heavy Welsh accent, "but I am no Englishman, thank Christ."

"Nor I," spoke up another voice. This one was more guttural, with an accent I didn't recognise.

"Take your place among us," said the West Country voice,

who was the nearest, "there is straw to sit on, if you don't mind it infested with rat turds."

I looked to my left, and spied the outline of a man sat against the wall. He shifted aside as I trod carefully across the slimy flagstones to join him.

"Sir Thomas Braham," he said, offering me his clammy hand, "of Wimborne in Dorset. Honour to meet you, Sir John."

He raised his voice a little. "Friends, introduce yourselves to our new comrade."

One by one, the other prisoners croaked out their names and places of origin. The Welshman was Grono ap Grufydd ap Hoel of Brecon, and a kinsman of Sir Dafydd Gam, who was famously knighted by King Henry as he lay dying on the field at Agincourt.

The others were all English, save for the man whose accent was unfamiliar to me. To my surprise, he turned out to be German.

"Herr Hartmann von Arnsberg," he rumbled, "of Westphalia. If I only had the sense of a goat, I would have listened to my father and stayed there."

"*Bitte,*" he added wearily, "do not ask me how a German knight managed to get mixed up in a war between England and France. I have repeated the story many times. Suffice to say I was a younger brother, and required to sell my sword to earn a living. At first I served under the Duke of Burgundy, but the pay was a bad jest, so I broke my indenture with him and took arms under King Harry."

He paused for breath, and to hawk up some phlegm. "Fool that I am, I got myself captured by the leper's villains after the fall of Louviers. Now I sit in the shadows and wait for him to tire of the game."

"So do we all," said Sir Thomas, to a murmur of groans and sighs.

"What game?" I asked. My eyes had grown accustomed to the gloom, and I strained to make out the faces of my fellow prisoners. The few I could see were grey as death, dirty and bearded, lank-haired and hollow-eyed.

I recoiled in disgust as I saw lice crawl through one fellow's hair. He made no effort to remove them, but sat listlessly staring at the floor, weighed down by the thick iron shackles on his ankles.

"The lepers claims to have sent ransom demands to King Henry," said Grono, "it is a cruel trick he likes to play, to make us hope we might one day be set free. I think he has done no such thing. He amuses himself by torturing us."

It was uncomfortably warm in the dungeon, thanks to the press of bodies, yet a chill stole over me. "What," I croaked, struggling to force out the words, "what kind of..."

I couldn't bring myself to finish the sentence. "Flogging, mostly," replied another prisoner, "the sight of men being flogged gives him great pleasure. Every morning his guards take a few of us up to the courtyard, strip us naked and beat us bloody. All the while that diseased monster sits in his chair, grunting and shivering."

"He won't kill us," said Sir Thomas, "unless we displease him."

A heavy silence fell over the dungeon. "I...I saw a man being tortured," I said, "in the courtyard."

"Richard Goldesburgh," replied Grono, "he was taken from us two days ago. The poor fool was being flogged, and dared to curse the leper to his face, or what remains of it under the mask."

"I was there," the Welshman added, "the leper was so enraged he almost fell out of his chair, and vowed to make Richard beg for death."

I sensed them all looking at me expectantly. "Richard was still alive," I said, "just. I will not describe what the guards were doing to him."

This met with a few muttered curses, and someone sobbed in the darkness. It struck me that the prisoners had given up. The monster upstairs had broken their spirit, and reduced proud fighting men to mere husks.

I did my best to revive their dormant spirits. "There are fifteen of us," I cried, "has the Baron cut off your limbs? Why don't you fight?"

"Because there are thirty-two men in the garrison," Herr Hartmann said gloomily, "their master feeds like them fighting cocks, and they have armour and weapons. We have nothing save our bare hands. Some of us are loaded down with irons. *Allmächtiger!* It would be a slaughter."

I gazed at his lumpen silhouette in despair. "You are a knight," I said forcefully, "and every man here is a soldier, or was. Where is your pride? Your sense of honour? Surely it is better to die with some honour than sit in this filthy hole and wait meekly for death?"

I sought to insult them, to rouse a flicker of indignation. At first there was no response, and then Sir Thomas laid a frail hand on my shoulder.

"Wait until dawn," he said in a kind voice, "then you will understand."

21.

I drowsed a little that might, caught between sleep and waking, my mind full of obscene images of the torments that awaited me.

The conversation of my fellow prisoners didn't help. Most slept the sleep of the damned, victims of sheer exhaustion, despair and a foul diet. Their gaolers, I was told, only fed the prisoners once a day, and that was vile swill - potato peelings, rotten cabbage, bacon rind and the like, the sort of rubbish you would think twice before feeding to pigs.

"Just enough to keep us alive," Sir Thomas said, "and for refreshment we have water from the castle ditch. Sometimes the gaolers piss in the bucket."

He leaned closer, until I could feel his warm breath on my ear. "I've seen men lap the tainted water off the floor," he whispered, "it is incredible what we do to cling to life. I think it is part of the leper's game. He wants to see how far he can degrade us. He means to take away our manhood, piece by piece, just as disease has taken his."

"The leprosy has driven him mad," I said, "have you heard of his plans to raise an army of mercenaries with the money from our ransoms, and use them to destroy the enemies of France?"

Sir Thomas chuckled. "That old dream. I was brought here three months ago, and he was raving about it then. He fails to realise that none of us are worth much in the way of ransom.

The leper has failed to capture anyone above the rank of knight, and poor knights at that. Assuming our ransoms are ever paid, the money won't be enough to hire more than a few score beggarly routiers. The scrapings of the gutter. No, King Harry and the Duke of Burgundy have little to fear from the Baron de Rougemont, even if we do."

He was keen to know how the war progressed, and if the King had advanced on Paris. I was encouraged by his questions, and those of Grono and one or two others. At least they retained some interest in the world beyond La Tour Sombre, which suggested they hadn't given up all hope.

"Our army is still sat outside Rouen," I told them, "the Dauphin has sent no aid to the city, nor is he likely to. Sooner or later, Rouen must fall, and then the whole of Normandy will be in our grasp."

The news sparked some life into them. "I suspected as much," hissed Grono, "though the leper pretends that the Duke of Burgundy broke the siege weeks ago, and drove our army all the way back to the coast. He tells all manner of lies."

The next day, shortly after daybreak, I was given a taste of the Baron's other methods.

Faint from hunger and weariness, I had drifted into a stupor. Nothing was quite real, and the coarse voices and clattering footsteps of the guards outside seemed like part of the same bad dream.

Harsh reality intruded when the door swung open, grinding on its rusted hinges. Cries of pain and alarm broke out as light flooded into the musty pit of the dungeon. I shrank back against the wall and threw up my hands against the sudden glow of torches.

A troop of guards swarmed in and began to strike at us with cudgels.

"Where is the German pig?" I heard one shout, "show yourself, *herr* porker! Ah, there he is! Drag him out!"

"That one, too," snarled another, "and the fresh meat Sir Roland brought in yesterday. Where does he hide?"

I did my utmost to meld into the wall, but two of the rogues spotted me. One seized my arm, while his comrade grasped a handful of my hair and gave it a savage twist.

"Come with us, *goddam*," he growled, "milord wishes to welcome you properly to La Tour Sombre!"

Along with a few other luckless souls, I was shepherded outside with kicks and blows, and up the stair to the courtyard. The howls of my fellows echoed in the stairwell, though I gritted my teeth and refused to cry out. My pride ebbs and flows, often depending on the situation and how much money is involved, but I would not give these monsters any satisfaction.

I stumbled into the grey light of dawn, to find the Baron waiting for us. His shapeless bulk sprawled in its high chair before the entrance to the hall, twitching in barely suppressed excitement.

"Good morning, Sir John," he said in his hoarse whine, "I trust you slept well? That you are fully refreshed?"

A scaffold had been erected in the middle of the courtyard. It stood taller than a man, and in place of a noose three double sets of manacles hung on hooks from the cross-bar.

Sir Roland stood by the scaffold, along with five of his men. He looked pale and haggard, and had a feverish glint in his eye.

I looked at the smithy. The vat of blood was still there, but the unfortunate Richard Goldesburgh had vanished. I bit back a moan of fear when I saw the lumps of offal floating in the vat. More pieces of his body, cut from him while he yet lived.

"Hang them up!" rasped the Baron, and I was pushed towards the scaffold.

My two companions from the dungeon were Herr Hartmann and another man I didn't know. In the blue-grey light of dawn I saw them clearly for the first time, and was shocked by their condition. Both were emaciated from long imprisonment. Their filthy jerkins and hose hung loose off their fleshless bodies, and their faces were virtually hidden under long, greasy manes of matted hair and beard.

"Courage," Herr Hartmann said tome, "you will need it, *kamerad*."

What remained of my courage drained away as the guards forced me to stand under the middle of the cross-bar.

"Raise your arms," one ordered. I obediently raised them, and the manacles were snapped shut about my wrists.

The same was done to my fellow prisoners, until we all three stood on tiptoe under the scaffold, our arms stretched painfully above us.

So we were to be flogged. I thought I could stand that. Father Stephen never stinted with the birch when I was young, and a flogging was small beer compared to the agonies of Richard Goldesburgh.

"Bare their backs!" yelped the Baron. His voice was shrill with excitement now, and I could hear the rocking of his chair on the cobbles. I offered up a silent prayer that he would overturn it and smash his rotten head on the cobbles.

I shuddered at the cold kiss of a dagger. It ripped down the length of my spine and cut my jerkin in two. The shreds were torn away, leaving my back exposed to the dawn chill.

A tall, broad-shouldered man emerged from one of the outbuildings. He was ugly as a mastiff, bald and bearded, and stripped to the waist. His belly hung down over his crotch like pale suet, and his long arms were thick with ropes of muscle.

My companions started to mumble prayers. I might have done too, but the words stuck in my throat when I saw the instrument of torture in the man's right hand.

It was a whip or scourge, of a kind devised by fiendish minds to cause the utmost fear and pain in its victims. Three lashes made of twisted and plaited leather, each some ten feet long, were attached to a long handle. The thongs ended in a trio of perfectly round lead balls.

I gasped at the sight of the evil thing, and for a moment lost my composure. The guards laughed and jeered as I strove desperately to wrench my wrists free of the manacles.

"Heave, *goddam*!" they yelled, "heave, and call on Saint Crispin! Perhaps he will descend from the heavens to release you!"

Agincourt, of course, was fought on Saint Crispin's Day. These French devils knew that, and mocked me with the saint's holy name.

The scaffold trembled slightly with my efforts, but the

manacles only became tighter as I struggled.

"Be still, you fool," murmured Herr Hartmann, "do you think you are the first man to try his strength against these bonds? You will achieve nothing save broken wrists."

After a few seconds the madness passed, and I tried to compose myself for the ordeal to come.

The brute with the whip paced slowly before us, and laughed softly as he trailed the lashes on the ground. I can still hear the noise of the lead balls rolling across the cobbles, and the little moan of the man to my right - Edmund Grey, I think his name was - as his body went limp. He had fainted.

He was revived by a pail of water upended over his head. The poor wretch had clearly been flogged before. I saw a series of purple marks and ridges on his back, like the claw-marks of a wild beast, and the memory was enough to rob him of his senses.

"Enough of this delay," cried the Baron, his voice choked with phlegm, "begin!"

I closed my eyes and bit down hard on the silk of my father's old pennon, the rag-end of which I still wore about my neck. It would, I hoped, muffle my screams.

"Five strokes each," I heard Sir Ronald say in a quiet voice.

Those five strokes are seared forever into my mind and body. The bald torturer cracked his whip with expert skill, and was able to ply the lashes across the backs of all three of his victims at the same time.

Screams burst from the throats of the men either side of me. Mine was stifled by a mouthful of silk, but I was unable to stop the flow of tears.

My left side was still tender from the battle in the mines outside Rouen. The torturer must have noticed the bruise, and aimed for it. Three times I howled in silence as the lead ball whipped across my ribs.

Somehow they withstood the impact. On the fourth stroke, I felt and heard something snap. Pain, pain like I had never known, flowered inside me like a white-hot rose. Half my body was set on fire.

No man can endure such agony for long. My vision went red, and then black, and I knew nothing more.

When I regained my senses, I was still in darkness. Panic swept through me, and I stretched out my hands. Feeble whines escaped from my throat.

Blindness is another of my great fears. I sobbed like a child, fearing the leper had torn out my eyes.

"Peace," said the blessedly familiar voice of Sir Thomas Braham, "lie him down. Careful, now."

I allowed myself to be gently lowered onto a heap of straw. They set me down on my right side, which was undamaged. Pain flared as cold fingers probed delicately at my bruised flank.

"No," I whined, "please, no more...leave me be, I beg you..."

A voice cursed in Welsh. "Damn the Baron. May be burn forever in the deepest circle of Hell."

"Let God take care of the leper's soul, if he has one," said sir Thomas, "what are Sir John's hurts? Are the ribs broken?"

"Yes," answered Grono, "one, certainly. Maybe two. He was already carrying a wound before the flogging started. It will take weeks to heal."

Sir Thomas sighed. "At least he will be spared further torment. Even the leper can see Sir John would not survive another dose of the whip."

Grono snorted. "As if the whoreson cares if any of us live or die! Do you believe his talk of ransoms? I wager he has not even sent the demands to King Harry. He only mentions them to give us false hope. Another of his games."

I could not see either man, only listen. Gradually, my eyes grew used to the darkness of the dungeon again.

"What...what happened?" I whispered, gasping as the mere effort of speech caused an invisible needle to pass through my flesh.

"You fell unconscious when the whip broke your rib," replied Sir Thomas, "the guards wanted to revive you for the fourth and fifth strokes, but Sir Roland persuaded the leper to spare you further punishment."

"Aye," Grono added caustically, "according to Hartmann, he said there was poor sport in killing wounded birds."

"It pains me to say anything of good of Sir Roland," said Sir Thomas, "but you should be grateful to the leper's kinsman, Sir John. If not for him, the final two strokes could have broken your spine."

It was hard to feel much gratitude "What of Hartmann?" I gasped, "and Edmund Grey?"

At first neither man spoke. "The German lives," Grono

replied shortly, "he's made of tough metal, that one, and not easily broken. Edmund Grey is dead, alas. He was already weak from a previous flogging. His heart gave out on the fourth stroke."

"One less ransom," remarked Sir Thomas.

"Aye, one less ransom," spat Grono, "for the leper to fund his mighty army. Every one of us will die under the whip before the sickness kills him."

22.

I lingered for weeks on end in that nightmare dungeon, hovering between life and death. A fever took hold of me, and for a long time I knew little of who or where I was.

It was near Christmas before I was fully myself again. I owed my life to Grono, who had some skill in medicine, and the tender care of the other prisoners. The strongest gave their food to me when I needed it most, and took pains to ensure I was always warm and comfortable, or as comfortable as any man could be in such a place.

Outside the war continued to rage. The Duke of Burgundy chased the Dauphin out of Paris, seized the person of the mad King Charles and declared himself protector of the realm. Meanwhile the Dauphin scrambled from one place to the next, trying and largely failing to whip up support, before setting up a new court at Bourges. His enemies mocked him as the King of Bourges, since it was the only part of France he truly controlled.

King Henry, who still hoped to recruit Burgundy for an ally, remained camped outside Rouen. The citizens had managed to sneak out a couple of envoys to beg for aid. They failed: neither

Duke John the Fearless, nor his rival the Dauphin, were able or willing to set aside their quarrel and march against the English.

No city, however bravely defended or well-supplied, can hold out forever. Trapped in our dungeon, cut off from the outside world, we prisoners could only speculate as to when Rouen might fall, and King Henry's next move.

"He won't march to our aid, of that you may be certain," said Grono, ever the pessimist, "this castle is just a fly-speck on the maps of France. I doubt Harry even knows it exists."

Salvation arrived in the unlikely person of Sir Roland. Late one night, my uneasy sleep was disturbed by the scrape of a key in the lock of the prison door.

It also woke my companions, such as remained. By this stage our number was reduced to twelve. Two more of us had given up the ghost, one to injuries caused by the leper's whip, the other to sheer misery and exhaustion.

The heavy door creaked open to reveal the figure of Sir Roland, framed in the archway by the night lantern that burned at all hours.

I shifted in the corner where I spent my nights, barely noticing the familiar ache of cramp and the dull pains in my injured side. The ribs had knitted together, eventually, but I was still weak. Like the others, I also suffered from the lack of fresh air, exercise and decent food.

"How now, Sir Roland," croaked Sir Thomas Braham, "hast thou come to pour scorn on us? I wote well thy mother and father would weep for shame at thy conduct. False knight I call thee, a base craven, unworthy of the honour of knighthood."

He spoke the ancient High Language of chivalry. It lends a man a superior kind of dignity, no matter how pitiable his condition, and there is nothing quite like it for insulting fellow knights.

Sir Roland stepped inside the dungeon. I saw no guards in the stairwell beyond.

"Your words sting, Sir Thomas," he said gravely, in his fluent English with the lilting French accent I had come to know and despise, "though I understand your bitterness. None of you have any cause to love me."

Grono stumbled forward. His wrists were loaded down with chains, attached to stout iron brackets in the walls, else he might have sprang at our visitor. "Love you?" he hissed, "come closer, my hero, and let me fold you in a warm embrace."

The Frenchman kept his distance. "Listen to me," he whispered urgently, "I came here alone, of my own free will. My kinsman has treated you shamefully, and I have aided him in his work. Now I wish to make amends."

There were some angry murmurs among the prisoners. Sir Thomas raised his hand to still them. "Amends?" he said, "three of our number have died in this place. How can you amend what was done to them?"

Sir Roland hung his head. "I know," he admitted, "their deaths lie on my conscience. I might have acted sooner, but I needed time. It wasn't easy to turn my cousin's soldiers against him."

This was met with silence, and Sir Roland hastened to explain. "Rouen is on the brink of surrender," he went on, "no French army will march to its relief, and the people of the city

211

will soon be reduced to eating each other. Rumour has it that the burghers are discussing terms with your king."

"Once Rouen falls, all of Normandy will be in English hands. The Duke of Burgundy, that treacherous dog, will throw in his lot with King Henry."

Grono broke in. "And this castle will suddenly be in English territory," he sneered, "which means that everyone inside it will become a subject of the English crown."

The Welshman bared his broken teeth. "I see your thoughts, coward. Sooner or later King Harry will learn of the torments inflicted upon his soldiers in this God-cursed castle. You hope to save yourself from his justice by turning traitor, and helping us to escape."

"Not just to escape," the Frenchman answered, "I offer a bargain. Help me to slay my cousin and those who remain loyal to him. Once we have taken control of the castle, I shall escort you safely to your king."

Grono looked away in disgust. He was a man of honour to his finger-bones, that one, and clearly wished to have nothing to do with such treachery.

The same could not be said for the rest of us. Not every man is born to play the hero, and embrace a martyr's doom. I for one was happy to clutch at any straw, if it meant I would see the sun again, and feel the wind on my face. Sir Roland's conscience, or lack of it, was his affair.

Sir Thomas was of like mind. "Go on," he said, "how might this be achieved?"

"Eighteen of the men in the garrison have agreed to join me," replied Sir Roland, "and betray their lord when I give the signal. I can also count on my esquire and servants. Along with yourselves, that makes thirty-three of us, against fourteen soldiers and my cousin. We need not worry about him. He has not lifted a sword for years. I doubt he could now."

"Nor can we," I said, "look at us, Frenchman. Look at the fruits of your tender care."

This gave him pause. Weeks of torture, confinement and poor diet had made us the pale husks of men, dirty and emaciated and feeble as mice. I could barely stand without aid, let alone wield a sword, and there were others in even worse state.

"I can help you recover your strength," he said, "from now on, you will be fed by men loyal to me. No more slops or tainted water. Instead, ale and wine from my cousin's own cellars. Meat, bread and ale from his larder. Fresh clothes shall be provided, and medicine for your hurts. In a month's time, you will be like new men."

"Why not toss us a few whores, while you're about it?" sneered Grono, "I like mine fat and ginger, if you please."

His cynicism was understandable. Sir Roland's offer could well have been a sham, another cruel trick devised by his unspeakable cousin.

Sir Roland sensed our doubts. "Let my prove I am as good as my word," he said, "tomorrow night, after my cousin is safely asleep, you shall receive gifts. Wine and food and clothes. Later, when the time is right, I'll supply you with weapons. Are we agreed?"

"The word of a traitor," replied Grono, "is worth less than the contents of his privy."

His was a lone voice of dissent. Sir Thomas glanced at me, and then at the rest of the prisoners. Every one of us gave a nod of approval. This was our last hope.

"Agreed," he replied.

23.

Sir Roland kept to his promise. The next night, after three of our number had been dragged upstairs for the leper's entertainment, and returned bloody and insensible, the first of his gifts arrived.

The floggings were less frequent, whether due to Sir Roland's influence on his kinsman, or the Baron's worsening condition, I cannot say. There was no longer any talk of ransoms. The demands had almost certainly not been sent, and if they had King Henry chose to disregard them. He was ever careful of money, and unlikely to part with considerable sums in order to ransom a few lesser knights.

We drank down the ale - it was the first drop I had tasted in weeks, and slipped like honeyed nectar down my throat - and mixed the wine with water to pour over the bloodied backs of our comrades. Their flesh was already criss-crossed with scars, and the leper's whip had opened up some old wounds on top of the new ones.

The victuals were brought by two guards, a couple of leathery, bearded oafs who had given us a fair number of kicks and blows in the past. It was difficult to believe they were now on our side, and I watched carefully from the shadows as they hastily dumped the baskets on the floor and fled. The door swung shut behind them with a crash that echoed through the stairwell.

"Not as stupid as they look, maybe," remarked Herr Hartmann, "they will soon be English subjects, and know it. Sir Roland must have explained that King Henry would hang them all unless they agreed to turn traitor."

Privately, I thought Sir Roland gravely mistaken if he hoped for a pardon. Henry's attitude towards traitors of any stamp, even those who did him good service, was the same as towards deserters and looters. Nor was he fool enough to take a turncoat into his service.

Nevertheless, the victuals continued to arrive. Sir Roland must have placed his men in charge of the cellars and the kitchens, else his cousin's loyal guards would have noticed the steady flow of rations vanishing down the stairs.

On the third night Sir Roland's esquire brought us a basket of bread and cheese. He was more talkative than the soldiers, and happy to answer our questions.

"The leper keeps his men close about him," the lad explained, "he lives in terror of assassination, and wishes to die at an appointed time, with a priest to hear his confession and absolve his sins. If he goes before he has time to prepare, he believes his soul is too tarnished for purgatory, and will be cast straight into the fire."

"He will burn, whether or not a priest agrees to mutter a few words over his carcase," snarled Grono, "I never met a likelier candidate for damnation."

Two weeks passed. We ate like pigs, drank like lords, and grew stronger by the day. Our spirits, cast down for so long, rose by the hour.

As well as the much-needed victuals, I was given a pot of

unguent to rub on my bruised and battered ribs. At the end of the fortnight, I was well enough to stand without aid, and my fingers itched to feel the grip of a sword again.

We had seen nothing of Sir Roland since he came to reveal his treachery. One day, perhaps midway through January, he paid us one final visit.

"Tomorrow at dawn," he said, "is our best opportunity. My cousin has rallied, and declared himself fit enough to watch a little sport. He sent me to choose the victims."

He nodded at me. "Sir John Page. You have not taken part in the entertainment for a while. Nor you, Grono. Sir Thomas Braham, you shall be the third."

We three, along with Herr Hartmann, were the strongest of the surviving prisoners.

"My men will pretend to fix you to the manacles," said Sir Roland, "when I give the word, they will turn on my cousin's guards. I have ordered them to show no quarter."

"Here," he added, producing three daggers from his belt and passing one to each of us, "hide these about your persons. You will have need of them when the slaughter begins."

"What of the Baron?" asked Sir Thomas.

"No quarter," the other man repeated solemnly, "he is my blood, and it falls to me to put an end to him."

The next morning Sir Roland's men came for us, as he had promised. We were all awake when they arrived, and breakfasted on the last of the previous night's victuals. To calm my nerves I drank too much ale than was good for me, especially at such an early hour, and my head spun as the keys turned in the lock and light streamed into the dungeon.

"Come," said one of the guards. This one was somewhat older than the rest, most of the hair rubbed from his scalp by decades of wearing a mail coif. He and his mate carried lanterns, and went first up the steps.

"They should curse us," whispered Herr Hartmann, "and knock us about a little, for the look of the thing. Else the Baron might think something is amiss."

"Speak for yourself," hissed Grono, "I've had my fill of hard words and blows from these clods."

He patted the sleeve of his filthy tunic, where he had hidden his dagger. "The next one to raise a hand to me will lose his eyes. I care not for the consequences. Today I shall win my freedom or go to meet my ancestors."

It was a suitably warlike oath, and warmed my blood a little. I exchanged looks with Sir Thomas, who had a look of grim purpose on his raddled features. A naturally big, fleshy man, weeks of privation had reduced him to a skeletal figure, gaunt and bearded and dishevelled. There was still considerable strength in his deep chest and broad shoulders, and long-banked fires smouldered in the pits of his sunken eyes.

After so many weeks underground, I was temporarily blinded by the sun. Unable to see, I reached out to support myself against the wall.

"Welcome," rasped the hatefully familiar voice of the Baron, "I see life as my guest agrees with you, Sir John. Why, you are as fat as butter. We must whip some of that unsightly weight off you."

When the glare of the sunlight had subsided, I opened my

eyes a crack to see the Baron seated at his usual place, under the expanded arch of his hall.

His condition had deteriorated since I last saw him. He sat with the poise and grace of an old sack, his head lolling forward, and was only held upright by two lengths of rope passed around his trunk and the back of the chair.

Most of his loyal guards stood either side of the chair, armed with spears and shields. One man stood ready with a crossbow on the battlemented roof of the hall. I wondered if the Baron had smelled treachery in the air, and taken steps to guard against it.

"Chain them up," he ordered, his voice hoarser and weaker than before, "chain them up, and let me see them dance."

Time seemed to slow as we were ushered towards the scaffold. Every detail of the world around me suddenly came into sharp focus. The battlements of La Tour Sombre were topped with snow, sparkling like crystals in the blue-grey light of dawn. More snow crunched underfoot, and I trod carefully to avoid cutting myself on the dagger hidden inside my left shoe.

There was no birdsong. There never was at La Tour Sombre during my time there as the Baron's prisoner. His evil presence filled the castle like a noxious cloud, driving away the essential goodness of nature.

I was made to stand under the centre of the scaffold. My breath came in short gasps as I remembered the agony of the torture I had suffered on that exact same spot. I started to shiver, not just with the cold, and my throat dried up. The pain in my side, which had ebbed in recent days to a dull, persistent ache, suddenly flared hot again.

The bald brute with the whip stepped out of his little hut. He had the temerity to wink at me. I ground my teeth in silent rage, and prayed he was not one of Sir Roland's allies. It was high time to settle old scores.

"What means this delay?" the Baron squealed irritably, "chain them up, I said! Let us be about our sport! I will not dine this morning until I see blood on the snow!"

"Then you shall see yours!" yelled Grono.

He stood to my left, where the guards pretended to fumble with the manacles on his wrists. They waited for Sir Roland's signal to attack, but Grono had other ideas. He ripped his hands free, drew the dagger from his sleeve and leaped towards the Baron's chair with a shrill cry.

The crossbowman above was alive to the danger. A shout of warning rose to my lips as he levelled his weapon at the unkempt, wild-eyed Welshman charging straight at his master.

I shouted in vain. The bolt flew straight and true and thumped into Grono's breast, lifting him clean off his feet. He landed heavily and coughed blood as he struggled to pull out the missile embedded up to the quarrels in his flesh.

Bright steel flamed in Sir Roland's hand. "Now!" he bellowed. "Avaunt! Avaunt! No quarter!"

'Avaunt' was his watchword, the signal for his men to tear off their masks of loyalty and set about their comrades.

Shouts of rage and alarm filled the air. The Baron's guards closed around their master and locked shields, forming a protective half-circle. Two of Sir Roland's turncoats had fetched crossbows from the armoury, and took aim at the man on the roof.

The guards near the scaffold charged at the wall of shields, leaving myself and Sir Thomas free to seek our own quarry. Like me, he had hidden his dagger inside his shoe. We both knelt and fumbled for the blades while the war-yell rose around us, and the ancient walls echoed to screams, oaths and the clash of steel.

Our chief tormentor, the bully with the whip, proved himself craven as well as sadist. As the courtyard erupted into violence, his face changed colour and he fled back inside his bolt-hole.

"Mine!" I shouted at Sir Thomas, and gave chase as fast as my legs could carry me.

I should have known better than to dive recklessly through the narrow doorway of the outbuilding. My blood was up, and I gave no thought to danger. All I wanted was to lay hands on the villain who had broken my ribs and murdered my friends, and tear him limb from limb.

Even a rat, when cornered, will show fight. His whip cracked in the shadows, and my face exploded with pain as one of the lead balls caught me across the jaw.

Blood filled my mouth, and red lights spun before my eyes. The ball had broken a tooth. I reeled against the fragile timber wall and knocked over a barrel. My foe launched his weight at me, roaring like a crazed bull.

We went down together, our bodies rolling over and over on the dirt floor. One powerful hand clutched at my throat, while the other tried to gouge my eyes.

The sergeant-at-arms at Kingshook had trained me in all the knightly arts, including unarmed combat. Against a bigger and stronger opponent, the trick was to use guile, and turn his advantages against him.

Easy to say, harder to execute when fighting for your life in darkness, pressed down on the floor with a raging monster on top of you. His sheer weight crushed the air from my lungs, and I was still dizzy from the blow to my jaw.

I managed to extricate my right arm. He might have pinned my wrist to the floor, but the oaf had lost his head completely, and seemed intent on stifling me to death.

My dagger slid home, angled through the back of his neck, sliced through layers of well-padded muscle and flesh. He gasped, treated me to a final blast of his pungent breath, scented with garlic, bad wine and meat larded with spices, and started to go into spasm.

With a grunt of effort, I rolled his enormous body off me. While he twitched and jerked his last, I lay on my back for a moment, waiting for my heart to stop racing. I gingerly explored my tender jaw, and spat blood as I worked loose broken bits of tooth.

When I felt able, I crawled over to the dead man and tugged the dagger out of his neck. The blade was dark with his blood, so I wiped it clean on the back of his jerkin.

The sounds of battle still raged outside. I was tempted to lie low until all was over. Dazed and bleeding, still weak from long imprisonment, and armed only with a pig-sticker, I could be of little use.

There were gaps in the planks of the shed wall. I peered through one to see how Sir Roland's men fared.

They had the upper hand. Several of the Baron's men lay

strewn about the courtyard, staining the snow with their lifeblood. As yet the turncoats had suffered no casualties, save one man who stood leaning against the wall of the tower, nursing a wounded arm.

The Baron was hidden behind a mob of fighting men, though I could see the peaked top of his chair. Incapable of defending himself, he could only sit and curse.

Once again I felt a twinge of pity for him. Villain though he was, bloodthirsty lunatic who had long since forsaken his vows of knighthood, he should at least have been able to die on his feet, like a man, sword in hand. The curse of leprosy had robbed him of dignity as well as pride.

His end was not long in coming. Sir Roland's esquire had run down to the dungeon to release the rest of the prisoners, and these ragged, vengeful ghouls snatched up fallen weapons and streamed into the fray. They set about their tormentors with frenzied relish, hacking the Frenchmen to pieces as they lay helpless on the ground, smashing in their skulls with maces and flails.

Aided by these reinforcements, Sir Roland and his turncoats made quick work of the thin line of shields. The outnumbered loyalists were cut down, dragged aside and butchered, while four men laid hands on the leper.

He squealed, he writhed, even as they severed the ropes that held him upright in his chair. Sir Thomas Braham, it grieves me say, was one of those who pulled the helpless Baron from his chair and flung him to the ground.

At no point did the Baron ask for mercy. His shouts were borne of pure indignation, and he roundly cursed those who had served him, ate his bread and drank his wine and took his wages, and finally turned on him.

Sir Roland reached down and whipped off the hood covering the Baron's face. A cry of horror went up, and my eyes caught a mercifully brief glimpse of what lay beneath: a skull, essentially, still with a thin cover of grey flesh, the hair mostly fallen away, one eyeball rotted to nothing, the nose gone, most of the upper lip rotted, exposing black teeth and black gums.

He should have been granted a quick death. Instead Sir Roland chose to make a ritual of it. At his command, some of the guards fetched the vat of blood from the smithy.

"He lived by blood," cried Sir Roland, "let him end in it!"

They picked him up, thrust him head-down into the vat and held him there until his hideously swollen legs ceased to quiver. The turncoats cheered and laughed, echoed by the feeble shouts of the prisoners. One or two danced in celebration of the Baron's demise.

I watched awhile, and was then violently sick in a corner.

24.

"Tell me, sir knight," said King Henry, "what would you ask of me?"

His voice was soft and steely, and his eyes full of disdain as they looked upon Sir Roland.

The Frenchman failed to heed the royal mood, and rushed straight in among the stakes and caltrops. "If it please you, sire," he replied with an enthusiasm that made me wince, "I would renounce my fealty to King Charles and swear loyalty to

Your Majesty. In return for my service, I would request to be confirmed in the barony of Rougemont-sur-Seine."

"The barony is my right," he added when Henry didn't respond, "I am the previous Baron's only living kin."

Myself, Sir Roland and Sir Thomas Braham knelt inside the royal pavilion outside Rouen. We had just returned from La Tour Sombre. It was a strangely mixed fellowship that journeyed north to Rouen, prisoners side by side with French soldiers and servants. The latter were Sir Roland's turncoats, who accompanied their new master in the hope of reward from the English king.

Sir Roland had the luxury of a horse, while Sir Thomas rode the late Baron's charger. There were no other mounts in the castle stables, so the rest of us had to slog on foot.

Not far outside Louviers we met with an English patrol, who furnished us with horses and as much of their rations as could be spared. I had not ridden for months, and sat athwart the saddle of my borrowed rouncy with all the grace and skill of a bag of coal.

The English pickets were astonished to see such a beggarly company of men, and even more so when Sir Thomas told them   of our recent history. One hastened to inform the king, another to arrange food and clothes and medicine for us. Meanwhile we gratefully collapsed onto the grass and lay strewn about like so many corpses, our ordeal finished.

The Frenchmen sat apart in a huddle, casting fearful glances at the distant sprawl of Rouen, and the forest of English banners and tents that had grown up around it.

King Henry sent a herald and a troop of archers to summon

myself and Sir Thomas into his presence.

"Can it not wait until morning?" I groaned, "look at us. None of us are in any fit state to meet the king."

The herald was the same sly, fair-haired young man who had escorted me to the royal pavilion, half a lifetime ago.

"That is for His Majesty to decide," he said firmly, "come, on your feet. The King has much business to attend to, and does not like to be kept waiting."

Sir Roland strode over. "I shall come too," he announced, "Sir Roland de Rougeville, at your service."

The herald looked him up and down. "I don't know you, sir knight," he said coldly, "the king said nothing about a third party."

Sir Roland smiled. "Perhaps not, but these men owe me their lives. King Henry will, I am sure, be pleased to hear my story."

"Follow, then, if you wish," the herald said, with a shrug of his narrow shoulders, "though you had best make the tale a good one."

"Good luck, *mein kamerads*," said Herr Hartmann as we trooped off, escorted by a double file of archers, "if you can, put in a kind word for one poor German *knechte,* who has fallen on hard times."

The king sat in his loose black gown, just as he had in my last audience with him, and listened intently to Sir Roland's account of what had passed at La Tour Sombre. If he was pleased to see me alive and relatively whole, he didn't show it. Instead his attention was fixed on the French knight and his testimony.

Sir Robert Umfraville and Richard Beauchamp, Earl of Warwick flanked Henry's chair. Umfraville was as grim and taciturn as ever, and Warwick a tall, lordly man with a coffin-shaped face, full of stern disapproval. The three of them were as formidable a trio as could be imagined, and made me feel like some miserable sinner, brought for judgement before a court of Old Testament prophets.

"Am I to understand," said Henry, slowly and deliberately, "that having slain your cousin, and broken faith with your liege lord, you now expect me to accept your oath of fealty? To set you up as a baron?"

Sir Roland paled a little. "Sire," he began, stumbling over his words, "my cousin was a beast in human shape. He tortured your soldiers after taking them prisoner, and would have killed them all if I hadn't intervened. I..."

Henry held up a hand to silence him. "I am aware of that. Sir Thomas has already told me of the debt he and his fellow prisoners owe you. For my part, I am pleased my men were rescued. Those that survived."

He leaned forward. "Do not imagine, traitor," he went on in a voice as cold as the grave, "that you can place the King of England in your debt, and barter with him over the corpse of a murdered kinsman. You came here seeking a reward for your crimes. You have found justice instead."

"Take this man out," he commanded, "and hang him as he deserves."

Sir Roland half-stood, red in the face, as two halberdiers stepped forward to lay hold of him.

"Wait...wait!" he spluttered, "this is not just! I never swore fealty to Your Majesty. You cannot be my judge. Send me to King Charles in Paris, or the Dauphin at Bourges, so I might stand trial before my peers."

Warwick uttered a short bark of laughter at this desperate line of defence, and Henry's full mouth twisted in contempt. "I am the rightful King of France," he said harshly, "not the madman Charles de Valois or his idiot son. There is no question of fealty. You are my subject, as all Frenchmen are, and mine to judge as I see fit."

The halberdiers roughly seized Sir Roland's arms and dragged him outside to meet his fate. Sir Thomas and I made no effort to speak up in the French knight's defence, even though we owed him our lives. The king had spoken, and it was a brave man who questioned his judgements.

"Now, we may turn to more pleasant matters," said Henry, with one of his rare smiles, "I congratulate you both on your survival. From what Sir Roland told me of his cousin's behaviour, you and your fellows were treated with great cruelty."

"The Baron de Rougemont was a madman, sire," replied Sir Thomas, "disease robbed him of his wits."

Henry relaxed slightly, and folded his hands on his lap. "France appears to be rife with madmen," he said, "I think God has seen fit to make their leaders insane, so we may conquer them all the more easily. What say you, Umfraville?"

The Border knight, who until now could have been mistaken for a statue, stirred into life. "The French choose their leaders poorly, sire," he said in his thick Northumbrian accent, "and there is no du Guesclin to save them this time."

He referred to Bertrand du Guesclin, the great French mercenary captain who had almost single-handedly reversed the tide of English military successes in France, back in the days of Henry's great-grandsire.

My father, according to the ballads, fought alongside and against du Guesclin during the wars of Pedro the Cruel in Castile and León. This was by no means uncommon among routier captains. Both men were professionals who sold their swords to the highest bidder.

Henry nodded in agreement with Umfraville. "Indeed," he said, "our enemies are badly led. I mean to show better judgement."

"Sir Thomas Braham," he added after a moment, "what lands do you hold in England?"

"Three manors in Suffolk, Your Majesty," my companion answered.

Henry turned his attention to me. "What of you, Page?"

"No lands, sire," I replied, "I am bastard-born, and my mother's manor of Kingshook, where I grew up, was stolen by her kin before I came to France."

Sir Thomas glanced sidelong at me. I hadn't yet informed him that I was a mere esquire, and that my claim to knighthood and a barony were convenient fictions.

Henry gave another little smile. For the first time I wondered how much he really knew of my background. Had my uncle sent a message across the Channel, informing the King that I was wanted in Sussex for homicide? Then there was the list of other offences I committed in the company of Robert Stafford and his outlaws. Enough, all told, to hang me several times over.

First and foremost, Henry was a practical man. He cared for justice, true, but only when it suited him. Even if he was aware of the full extent of my crimes (and I never discovered how much, if anything, he knew) I was too useful to be given over to the hangman just yet.

"No lands," he said, "and the castle and manor of Rougemont-sur-Seine will shortly be in need of a new lord. Until the French have come to their senses, and accepted as as their rightful liege, I must set good Englishmen to rule over them."

I must have looked baffled, for he neighed with laughter, a most unexpected noise coming from such a self-possessed man. Umfraville and Warwick joined in, as wise nobles do when their king laughs.

"You did not expect such bounty, eh?" cried Henry, "tut, man, you deserve no less. The hero of Caen, the poet of Rouen, and now the survivor of - what was the damned place called?"

"La Tour Sombre, sire," said Sir Thomas, "or so the local villages termed it."

Henry snapped his fingers. "That's it. The Dark Tower. Ha! They will be singing ballads of you before long, Page."

"Unless he writes them himself, sire," remarked Warwick with a thin smile, to another burst of royal mirth.

The tension inside the pavilion evaporated. This was the first and only time I saw the human face behind the stern iron mask Henry presented to the world. He seemed younger than his thirty years, and the burdens of kingship were briefly shrugged away.

It mattered little to him that I had failed in my mission, to escort the so-called Lady Constanza to Paris. I knew nothing of her fate. Nor did the King choose to enlighten me.

Warwick leaned down to whisper something in Henry's ear. "I am amiss," cried the king, thumping the arm of his chair, "my lord Beauchamp has reminded me, quite rightly, that one cannot be made a baron without first being dubbed a knight."

He flowed gracefully to his feet. "Robert," he said, "fetch my sword."

The king's sword rested in its scabbard on a stand next to the king's armour. Umfraville lifted out the blade with a smooth hiss of oiled steel on leather, and presented it hilt-first to Henry.

My soul raged with conflicting passions as the sword tapped me lightly on both shoulders: pride, embarrassment, relief, shock, joy, all jostled and fought with each other, like rats in a barrel.

"Rise, Sir John Page," said the King.

25.

Two days after my elevation to the baronage, Rouen surrendered. It was not unexpected. Henry had been discussing terms with the burghers for weeks, ever since it became obvious that no relief would be sent to the city.

On the Feast of Saint Wolstone, a Thursday, the King went to meet the burghers at a religious house outside the walls. There they knelt before him and delivered up the keys to Rouen.

That night Henry sent the Duke of Exeter with a strong guard to enter the city, and formally claim it in the name of the King of England. I watched the Duke ride through the gates with great pomp and ceremony, preceded by a troop of mounted esquires carrying banners that displayed the lions and lilies of England and the cross of Saint George. The French were ready to greet our men, and heralded them with much playing of brass trumpets, pipes and clarions, as though we came as friends rather than conquerors.

"Saint George! Saint George!" cried the people gathered in the streets, a right scarecrow crowd, half-dead from months of hardship. The expulsion of the poorest citizens had enabled them to eke out their supplies a while longer, but now they were reduced to the final extremity. Even the wealthiest burgher resembled a living skeleton, fleshless and sunken-eyed, almost lost under his rich robes of office.

"Much of the folk that were therein,

They were but bones and bare skin,

With wan colour as unto lead,

Unlike to living men but unto the dead..."

These lines are part of the final verse of The Siege of Rouen, the poem I had left unfinished when the King sent me to Paris. After my escape from La Tour Sombre, and my unlooked-for promotion, I decided to complete it.

Exeter rode through the city and gave out bread and alms to the starving rabble. This was done on the order of the king, who well knew how to win the love of the people he intended to rule. The Duke then took possession of the castle, and set up the banners of England, France and the Holy Trinity over every major gateway.

After sitting outside Rouen for so long, I finally gained my first sight of the interior on the Friday morning after the Feast, when the King himself entered the city. He rode at the head of a formal procession, followed by a rabble of archbishops and abbots holding aloft richly decorated crosses (naturally, the high churchmen were first to the spoils) and a long line of nobles, knights and men-at-arms.

As a baron, albeit an extremely minor one, I was entitled to ride among the lesser knights and peers in the middle of the procession. I must have cut an impoverished figure among so many richly dressed men in my plain, battered half-armour, with no esquire to carry my pennon, but I cared little. The awesome splendour and majesty of the occasion overwhelmed me, and the stark contrast between the plump, well-fed look of our soldiers and the pitiful state of the French.

All eyes were naturally drawn to Henry. He rode on a black charger, and wore a mantle of black damask, black gauntlets, black hose, and a breastplate of polished gold. Golden pendants, stamped with the Plantagenet lions, overhung the flanks of his charger. His gold-hilted sword was tucked inside a scabbard of black velvet, and he rode with one gauntleted hand resting lightly on the pommel: an unsubtle reminder of where his real power lay.

The procession halted at the minster, where Henry dismounted and followed his chaplain inside to hear mass.

From the grand archway rolled the sound of plainchant. The hymn was *Qui est magnus Dominus?* or 'Who is the greatest Lord?' On that day, the question scarce needed to be asked. Henry was the victor, the favoured one of God, and no man present could deny it.

I had my own modest glory to celebrate. The Bastard of Kingshook, the Wolf-Cub, outlaw and homicide and fugitive from justice, had contrived to win a knighthood and a barony. Great good fortune had come my way, and in the final lines of The Siege of Rouen I paid tribute to Him who I owed thanks:

232

"They that have heard this reading,

To His bliss may He them bring,

For us He died upon a tree,

Say amen, then, for His charity."

Once Rouen had fallen, those towns and castles still in French hands rushed to make their peace with Henry. By early spring, the whole of Upper Normandy and the Seine valley was in his grasp. With the lion's share of the duchy secured, he set the seal on his conquest with another formal procession in Rouen, this time wearing his ducal robes.

Those were grand days to be an Englishman in France. Normandy was ours, the French were either in full retreat or fighting each other, and the opportunities for land and profit seemed almost endless. France is a huge realm, and Henry had need of loyal men to help him govern it. Any Englishman, no matter how low-born, could hope to stake his claim to a piece of conquered territory.

My share, the little barony of Rougemont-sur-Seine, was a fair beginning, the first rung on the ladder I intended to climb. It wasn't very large, consisting of just two knight's fees, and small ones at that. Less than fifteen hundred acres, though at least the land was fertile enough. Much of it was low-lying pasture and forest, watered by a tributary of the Seine.

The castle held evil memories for me, and I had no great desire to see the place again, let alone dwell in it. Still, only a fool snubs the offer of a castle and a lordship for the sake of a few nightmares.

My actual title was a vexed question, and one Henry, with characteristic attention to detail, wanted to settle according to French custom.

"Since you are bastard-born, with no claim to lordship in England," he informed me, "you may not call yourself baron.

That is a privilege reserved for nobles. Instead, as a commoner raised to rank and title, you are the *seigneur de la baronnie*, or lord of the barony."

Formal titles mattered little to me, and I happily accepted his judgement. What mattered was the land, the status, and the wealth that would (with God's grace) flow from both.

I soon realised that Henry's gift was not so generous after all. My pay of a shilling a day was enough to sustain myself, and perhaps one servant, but that was all. In desperation I appealed to the king for funds, and he reluctantly ordered his clerks to advance me the not very princely sum of four pounds.

This was rather less than the yearly income of the smallest manor in England. Kingshook had subsisted, barely, on five pounds per annum.

"His Majesty must favour you," sniffed the pinch-faced clerk who wrote out the receipt, "be careful you do not sacrifice that favour, Sir John."

His meaning was clear: use this money wisely, for if you come again, begging for alms, the king might take offence.

Four pounds was enough for my purposes, at least for the time being, and there was no shortage of labour. Now the campaign in Normandy was over, hundreds of men were discharged from the army. Not only soldiers, but cooks, carters, tailors, surgeons, huntsmen, grooms and all manner of camp followers. Just enough men were retained to fill the garrisons of the conquered duchy.

Most of the discharged soldiers were faced with the stark choice of finding new employment in some lord's retinue, or begging on the streets back in England. Thus I had no difficulty in finding five stout archers to take into service, along with a groom and a cook. I paid each of them a penny a day, roughly equal to half their pay in the army. A touch mean, perhaps, but they were desperate and I had to make my funds last.

After carefully studying a few maps, and talking to veterans who knew the country around Rougemont-sur-Seine - largely through having ridden over it, burning crops and slaughtering any peasants they happened to encounter - it became clear that my new lordship was a worthless ruin. The castle was most likely derelict, since the old Baron was dead and his only living kinsman executed on King Henry's orders. His followers had all been hanged with him, and I expected the few remaining servants had fled.

"The land is all burned and wasted," one captain of hobelars informed me, "it was in a bad position, see? Caught right in the middle of the fighting."

He jabbed his dirty thumb at a point on the map, near the north-west extremity of the lordship. "There's a village there," he added, "or was. A pretty little place, with houses made of pink stone and a church with a spire. Not much left of it now. My lads spent the night there, some five months gone. We had been badly cut up in a skirmish with some French men-at-arms, and were in a rough mood. The villagers took the brunt of it."

"Fire and sword," I sighed.

He nodded. "We torched the houses, and looted the grainstores before firing them as well. The villagers ran to the church for sanctuary. Fools. A couple of my lads stacked logs against the door to trap them inside. Then we shot fire arrows through the windows. Lord, you should have heard their screams, and got a whiff of the stench! Man-meat, when roasted, smells much like pork."

It was a familiar tale. The skyline of Normandy was black with the smoke of burned-out settlements. Both sides used fire as a principal weapon of war, and King Henry swore by its use:

"War without fire," he once remarked, "is like sausages without mustard."

I pinched the bridge of my nose. "You and your lads," I

snarled at the captain, "have made a beggar of me. If the land is wasted, and the villages depopulated, I will have no income."

"War is war, my lord," he replied indifferently.

The old Baron, it seemed, had done me no favours by failing to defend his territory against bands of marauders. No doubt he was too sick, or too busy with his vicious amusements.

There was nothing to be done save inspect the lordship for myself. My tiny household set out from Rouen on a bright, chill day in early March, to retrace my steps to the place where I had known so much pain and fear.

We were accompanied by Herr Hartmann, the German knight-turned-mercenary who shared my torments at La Tour Sombre. In my excitement at being knighted, I had forgotten to ask King Henry to bestow a favour on Hartmann. Oppressed by guilt, I invited him to join us.

"Back to that blasted castle?" he exclaimed when I found him, seated outside a tavern in Rouen market, "*Donnerkeil!* The scars on my backs have still not healed. I would as soon journey to the gates of Hell."

I noted his shabby appearance, and the cup of rancid ale he nursed in his swollen and callused hands.

"The war is over, at least for a time," I said, "bad news for fighting men who live by the sword, and have no other trade to follow. What will you do when your pay runs out, Herr Hartmann? Live on grass and berries?"

He sniffed, and upended his cup. "I had some thought of going to Italy," he answered as the piss-coloured liquid splashed on the cobbles, "there is always work for soldiers there. Or else go east."

"East?" I said, "you mean to fight the Turk?"

Herr Hartmann gave me a shrewd look. "No need to go so far as that, my friend. A war is brewing in the Kingdom of Bohemia. Such a war, as will eclipse this petty brawl in France."

I had some vague notion of what he meant. Rumours and snatches of news occasionally reached my ears, of rebellions and holy wars tearing through the complex patchwork of kingdoms that lay east of the Holy Roman Empire.

Along with most Englishmen, I paid scant attention to any of it. We were concerned only with France, and the lands Herr Hartmann spoke of were as distant and mysterious as the backside of the moon.

"Come with me to Rougemont-sur-Seine," I said, "and tell me more of Bohemia and your homeland on the way. At least I can provide you with food and drink, and a roof over your head, until you decide what to do."

He accepted, with a show of reluctance, and I was glad of his company. The big, fair-haired knight was quick to laugh and slow to judge, and kept me entertained with his inexhaustible fund of war stories. He was about twice my age, and had spent the best part of twenty years as a mercenary, mostly in Hungary and Poland, as well as the service of the Greek Emperor.

"This brand has lopped off a hundred Ottoman heads," he said cheerfully, swishing his broadsword through the air, "I used to carry the skulls of three Sipahi officers hanging from my saddle-bow, still wearing their spiked helmets. The Greeks and Hungarians thought it a great jest, but the Burgundians cried out in horror and said I was a barbarian. I had no wish to offend my new employers, so left the skulls impaled on stakes in a cornfield somewhere east of Paris. Useful scarecrows, I told the farmer. He agreed, and gave me fifty francs for them."

I laughed. "Twenty years of soldiering must have paid

well," I said, "have you no lands or castles of your own, then? Where has all the money gone?"

"Wine and women," he replied vaguely, "the usual things. Gambling debts. I had a wife, once. She was a whore from the Morea, and on the ninth morning I woke up to find her gone. I could stand that, save she took with her a jewelled reliquary and a diadem studded with gemstones. All my booty from the previous campaign."

He seemed reluctant to talk of his homeland, Westphalia. All I could gather from him was that it comprised a small duchy south of the Lippe River, mostly covered in dark forest.

"A gloomy place," he said, "I was happy to ride off to war, and leave my brother to die of boredom in our father's damp little *schloss*. I have never gone back. Never will."

We rode at a leisurely pace, undisturbed by fear of bandits or partisans. In this we were unwise, for plenty of dangerous men lurked in the woods. The roads were still empty of civilian traffic, and we passed a number of villages destroyed by the tides of war. Little remained of the houses save blackened gables, and the windows of the churches were dark and silent, sad eyes peering out at an evil world.

Eventually we reached the spot where myself and Lady Constanza had been ambushed. My thoughts once again turned to that mysterious woman as I gazed at the stretch of road, now empty and peaceful. What had become of her? Had she escaped the clutches of the Baron, only to succumb to some even worse fate in Paris? The Duke of Burgundy was still holed up in the French capital, and showed no outward sign of throwing in his lot with King Henry. Whatever message Constanza carried, assuming it ever reached the Duke, plainly had little effect.

We turned onto the side-road that led through deep forest to La Tour Sombre. Perhaps it was my imagination at work, or merely the onset of spring. but the wilderness seemed less dark and forbidding than before. The trees were in bloom, the shadows of winter had receded, and everywhere was new life and birdsong.

On the last stage of the journey Herr Hartmann's mood darkened. He was a little drunk, having polished off the contents of two flasks filled to the brim with strong ale.

"Tell me, my friend," he said thickly, between long swallows from a third flask, "does the name Jan Hus mean anything to you?"

I cudgelled my memory. In common with most of my countrymen, I was shamefully ignorant of anything that didn't directly concern England, and happy to be so. The doings of foreigners were of little interest unless they could be turned to our profit.

Jan Hus, however, was different. Like John Wycliffe, the English preacher and theologian, he was famous across Christendom for railing against the corrupt doctrines and practices of the church. Unlike Wycliffe, who had the good fortune to die a natural death, Hus was captured and burned at the stake. His execution occurred in the year of Agincourt, and his ashes were thrown into the Rhine.

Other than that bare handful of facts, I knew nothing of him, even where he lived and preached. I admitted as much to Herr Hartmann, who filled the gaps in my knowledge with drunken enthusiasm.

"You mind I spoke of the war in Bohemia?" he said, "well, Hus was a native of Bohemia. Educated in Prague, and ordained as a priest there."

The German brandished his flask at me. "Hus was still in Prague when the truth became apparent to him. He witnessed clergy, bishops, servants of the papacy, sunk in greed and every form of vice, abusing their privileges as churchmen, feeding like parasites off the poor and helpless."

I glanced nervously at my followers. Herr Hartmann was shouting, and I didn't want them disturbed by his crudely expressed heresies.

"My friend has sunk too much ale," I said with a forced grin, "pay no heed to what he says."

If any of them were offended or frightened, they didn't show it. The archers were cheerful, rough-hewn types from Warwickshire and the Marches, the groom a quietly polite northerner, and the cook a fat little Gascon who spoke little English and communicated largely via obscene gestures.

"The seeds Hus planted in Bohemia are ready to flower, my friend," bawled Herr Hartmann, "their roots shall spread and choke every damned priest between Prague and Constantinople!"

He stopped, and looked around guiltily. "I'm sorry," he whispered, "my tongue wags too freely when I am in drink."

"Much too freely," I replied, "that sort of talk will have the papal inquisitors after us."

I spoke harshly, but only for the benefit of my followers. Secretly I was intrigued by his talk of unrest in Bohemia. My own heretical views of the church were still intact, though I took care never to reveal them. The priests clustered around King Henry like flies, and any English soldier suspected of heresy would soon found himself chained to a stake, pleading for mercy while the stench of his burned flesh rose to the heavens.

Abashed, and possibly a little frightened at what he had said, my companion remained quiet for the remainder of the journey. I was content to ride beside him in silence, enjoy the balmy spring weather and mull over questions to ask him in private.

I broke out in a light sweat when the highest turret of La

Tour Sombre appeared over the trees to the east. The black pennon with the silver fish was gone - Sir Roland had ordered it torn down after we slaughtered the Baron and his men - yet an air of evil still seemed to hang over the place.

More of the castle gradually became visible through gaps in the trees. The road narrowed to a dirt track that wound through the edge of the woods to the fair open parkland beyond.

Squatting on its rise in the middle of the open country, just as I remembered, was the castle.

Herr Hartmann broke his silence. "Christ save us," he breathed, making the sign of the cross on his armoured chest, "I never thought to see this dung-hole again."

I shaded my eyes to get a better look at my new property. The drawbridge was still down, as we had left it, and the teeth of the portcullis raised. No helmets glinted on the battlements. The place appeared to be empty.

"How can you live there?" asked Herr Hartmann, "after everything we saw and suffered inside its walls?"

"By remoulding it," I replied, "to begin with, La Tour Sombre shall have a new name. An English name for an English lord."

"What name?"

I gazed at the single tower thrusting into the sky like an upright crimson lance. The castle was made of dark red sandstone, red as the blood its insane previous owner had spilled so freely.

"Red Keep," I said.

26.

I spent the next few days exploring the barony . My purpose was to let the serfs and tenants see their new lord, and to inspect the damage wrought by months of war.

It was just as bad as I feared. There were seven villages on the map, and all but two were utterly ruined. I rode sadly through empty settlements, where deer cropped at the grass in the deserted cemeteries and marketplaces and fled at my approach. With no-one to bury them, the bodies of murdered peasants lay rotting in the streets where they had fallen, cut down by English and French blades.

Herr Hartmann rode me with on these expeditions. I took three archers as a guard. Two were left to guard Red Keep and help the groom and the cook make the place habitable again.

None of the old Baron's household remained. We found the castle abandoned, though there were signs of recent life: the kitchens, buttery and wine cellar had all been ransacked, leaving just a few loaves and smelly cheeses.

The corpses of the Baron and his followers had also vanished, thankfully, and I could only guess that local peasants or brigands had raided the castle after we left. I never discovered what they did with the Baron's remains, nor enquired too closely either. It mattered only that his presence was gone from the castle, along with his foul spirit.

At last, near the eastern borders of my land, we found a village that had escaped the ruin of war. I could have shouted for joy when I saw the smoke of cooking fires rising over the hills, and spied a few men working in the fields. It was the time of spring planting, and here at least was some some good land that hadn't been burned or left fallow.

I had the Devil's own job to persuade the villagers to speak with me, or even venture out of their miserable little cottages. They saw me armed to the teeth, with four soldiers at my back, and naturally assumed the worst. To them, the presence of armed men on horses spelled nothing but death and disaster.

"Expect small welcome here," said Herr Hartmann as we guided our horses down the single muddy street, "these people are frightened. I've seen it before, many times. The innocent always suffer most in time of war."

He gestured at the rows of firmly barred doors and fastened shutters. "They will be huddled inside like so many mice, praying for us to go away."

I sighed, and goaded my horse towards the rough stone cross that stood in what passed for the village square.

"Listen to me," I shouted in French, standing up in my stirrups, "my name is Sir John Page. I am the new lord of Rougemont-sur-Seine. Your old lord, the Baron, is dead. He was an evil man. I promise to treat you better than he did, and to protect you."

My words went unanswered. Herr Hartmann gave me a nod of encouragement, so I tried again.

"I have taken up residence in the castle. Any one of you is welcome to come and speak with me. No harm will come to you. Do you hear me? No harm!"

Still no response. The doors and shutters remained closed. Somewhere a dog barked, and was swiftly silenced.

"God save King Henry," I said moodily, giving my reins a shake.

We got an equally cold response at the next village, though again I was cheered by the sight of the land being ploughed and sown.

"Take heart," said Herr Hartmann as we rode slowly back to the castle, "the people might get used to you, in time. Don't forget you are not only a foreigner but an Englishman, the natural enemy of their race. Peasants are a silly lot, ignorant as sheep and full of superstition. They probably think Englishmen are devils, sent from Hell to ravage and destroy their country."

"We're supposed to have tails," I replied, "didn't you know

that? Somehow the Scots got hold of the idea that all Englishmen have tails. For aught I know, the story may have spread to France."

The archers overheard me, and laughed when I lifted my rump from the saddle. "See?" I said to Herr Hartmann, "I am tail-less. Or else my mother snipped it off when I was born."

"Clear proof," the German remarked soberly, "that you are bastard-born indeed, and no true Englishman."

Our good humour lasted all the way back to Red Keep, where the cook had managed to scrape together some kind of feast. Rye bread and salt pork, mostly, the last of our rations washed down with the only two casks of wine left in the cellar.

The food was plain, and the wine far too sweet, but we made the best of it. I took my seat at high table in the cavernous hall, and filled my cup.

"Friends," I declared, "I ask you to drink in honour of Thomas Page, the Wolf of Burgundy. May he find peace."

My handful of followers, who sat together at one of the benches below the salt, obediently raised their cups in a toast.

"Thomas Page," we chorused, "the Wolf of Burgundy!"

That night we all slept on the floor of the hall. As the lord, I should have lain in the Baron's old bedchamber on the top floor of the tower, but I couldn't face sleeping in his bed. It would still smell of him, his putrid and decayed flesh, and the no less rotten odour of his soul.

Red Keep was full of ghosts that needed to be exorcised before I could think of the place as home, or hope to rest easy at night. In the following days my followers discovered some gruesome remnants of its recent history: a couple of broken skulls lying among the overgrown weeds in the ditch, and other scattered bits of bone and vertebrae.

"Bury them all together in the woods," I ordered the archers who found them, "and set up a wooden cross over the grave."

That was the nearest to a Christian grave I could provide for the wretches who had died there, tortured to death on the orders of a diseased madman.

They were almost the last, but not the worst, of Red Keep's grisly secrets. On the second floor of the tower, while rummaging through a battered old chest, I discovered a skeletal hand.

It was a pathetically tiny, claw-like object, and can only have belonged to a child. Revolted to my stomach, I ordered it taken into the woods and buried, this time with no marker. Some things are best forgotten.

While I laboured to mend and cleanse the barony, King Henry's star continued to wax. Alarmed by the loss of Normandy, the French rushed to make terms with him, and he spent most of the summer locked in negotiations with this faction and that faction, demanding much and conceding little.

Had they united against him, the French might yet have thrown his little army off French soil. For a brief time, this threatened to happen. The streets of Paris seethed with unrest, and the Duke of Burgundy was persuaded to open talks with his deadly rivals, the Duke of Orléans and the Count of Armagnac.

These high and mighty nobles had been sworn enemies for years, ever since the Duke of Orléan's father, Louis, was assassinated by the Burgundians. Entwined in their feud was the Dauphin, who favoured the Armagnac faction, and his mother, Queen Isabeau. She was rumoured to have bedded one or other of the dukes, or possibly all of them together, and repeatedly made a cuckold of her insane husband, King Charles. He, poor man, spiralled ever deeper into the pit of madness, and spent most of his days strapped down a table, screeching that he was made of glass.

Against the cool intellect and indomitable will of Henry of England, this band of quarrelsome, incestuous idiots had no answer. Throughout that summer he skilfully played one off against the other, all the while calculating the best terms for himself. The crown of France was still his goal, though he might have been content with Normandy and the restoration of all the lands ceded to his ancestor, King Edward, in the Treaty of Bretigny.

By this he stood to gain huge chunks of southern France, including Poitou and Guienne. Along with the duchy of Normandy and the crown of England, Henry would become one of the most powerful men in Christendom, on a par if not greater than the Holy Roman Emperor. Faced with this terrifying prospect, the Armagnacs and the Burgundians put away their knives and made an effort to overcome their mutual hatred.

Meanwhile France slid into ruin. The war had devastated much of Normandy, and the English-held towns were isolated outposts, surrounded by a hostile countryside. Bands of outlaws and partisans and dispossessed peasants roamed the land, robbing and murdering at will.

Royal government had all but collapsed in other areas of France, where supporters of the Armagnacs and Burgundians fought each other for temporary control of some patch of land. As Herr Hartmann said, it was the common people who suffered most. The sky was black with the smoke of burning towns, and the roads littered with slain innocents, like so many broken birds fallen from the sky.

In such a violent, unstable realm, with the threat of renewed war constantly on the horizon, every landowner needed plenty of money and swords about him if he wished to defend his own.

I had very little of either, and stood in the greatest danger. My lordship was uncomfortably poised near the border of Normandy and France, and had already suffered at the hands of roving bands of freeriders and common thieves. I could only pray that Henry would patch up some kind of a truce with the French, and that a lasting peace would ensue.

"We need time," I said to Herr Hartmann, "time to win over the tenants on my land, to rebuild the villages, to plough and plant the burned fields anew. Then, and only then, will this estate start to make any kind of profit."

"That will take at least a year," he replied frankly, "everything depends on the harvest. If God is merciful, there will be enough food to sustain everyone over the winter. If not..."

He spoke some unpalatable truths. I had barely enough money left to pay my followers for the next three months, and none at all to feed the villagers if the harvest failed. All I could do was wait, and pray for peace and good weather.

I was anxious to keep up with events in the wider world. To that end I sometimes despatched my groom, Ralf, to Rouen or Paris to fetch back the latest news. He was a soft-spoken Cumbrian with impeccable manners whom I suspected had once served in a noble household, possibly as a scribe, though he claimed to be illiterate.

Whether or not he could read and write, he knew how to digest information. Throughout the spring and into the summer he rode back and forth from Red Keep, bringing me word of the latest in the treaty negotiations, along with bits of scandal and vicious gossip. Most of the latter concerned Queen Isabeau, who seemed determined to cling onto power by opening her legs to every Frenchman of noble blood.

This was mere street gossip, of course, and for all I know the queen may have been as pure and chaste as a cloistered nun.

What it showed was the depth of the hatred the Paris mob had for her, and her rumoured bedmate, the Count of Armagnac.

The debauchery of the French court, the seething violence in the streets of Paris, and the delicately poised negotiations at Rouen: it all seemed a world away from the quiet woods and fields of Rougemont-sur-Seine. The countryside was not so very different from Kingshook, though the weather was balmier, and at times I longed for the overcast skies and gentle rains of Sussex. My little household survived by hunting in the woods, which were full to bursting with game, and fishing in the well-stocked rivers.

My efforts to win over the villagers met with little success. They continued to regard their new English lord with deep suspicion, and refused to come anywhere near the castle. I still had hopes of bridging the gulf between us. If nothing else, I could offer them shelter if they needed it, and protection if their homes were attacked.

Then, in midsummer, all my hopes were smashed by the arrival of the Bastard of Thian.

27.

The Bastard, Your Majesty may recall, had been one of the commanders of the French garrison at Rouen. During the siege he had taken special pleasure in beheading and flaying captured English soldiers, and hanging their mutilated bodies from the walls to taunt the rest of us.

After the city fell, King Henry severely punished some of the French commanders for their cruelty, executing some and sending others to captivity in England. The Bastard, however, was able to buy or talk his way out of trouble, and walked free while the heads of his comrades were impaled on pikes.

Since then he had roamed the French countryside with as many followers as he could attract to his banner, burning and looting and slaying at will. He claimed to act on behalf of his lord, the Duke of Burgundy, but in truth he attacked English and French alike.

This mad dog was naturally drawn to easy prey, and my ill-defended lands made a perfect target. With no scouts or watchtowers, I was caught totally unprepared.

I was in the smithy at Red Keep one morning in late September, whetting the edge of my sword on a grindstone, when a trumpet screeched on the roof of the tower.

"Banners to the south!" roared the archer who kept watch on the roof, "I see horsemen on the road. They come this way!"

I dropped the grindstone and ran across the yard into the base of the tower. The spiral stair was four storeys high, yet I galloped up them in less than a minute, hotly pursued by Herr Hartmann, Ralf and the rest of the archers. My cook, Pepin, was making venison stew in the kitchen, and it took more than the prospect of imminent danger to tear him away from his pots and pans.

"There," said the man on watch when I stumbled onto the roof.

His hand shook as he pointed to the south. I saw a trail of dust rapidly moving in the direction of Red Keep. They were less than two miles away, and a long row of bright pennons and banners could be seen through the haze.

"Raise the drawbridge," I ordered, "lower the portcullis and man the rampart above the gate. We will make a show of strength."

"Never fear," I added, trying to sound confident, "it could be an envoy from King Henry. The roads are unsafe, so it makes sense to travel with an armed escort."

"The roads are indeed unsafe," remarked Herr Hartmann as the archers clattered back down the stair, "thanks to men such as those riding towards us. They are brigands, John. Count on it."

As usual, his pessimism was both unwelcome and well-founded. While two of the archers frantically turned the windlass to raise the drawbridge, I raced down to the armoury to fetch my bascinet and quilted jack.

Herr Hartmann was already in his plate and mail, and waited for me on the walkway above the gate. Chains rattled and clanked in the room below as the teeth of the portcullis sank to the ground.

The German leaned his steel elbows on the parapet. "I knew this castle would prove the death of me," he said casually, "one way or another."

I looked at the field south of the castle, and my heart withered and died inside me.

Riders poured out of the woods. I counted heads as they spread out with impressive haste and discipline.

"Eighty-two," I murmured, "light horse, mostly, with a few men-at-arms at their head. Not just a pack of brigands, then."

"No," Herr Hartmann admitted, "a company of routiers, I would say. Well-led and organised. None of their banners show the arms of England or France. Look at that standard. Do you recognise it?"

He pointed a flowing pennon carried by one of the men-at-arms. It was by far the largest carried by the riders, and displayed the arms of their captain.

I strained my eyes to make out the detail. It showed a black hawk with folded wings against a white field topped with a red bar.

"I've seen that device before," I said solemnly, "at Rouen. Those are the arm of the lord d'Inchy, a French nobleman. The folded wings are a symbol of bastardy. Their captain can only be d'Inchy's half-brother, the Bastard of Thian."

Herr Hartmann's face was bleak. He knew of the Bastard's reputation, as did every soldier in France.

"You must try and bluff it out," he said, "they have no siege equipment, and his men will be none too eager to assault the walls. If the Bastard doesn't know how few we are, he may turn around and ride off to look for easier meat. If..."

In a bid to make our numbers appear greater, I told the archers to spread out along the walkway.

"Let me fetch some helmets from the armoury, my lord," suggested one, "we could balance them on top of our bowstaves, and prop the staves against the wall. From outside, the Frenchies will only see the helmets, and think we have twice the number of men."

Herr Hartmann nodded in approval. "I've seen it done before," he said, "at a siege in Hungary. The garrison were starving, and dropping like flies from the plague. They set up dummies on the wall. Helms on broomsticks. Anything to fool us, and ward off the final assault."

"Did it work?" I asked eagerly.

The big German shook his fair head. "No. We stormed the castle in a single night and put the lot of them to the sword."

Discouraged, I gazed out in despair at the enemy. The Bastard had formed his horsemen up into three neat companies, each two ranks deep. They waited, stock-still as if on parade, their pennons and streamers floating gently in the summer breeze.

The Bastard himself, a bulky figure in a suit of modish German-made armour, painted black and gold and richly decorated with elaborate patterns and devices, cantered forward to the gate. Behind him rode his standard bearer and three men-at-arms.

"He comes to parley," whispered Herr Hartmann, "be ready to bluff him out."

I readied myself, and looked over the parapet while the Bastard and his entourage halted, just inside bow-shot of the gatehouse.

"My lord," the nearest of my archers hissed urgently, "let me a try a shot at him. I could fell him from here. Please, my lord! I have a good eye and a steady hand."

I shook my head. The consequences if he missed were too dreadful to contemplate.

The Bastard raised his visor. I had never seen his face before, and it wasn't a pretty sight: fleshy, empurpled and pop-eyed, with thick lips and a broken mess of a nose. He went clean-shaven, and put me in mind of a furious infant.

"Sir John Page," he barked, "is that you I see on the wall?"

"It is," I shouted back, "come no closer, bastard, unless you want an arrow for breakfast."

He grinned. "I've already eaten, Sir John. Let us not chop words. Surrender your castle to me without a fight, and I promise to grant you and your men a swift death."

His grin widened into gap-toothed snarl. "Swifter, at any rate, than if you choose to resist. I believe you were at Rouen, Sir John. You know me."

I was briefly lost for a reply. The terrible memory of flayed Englishmen, dangled upside down over the walls of Rouen and shrieking in agony while the Bastard chortled over them and brandished his flaying knife, robbed me of words.

Herr Hartman's steel elbow nudged me in the ribs. "Speak!" he hissed, "don't let the *schwein* know you are frightened.."

I swallowed, and did my best to work up some defiance.

252

"There are forty archers inside this castle!" I cried, "all of them veterans of Agincourt. We are well-stocked for a siege. You have no guns, bastard, no rams or siege towers. I suggest you run away and seek a few defenceless peasants to molest."

The Bastard laughed - a fat, snorting noise, like a merry pig - and pointed to his left. "Forty archers, is it?" he grunted, "these men tell me otherwise. They say you have just a handful of followers, Sir John, barely enough to boil your porridge and wipe your backside in the morning. Do they lie?"

He gestured at a dozen or so ragged youths mounted on ponies. My blood ran cold when I recognised a couple of faces. I had seen them before, working in the fields outside my villages.

"Betrayed," I growled, "by my own folk! I offered to protect them, and be a good lord to them, and this is how they repay my kindness."

Herr Hartmann puffed out his cheeks. "I warned you," he said, "they want no foreigner to rule over them. The old Baron may have been a bad man, but at least he was French."

The treachery of the villagers took me between wind and water. I was struck dumb, and could summon up no more empty noises to hurl at the Bastard.

"Lost your tongue, Sir John?" he mocked, "tomorrow at dawn you shall be silenced forever. Say your prayers, and make peace with God."

"One more thing," he added cheerfully, "the helmets on sticks made me smile. They will make for a good story when I present your head in a basket to the Dauphin."

With that he turned and rode back to his men, laughing as he went.

The Bastard had given us another twenty-four hours to live. That gave his men time to cut timber from the nearby forest, and use it to make crude scaling ladders.

They were soldiers, not labourers, and made the peasants who had betrayed me do most of the work. The boys needed little goading, and I was disgusted and angered to see more men come in from the villages to help.

Their treachery, as I saw it, cut deep. Had I not rescued them from an evil master, and done everything in my power to win their trust?

In fairness I was still young, and had many hard lessons to learn. I was part of an army that had invaded their country, trampled and destroyed their crops, murdered their kin, drowned their homes in fire and blood, and expected gratitude in return.

Herr Hartmann tried to explain. "Imagine your roles were reversed," he said, "and you were an English peasant, asked to swear fealty to a new French overlord. Meantime, a few miles to the north, the King of France and his army are camped on English soil. You would be faced with a stark choice of submission or defiance. These men have chosen the latter. I salute them for it."

"As you wish," I spat, "I will hang them for it, when the time comes."

I turned my mind towards the defence of Red Keep. We were outnumbered ten to one, but I was determined to go down fighting. The alternative was to surrender to the Bastard, and I didn't believe his promises of a swift death for an instant. He would torture us to death, as he tortured his prisoners at Rouen, and draw out our agony for as long as possible.

Herr Hartmann and I sat in the hall and drew up a battle-plan. "If the Bastard has any sense," said the German, using his finger to draw a rough outline of Red Keep in a puddle of wine, "he will attack from several points at once. We don't have enough men to defend the length of the wall."

"The ditch will stop them," I said, "when it grows dark, we can fill it with caltrops."

Herr Hartmann nodded. "That will hurt a few of them, at least. Many routiers are none too brave, especially when there is little plunder to be had. If we stop them in the ditch, they may fall back."

He plucked at the bristles of his short yellow beard. " The only part of the wall not defended by the ditch is the gatehouse. He could throw all his strength there."

"I told Pepin to boil up as much porridge as he could, and keep it scalding hot," I said with an evil grin, "if they try to storm the gate, we can pour the stuff down on their heads. Ralf and the archers are gathering rocks and loose masonry to drop through the murder-holes."

"How many arrows do the archers have?"

"Twenty-four apiece. All our men are good shots, and should thin out the Bastard's numbers."

Herr Hartmann stuck his finger in the centre of the puddle. "If the walls are overrun," he said, "then we retreat to the tower and barricade the door. We should be safe in there, for a while."

For a while. How long? Until we starved, or King Henry sent a relief force to save us? Both were unlikely. The Bastard would be reluctant to linger at Red Keep, wasting time and supplies in a lengthy siege.

Henry had greater things on his mind than the siege of one small castle. After spending two months at Rouen, repairing the defences and reorganising the government, he marched east on Paris.

His decision was triggered by the news that the Armagnacs, and their friend the Dauphin, had met the Duke of Burgundy at Corbielle. The meeting was all smiles and good fellowship, without a hint of treachery, and suddenly Henry was faced with the prospect of the French nobility united against him.

He reacted to the threat with typical speed and resolve. In July he took Pontoise, to the north-east of Paris, and prepared to lay siege to the capital. Even if I had managed to send word to the king, pleading for aid, he could have sent none. Every spare man was needed for the assault on Paris.

I knew that our army had marched down the highway from Rouen, just a few miles west of my lands. King Henry sent no order for me to join him, and may well have forgotten my existence. Kings have short memories, especially with regard to subjects they have no further use for.

That night, while our enemies feasted and caroused outside, I had cause to regret my decision not to rejoin the army. I might have taken my place among the King's knights at Pontoise. Instead I was trapped inside Red Keep, wondering how best to spend my last few hours on earth.

Pepin, the fat little Gascon whose spirits were impossible to suppress, emptied his stores to provide the condemned men with a good dinner. My archers had recently shot and killed a fat buck in the woods, so there was no shortage of roast venison. There was only mead to wash it down, since we had finished off the last of the wine. Pepin made sure it was strong stuff, and after I had downed three cups of the thick, sickly sweet liquid I started to feel bullish, ready to take on the Bastard and all his villains single-handed.

"Let them come on the morrow," I declared, "I'll show them I am my father's son."

"A gold florin," I added, rapping my sword on the table, "to the man who brings down the Bastard. Shoot him full of arrows, or cut off his ugly head. It makes no odds. Just kill him."

My followers, who sat clustered at their table, greeted my

offer with apathy.

"What need have I of gold florins in Heaven, my lord?" asked one of the bowmen. Jenkin was his name, I think. Or Jack. Remembering the names of commoners has never been my strong suit.

"You ain't going to Heaven," rasped his mate, "not unless the angels need someone to shovel the dung."

There was a brief burst of laughter, and Jenkin or Jack responded by throwing a morsel of bread soaked in mead at his mate's head. The other man snatched it out of the air and greedily swallowed it, smacking his lips in relish.

"You need not argue, lads," I said, leaning back in my chair, "I haven't got a gold florin anyway. Truth to tell, I only have enough money left to pay you for another fortnight."

"Can we have the remainder now, my lord?" asked Ralf in his soft northern tones, "I owe fourpence to a tailor in Paris, and should hate to die in debt."

More laughter. Their gallows humour gave me cause for hope, and I regretted the absence of Herr Hartmann. He had volunteered to take first watch on the gate, ready to sound the alarm in case our enemies attacked under cover of darkness.

Now that danger threatened, the German mercenary was all business, and disapproved of us getting drunk. I told him lightly that we had rather die in drink than despair, at which he shrugged his heavy shoulders and strode off to the gatehouse.

A thought struck me, and I scraped back my chair and staggered out of the hall, leaving the rest to finish off the mead and venison.

I weaved my way across the torch-lit courtyard, grinning foolishly at the silhouette of Herr Hartman on the walkway above the gate. He was huge in his black armour, mace in one hand, short sword in the other. I almost pitied the men who would shortly face him in battle.

His attention was fixed on the enemy, and he failed to notice me as I pushed open the door of the tower. I soft-footed inside and started to climb the stair. Strong drink does nothing for a man's fitness, and I was labouring for breath by the time I reached the top.   Below me, to the south, the scattered fires of the Bastard's encampment glimmered like a field of stars. The sound of music and laughter drifted up from the field. They had a lute, along with pipes and drums.

I seethed with anger. My tenants were down there. They mingled with the enemy, gave them food and drink, laughed at their coarse jests.

"They shall hang," I muttered, "every mother's son."

I untied the scarf about my neck. At least I could keep one of my vows before the end.

By now the scarf was a fairly tattered and greasy object. I hauled down the rope attached to the pole from which the Baron's standard used to fly, and tied the ragged pennon around it. Then I winched the rope back up, so the remnant of Thomas Page's ancient wolf banner fluttered in the chill night air.

"Your standard flies again, father," I said, glancing up at the heavens, "as I promised it would. Though maybe not for very long."

I looked north. Somewhere over the far horizon, across the sea, lay England. The land I would never see again. Almost eighteen months had passed since I left my cousin bleeding into the dirt at Kingshook and fled on his destrier.

My father had also fled from Kingshook on a stolen horse. We were born fugitives, forever scrambling from one bolt-hole to the next. He had failed in his bid to outrun fate, and ended his days in a cage, despised and dishonoured. What indignities would the Bastard of Thian heap on my corpse, once I lay dead at his feet? Would he impale my head on his lance as a trophy? Maybe he would copy the example of Herr Hartmann, and tie it to his saddle-bow.

I couldn't afford to wallow in such dark thoughts. The men in the hall below looked to me, their lord, to set an example. If I gave way to fear, so might they.

More mead, I thought, might stiffen my courage. With a final salute to the wolf banner, I started back down the stair.

Shortly after midnight I took Herr Hartmann's place on watch. I was very drunk, while the Bastard's men showed no sign of going to sleep. Their campfires still burned, and the music and laughter was louder than ever.

There was an unrestrained, chaotic edge to the noise. Perhaps they also drowned their fears in alcohol.

"Do they mean to keep up that hellish din all night?" I muttered thickly, leaning against the parapet. The mead caused my head to pound, almost in time to the drums in the Bastard's camp.

"It's a deliberate strategy," said Herr Hartmann, "they want to intimidate us, and deprive us of rest. An old trick."

"They won't get any sleep either," I pointed out.

He shrugged. "So? The Bastard has the advantage of numbers. I know his kind. I've served under captains like him before. He won't waste too much concern on the welfare of his men. They may be exhausted in the morning, and we may kill a few before they overwhelm us. What is that to him? A few less mouths to feed, that's all."

The German left me, to warm himself by the fire in the hall and get something to eat. I wrapped myself up in a woollen cloak and watched the enemy for the best part of two hours, though it felt like eternity.

Slowly, slowly, the sands of time trickled away. Ralf was next on watch, and took my place while I staggered off, sleepless and frightened and still mazed with drink, to say my final prayers in the little chapel next to the hall.

I lay full length on the cold stone floor, and spread out my arms to form a crucifix with my body. The face of Christ, who writhed in agony on a small wooden cross resting on the altar, stared down at me. Whether in sorrow or pity or anger, or all three, I cannot say.

For some time I prayed, mostly for forgiveness, the salvation of my soul and the souls of my followers. I hoped the cool touch of the stone would keep me awake, but sleep was irresistible.

The flagstones seemed to dissolve and fall away beneath me. I sank into the pit.

A mailed hand shook me awake. In the confusion of waking, I thought it was the Bastard's hand, and yelled out in fear.

"Peace, my lord," said Ralf, "all is well."

His gentle voice was like a balm. He grasped my forearm and helped me stand.

Pale morning sunlight streamed through the narrow window above the altar. "The Bastard," I whispered, "has he...God's blood, get my sword!"

My throat was raw and dry, and my head roared as though the Devil's drummers were at work inside it. Ralf obediently picked up my sword, which I had placed next to me on the floor, and pressed the hilt into my hand.

"There is something you should see, my lord," he said.

He supported my weight as we left the chapel, as though I was an old man or an invalid. The hall beyond was empty, the fire burned down to a pile of ash in the hearth, and the benches and tables littered with the remains of last night's meal.

I shrugged off Ralf before we stepped outside. My men, if they still lived, couldn't see their lord in such a state. I paused a moment to gather up the tattered threads of my dignity, then strode out to meet the world.

All was quiet. The music had fallen silent, and the voices beyond the wall were stilled. An unearthly calm had settled over Red Keep.

My men, including Herr Hartmann and Pepin the cook, stood on the walkway of the southern wall. They broke the silence with a cheer when they saw me, and the archers waved their bows in the air.

Dumbfounded, I limped up the steps to the gatehouse and looked over the parapet.

Save for a few burned-out campfires, the field beyond was empty. The Bastard and his men had vanished - tents, horses, ladders and all.

In their place was a single white tent, and beside it a slender figure, hooded and cloaked, mounted on a sleek black courser.

The figure pushed back its hood, to reveal the tumbling tresses and strong, dark-skinned features of the Lady Constanza de Santaella.

28.

Constanza turned over in bed to face me. "John," she said, "what will you do next?"

"Next?" I murmured drowsily, "a little more sleep, a very large breakfast, and then..."

She gave my chest a playful tap. "Don't avoid the question," she said, mock-offended, "you know well what I meant. What are your plans for the future?"

I gazed at the ceiling and tried to think. It was difficult. The joy of my unexpected rescue from the Bastard of Thian, the consequent physical pleasure and lack of sleep, all conspired to stuff my head with straw.

"That depends." I said after a while. "I should do my duty, and ride to Pontoise to join the King. There is little enough to keep me here. This castle is full of evil memories, the land is mostly waste, and the people hate me."

We lay together in one of the smaller bedchambers inside the tower. I still refused to sleep inside the Baron's old chamber on the top floor. Sometimes I imagined his angry spirit stalking the room above me, and fancied I could hear slow footsteps dragging across the floor.

I had considered asking an honest priest (that rare breed) to exorcise the dead man's presence with bell, book and candle, though it would mean sending Ralf to Paris to fetch one. The local priests had either been driven out by the Baron or slaughtered in the wars. My lordship was a truly godless place.

Constanza chewed her bottom lip. Her long brown fingers delicately stroked my midriff. If I had any doubts of how extraordinary a woman she was, her account of the past few hours had laid them to rest.

Somehow she had learned of the Bastard of Thian's invasion of Rougemont-sur-Seine, and ridden straight from Rouen to persuade him to leave.

The Bastard was not a gentle or chivalrous man. I would have expected him to laugh in Constanza's face, and either rape her or have her flogged out of his camp.

Instead he received her in his pavilion with something akin to courtesy, listened to her words, and finally acted on her advice. Or threats. An hour or two before dawn, while I lay unconscious on the chapel floor, he gave orders for his men to break camp and ride away.

Constanza had explained this much to me in a breathless rush, while I hurried her up the steps to my bedchamber. My physical longing for her had grown in the months since we parted.

She returned my passion, or pretended to. I could never be sure of her true self. Constanza was too good an actress, and had lied and deceived for too long, to ever reveal it. I suspect her late husband, the knight of Castile, was her only true love.

Perhaps I do her an injustice. She must have felt something for me to confront the Bastard on my behalf. Then again, perhaps King Henry kept me in mind after all, and she acted on his orders.

"King Henry will not lay siege to Paris," she said suddenly.

Startled, I turned to look at her. "Why not?" I asked, "once the capital is in his grasp, the whole of France will follow."

"Think of it as a game of chess, John. The pieces on the board have moved, and one has been taken. Or rather, betrayed. The Duke of Burgundy is dead."

I sat bolt upright. "Dead? How can that be? Explain!"

She pushed a hand through her unruly mane and blinked up at me. In the half-light of morning, I could see how tired she looked. There were dark smudges under her eyes, and little creases at the corners. I wondered what those eyes had seen since we last met. What secrets they had absorbed.

"You know Duke John wished to forge an alliance with the Dauphin," she asked, "and put an end to the Armagnac feud?"

I nodded, and she continued. "When Henry advanced on Paris, the duke had the royal family, mad Charles and all, bundled away for safe keeping to Troyes, east of the city, where the English couldn't get at them there. Then he renewed his talks with the Dauphin."

"They had never met in person before. Special arrangements had to be made for their meeting, since there was so much hatred and distrust on all sides. After much argument, it was agreed that the Duke and his retinue would go to the bridge of Montereau, on the banks of the Seine, and there discuss terms with the Dauphin and his retinue. Carpenters were employed to build a cage in the middle of the bridge, with doors in each side."

"The duke and the dauphin both entered the cage, each with an escort of ten men who had sworn sacred oaths not to do each other harm. This was their method of guarding against treachery."

It sounded farcical, two of the most powerful nobles of France packed inside a cage with twenty other men, attempting to patch up some form of truce. Meanwhile their armed retainers eyeballed each other from the opposite banks of the Seine, keen to drown a few old scores in blood.

"Were you there?" I asked, "did you witness Burgundy's death?"

True to character, she ignored the question. "The duke was warned beforehand that his life was in danger if he entered the cage. However, he was not called John the Fearless for nothing, and went in regardless with his escort."

"He knelt before the dauphin, who refused to look at him. This offended the duke's pride, and he put a hand to his sword. One of the dauphin's supporters, Robert de Loire, accused him of daring to lay hand on a weapon in the presence of His Highness the Dauphin."

Any fool could predict what happened next. I groaned and put a hand over my eyes.

"The duke turned to his own men," Constanza went on, "what he might have said to them shall never be known. Tanneguy de Chastel raised his axe and shouted "kill, kill!". He hit the duke in the face with his axe."

"Wait," I said, raising my hand, "who in God's name is Tanneguy de Chastel?"

"The provost of Paris," she replied, "a great favourite of the Dauphin. He may have been told beforehand to strike down the duke. I'm not certain. In any case, his cry was the signal for the dauphin's escort to draw their knives and stab Burgundy as he lay on the ground."

"The door on the dauphin's side of the cage had been left open. As the duke was being stabbed, more soldiers piled through and finished him off with axes and swords. They cut off his right hand, just as his assassins had cut off the left hand of Louis of Orléans, twelve years ago."

"What of the duke's escort?" I demanded, "didn't they try to defend him?"

"It seems not. There was treachery in the air that day. Perhaps the Dauphin or his allies had bribed them to stand back while their master was cut to pieces. Whatever the truth, John the Fearless is no more."

My tired mind spun as I tried to make sense of it all. "I don't understand," I said, "why would the Dauphin plan or agree to such a thing? Murdering the duke will only drive the Burgundians into King Henry's arms. Burgundy's heir will never forgive the men who slew his father."

The late duke's son and heir was Philip, later known as Philip the Good. He was nineteen, still young, but old enough to avenge his father. It appeared to me that the Dauphin, and his allies among the Armagnac faction, had signed their own death warrants.

They had also sealed the fate of their country. With the new Duke of Burgundy for an ally, hot for revenge, Henry would sweep all before him.

Constanza swung her long limbs out of bed and crossed to the window seat. She sat down and gazed out at the morning sunshine. There was an enigmatic half-smile on her face, and she looked far too pleased with herself.

"The Dauphin is a strange creature", she said, "easily roused to action, and easily frightened. He will carry the blame for the murder, and deserves to. It was he who arranged it, with the connivance of his father-in-law, the Count of Armagnac, and certain members of Duke John's entourage."

None of this surprised me, nor that Constanza should know so much about it. "Why, though?" I asked, "what compelled Charles to do it?"

"He received a letter, delivered to him at Bourges by a certain friar. It carried no signature, and the seal was blank. The letter warned Charles that Duke John was in secret negotiations with the English. That he had promised them arms, troops, siege equipment and a ready supply of funds. This was enough to persuade the Dauphin to act."

I sank back against the pillows. "An anonymous letter," I said, "what a fool the Dauphin is. He should have held his nerve. At a stroke, he has delivered his realm into our hands."

"You seem to know most things, Constanza," I added after a moment's reflection, "do you know who wrote the letter?"

Maybe it was just the shadows playing on her face, but her smile took on on a sinister aspect.

"Who do you think wrote it, John?" she said. "Duke John played a double game for too long. We couldn't rely on him."

"*You...?*" I whispered, "you wrote the letter, on Henry's orders?"

Constanza gave a slow nod. "I prefer not to reveal secrets," she said, "take this one as a measure of my regard for you."

She was cold, Constanza, almost as cold as her royal master, and this revelation was the nearest to an expression of true warmth or affection I ever got from her. Even when we made love, if it could be called that, there was a part of her that remained absent.

Great Sultan, you may be surprised to hear that the hero-king of the English, Henry the Fifth, would have stooped so low as to arrange the murder of so high and puissant a nobleman as the Duke of Burgundy. Remember, Majesty, that Henry thought of himself as the scourge of God, sent by divine will to chastise the French nation for their sins. For him the laws of chivalry did not apply to France, and no stratagem was too base or ignoble to bring his treacherous subjects to heel.

Once I had rested, and recovered from the shocks and alarms of the previous few days, I was able to take stock. Constanza informed me that King Henry intended to take full advantage of his new alliance with Burgundy, and press on with the conquest of France.

"He plans to offer his hand in marriage to Catherine, King Charles' daughter," she said, "on condition that her father agrees to disinherit the Dauphin and make Henry regent, as well as heir to the French throne."

"King Charles is mad," I replied, "how can he agree to anything, when he doesn't even know who he is most of the time?"

Constanza waved that aside. "We only need his seal on the documents. Queen Isabeau and the royal council will do the actual negotiations on his behalf. By all accounts, the queen is willing enough to sell her daughter to Henry in exchange for peace, and the guarantee of her own position."

"The Dauphin will fight," said Herr Hartmann, "he is not

finished yet, even if his own father agrees to disinherit him. Henry has much work left to do."

The three of us were at breakfast in the great hall. Sunlight poured through the high windows and reflected off the silver platters and goblets Pepin had fetched from the buttery. This was the old Baron's best silver, which I had ordered to be broken out to celebrate our deliverance from the Bastard of Thian.

Our platters were heaped with porridge, the same porridge Pepin had intended to pour on the heads of the Bastard's men. There was also some rye bread, and venison left over from the feast two nights gone. A plain enough meal, but I savoured every mouthful, grateful and relieved to be alive.

This was the first time Constanza and Herr Hartmann had met. The German, who was a shrewd judge of character, plainly distrusted my bedmate. He gave her suspicious glances, and only spoke to her through me.

"John," said Constanza, "you never answered my question. What do you plan to do next?"

"The war looks set to continue," I replied, "I cannot hope to avoid it. Perhaps God sent the Bastard of Thian to teach me that lesson."

"I will go back to the the army. There is little option. I am down to my last few pennies, and cannot afford to run even this meagre household without more funds. My only trade is war."

"First," I added, "there is an oath I must fulfil. I vowed to hang the peasants who betrayed me and gave food and aid to the Bastard."

"That oath shall not be kept," Constanza said firmly, "hanging able-bodied men will achieve nothing. You need them to till and sow your fields."

She pointed her knife at me. "The King has not forgotten

you, John. He has a prodigious memory, and never forgets those who have rendered him good service in the past. If you want to earn more royal favour, more lands and castles, then you will not destroy the only estate he has given you so far."

"Henry would not forgive them," I said forcefully, "he has a short way with traitors, as Sir Roland found out. So do I."

"He has an even shorter way with fools," she retorted, "I warn you, do nothing rash."

Another man might have done it, hanged the villagers, and left their bereaved families to starve.

I was not that man. Yet. In spite of my hard words, there was still enough goodness left in me to overcome the base desire for revenge.

"To the army, then," I sighed, "let the traitors live."

29.

Great Sultan, I shall not weary you with a lengthy account of the war that followed. As in Normandy, King Henry fought no great battles, but wore the French down in one bloody siege after another.   I believe his true genius for warfare lay in siegecraft rather than pitched battles, which presented too great a risk. It should be remembered that Henry only fought at Agincourt because he had to, and would have gladly avoided the French army in return for safe passage to Calais.

His skill at reducing French towns to rubble was equalled by a talent for careful diplomacy. I was there at Troyes, the great cathedral town east of Paris, when he signed the Treaty of Troyes, whereby the madman King Charles agreed to disinherit his son and marry his daughter to Henry.

How much Charles knew about the treaty is debatable. He was present, in body at least, a frail, sick-looking man with scanty white hair, who had to be held upright by two French knights when he tried to stand. He remained silent, his eyes vacant, while Queen Isabeau conducted the negotiations. She was a tall, imposing woman, her high beauty marred by a lifetime of debauchery and politics.

Isabeau was as ruthless as any of the men about her. She justified the exclusion of the Dauphin, her own son, by claiming that he was in reality a bastard, the illicit product of one of her many affairs. His real father, so she claimed, was Louis, the Duke of Orléans murdered twelve years previously by supporters of John the Fearless.

Consider, O Sultan, the shamelessness of this woman. She was reader to sully her reputation, such as it was, in public, and admit to having cuckolded the King of France with a host of lovers. Not only that, but she also cast dirt on her son, stripped him of his princely status and dignity and humiliated him in the eyes of Christendom.

Perhaps I judge her too harshly. As a woman, she could not take the field and lead armies into battle. Isabeau sacrificed her reputation, and the interests of her son, for the sake of France. Her husband was a lunatic, her country was in tatters, her nobles a pack of worthless fools, more inclined to plunge knives into each other than unite against a common enemy.

In her eyes, the only man who could save the realm was King Henry, who had done so much to bring misery and destruction to it. By giving Henry her daughter, she hoped to end the war, and ensure that the royal blood of the Valois would run in the veins of future Kings of France.

The supporters of the Dauphin, who had declared himself the true regent and heir in opposition to Henry, still held many towns and castles south of Paris. Henry was keen to hurl himself back into the fray, but first had to go through the tedious business of wedding and bedding his new Queen.

With typical economy, he combined war with pleasure. A few days after the wedding he marched to lay siege to Sens, sixteen leagues from Troyes, and took his bride with him.

I was among the knights of the rearguard, and caught occasional glimpses of Queen Catherine, who rode in a covered litter, guarded by an escort of her own knights. She was a pale, slender little thing, with far too much of her father in her for my liking. The same watery blue eyes, milky complexion and silken fair hair.

"She is Valois through and through," remarked Herr Hartmann, "and may have inherited the taint of their blood."

I made a half-hearted attempt to defend her. "She is only half-Valois. Her mother is as sane as you could wish, if not very moral."

Herr Hartmann batted away the flies dancing around his destrier's muzzle. It was a hot, sticky summer, and the heat threatened to bake us alive in our armour.

"For your country's sake," he said, "I shall pray the maternal blood proves the stronger."

The Armagnac garrison at Sens surrendered almost as soon as our banners appeared before its walls, and King Henry was able to parade his wife before the citizens. We marched on to Montereau, where the garrison refused terms of surrender, and held out with desperate valour against our efforts to take it by storm. When the town fell, Henry had the surviving men of the garrison marched out and butchered like so many sheep in front of the gates.

He ordered a band of Welsh archers to do the throat-slitting. I was near his side while the men were slaughtered, and overheard him explain his reasons to the mayor of the town, who begged the King to show mercy.

"They die to atone for the murder of the Duke of

271

Burgundy," he said, "as all such traitors and assassins must perish."

This was a flat-out lie. The garrison of Montereu had nothing to do with the Duke's death, and Henry was in no way obliged to avenge it. He killed those men to provide another example of his severity, and terrify his enemies into submission.

The summer of blood wore on. Siege after siege. One town after another engulfed in smoke and flame. At Melun our artillery smashed through the walls, while our engineers undermined the foundations. It was Caen all over again, and we fought hand-to-hand on the ramparts and in the tunnels.

Once again Henry risked his own person in combat. In the stifling hell of the mines I saw him fight hand-to-hand against the French commander, a knight named Arnaud Guillaume de Barbazon.

Henry failed to kill Arnaud, which gave him a problem after Melun was conquered. He was furious with de Barbazon for putting up such a stout resistance, and wanted to execute him. The laws of chivalry forbade this, since he had engaged the man in single combat. Henry contented himself with hanging the man alive in an iron cage. The garrison met the same fate as their comrades at Caen and Melun.

Herr Hartmann, I am sorry to say, was killed at Melun. A sharp-eyed marksman on the walls shot him while he stood outside his tent and drank his morning ale.

The arrow hit my friend in the neck, just above the collarbone. Two archers carried him to a surgeon, who did his best to extract the barbed head with the aid of a knife and a red-hot iron.

Surgery, especially battlefield surgery, is sheer butcher's work. The surgeon was of the worst sort, a self-trained drunkard with an unsteady hand.

Herr Hartmann was strapped down down to a wooden pallet inside a pavilion full of other wounded men, and subjected to the most appalling torture, worse than anything he suffered at the hands of the Baron at Red Keep.

One of the archers who carried him to the pavilion knew he was my friend, and came to fetch me before the end. I hastened to the pavilion, and stood by while the wall-eyed fool who called himself a doctor poked and prodded at the arrow. He had broken off the shaft in his clumsy efforts to cut it out of my friend's neck, and left a jagged fragment firmly stuck in the wound.

There were far too many wounded for our surgeons to cope with, and many were simply dumped on the grass and left to die. A few of the lucky ones were dosed with poppy juice against the worst of their pain. Others shrieked and writhed on their blood-slathered pallets as surgeons and attendants laboured to saw off shattered limbs before they could turn bad.

The pavilion stank like a charnel house, rank with the odours of sweat and blood and fear, mingled with something else, a sweet-rotten stench that is every soldier's worst nightmare: gangrene.

Herr Hartmann was semi-conscious. "Where am I?" he murmured, "something hit me....I fell...I knew nothing more..."

I caught his wavering hand. "You were stung by an arrow," I said gently, "take heart. You are in the best of care."

This was a lie, and he was too experienced a soldier to believe it. "No surgeons!" he moaned, "I'll not have some wine-breathed sawbones cut me up like a side of beef! Let me die on my feet!"

The pallet jumped as he strained against the leather bonds that held him down. At a sign from the surgeon, two pale young attendants laid their hands flat on his chest and forced him to lie still.

"Bloody German," growled the surgeon, "I have plenty of good Englishmen to tend to. If he doesn't want to be treated, I'm happy to leave him be."

"No," I said urgently, "he is in pain, and doesn't know what he says. Please, for my sake, do what you can."

Muttering under his breath, he passed his knife to one of the attendants and reached for the cauterising iron, which lay among a heap of hot coals in a brazier.

"Failed to cut the arrow out," he muttered, his hot wine breath hanging in the air like a fume, "have to try and burn it out instead."

I looked away as he pressed the sizzling tip of the brazier against Herr Hartmann's neck. My friend shrieked, and my throat and nostrils filled with the smell of roasting flesh.

The agony caused him to swoon. He never woke, thank God, for the surgeon made an unholy mess of it. The arrowhead was finally extracted, a bloodied lump of iron, but by then the shadow of gangrene was already stealing over the ragged lips of the hole gouged into Herr Hartmann's neck.

"A pity," said the surgeon, throwing the arrowhead into a bucket, "I thought I had saved him. Ah well, *Decipimur speci recti*, as Horace has it."

He patted me on the arm with his hand, still rank with Herr Hartmann's blood. "To translate very roughly - we are deceived by the appearance of rightness."

It was tempting to knock the incompetent dolt to the floor, but my friend deserved some dignity in death. Brawling over his corpse would have been an insult to the memory of the only true friend I had made in France.

I sat by him awhile, thinking on the times we had known. Often, when we were alone together in the great hall at Red Keep, he had spoken of his heretical beliefs, and his admiration

274

of the Czech preacher, Jan Hus.

"You are the only living soul I have told of my heresy," he would say, "I trust you, John, more than I trust my own brother."

Now he was dead, and his secret would go with him to the grave.

"It is my fate," I murmured, folding his big, lifeless hands over his breast, "to be left alone in the world. My comrades die like flies, and yet God insists on keeping me alive. To what end? What purpose?"

God sent no answers. In truth, I knew them already.

30.

Herr Hartmann was laid to rest in the cemetery of a little church outside Melun. The padre was dead or fled, so there was none to object as his body was lowered into French soil.

The only mourners were myself and my household - Ralf, Pepin, and the five archers, all of whom followed me back to the wars. We had left Red Keep deserted, and the people to prosper or perish. I had ceased to think of them.

Once my friend was buried, there was the question of what to do with his few possessions. His suit of heavy plate was far too big for me, so I sold it to a French armourer in Melun.

"One cuirass with spaulders," he muttered as he carefully inspected the ironmongery laid out on a bench in his shop, "one bascinet with visor, a pair of gauntlets, one mail corselet, a pair of greaves, a pair of sabatons..."

He droned on, listing all the parts of the dead man's harness, while I gazed sadly at the hollow metal shell that had once contained Herr Hartmann.

"Part of this suit are old," said the armourer, "and damaged in places. See the scars on the cuirass?"

"The previous owner was a veteran of many wars," I replied absently. He shook his head and muttered something unintelligible in French. In other circumstances he might have quibbled over the cost, but I was armed, and Melun had barely recovered from the slaughter and damage inflicted by our army in the recent siege. The evidence of English cruelty was all around him, and he was too sensible a man to risk becoming another casualty of war.

"Twenty livres," he said, "you won't get a better price anywhere else."

Twenty livres at that time was roughly the same as fifteen English pounds, five times the amount King Henry gave me to set up a household at Red Keep. I accepted the offer, and left his shop with my saddle-bags bulging with coin. There was too much money for one horse to carry, so Herr Hartmann's destrier had to carry some of the weight.

The money was safely locked away in an iron chest, kept in the cellar of a guildhouse in the town centre, with my archers to guard it. I raised more funds by selling my late friend's destrier to one of the Earl of Warwick's knights. The beast was getting on in years, but still strong and hale, with good wind, and after some argument I got fourteen livres for him.

It might be said that I profited from Herr Hartmann's death. What of it? He had no more use for earthly chattels, and his kin were in far-off Westphalia. I had signed a new indenture with the army, and couldn't travel to his brother's damp little castle, high in the forested German hills, even I was so inclined.

With the new-found wealth I was able to buy new gear for myself, and to draw up serious plans for the resurrection of the Company of Wolves. That had been my ambition, ever since I discovered my father's old banner at the bottom of a strongbox at Steventon. Fate, and a chronic lack of cash, had conspired to undermine that ambition, but now I was in a position to realise it at last.

First I bought some black silk and red and gold thread, and hired a seamstress to create a new pennon, based on my father's.

"I want the same arms as these," I instructed her, tossing the ragged bit of fabric on her lap, "a red wolf's head, with golden eyes. Exactly the same. Understand?"

She nodded and creased her toothless mouth into an ugly smile. I left her to it, and went off to buy a new bascinet and a breastplate of Milanese design.

I had the breastplate inscribed with the word 'Avaunt', which Sir Roland had used as the signal to murder his cousin. His betrayal saved my life, and I had the word chiselled onto the steel as a constant reminder of the whims of fate, and the faithless nature of mankind. I wore the breastplate almost to this day, O Sultan, until your servants took it from me after my capture in the Hagia Sophia.

Before I could leave the army and carve out a career as a mercenary captain, I had to fulfil the terms of my indenture. That Christmas was spent in Paris, where King Henry, his new ally Philip of Burgundy and the mad King Charles, entered the city with great pomp. The Paris mob, thinking this an augury of peace, welcomed us with cheers, and showered rose petals on our heads from the upper storeys of shops and houses.

Henry left them in no doubt as to who was the master. He took the Louvre for his lodgings, where he kept the feast in royal splendour, while Charles and his threadbare household were packed off to the far less grand surroundings of the Hotel de Saint-Pol.

I heard that Charles' remaining servants chose to abandon their master, and left him alone to celebrate Christmas with a bowl of gruel and a single page for company. Consider, O Khan of Khans, the fate of this man, once the most feared and admired monarchs of Christendom, and have pity on his memory!

There followed a lull in the war, due in part to the season, and to King Henry's decision to return home and show off Queen Catherine to his English subjects. He left the Duke of Exeter in command of Paris, with a garrison of five hundred archers.

While we waited for the King to return, I made the best use of my money. I had it fetched from Melun in a covered wagon, guarded by my archers, so I could hire more men. There were plenty of masterless soldiers in the capital - deserters, some of them, along with mercenaries of all Christian nations, and men who had either lost their old captains as a result of war or sickness.

I was able to afford another thirteen hobelars, which made eighteen in total. Along with Ralf and Pepin, I now had the beginnings of a company. I was still a knight of the royal household, and my recruits had to sign formal indentures to join the king's army. As soldiers of the King, they were paid out of army funds, and to ensure their loyalty I added a penny a day out of my own war-chest.

"Don't worry, lads," I assured those who were reluctant to sign up for another year's service, "this war will soon be over. Once we have the Dauphin's head on a pikestaff, and King Harry has his rump on the throne of France, we can ride away and look to make our own fortunes."

"Where to, John?" was the question put to me by Constanza. She occasionally visited me in Paris, when she could spare the time from her various mysterious errands.

I never asked my occasional lover about her work, and she rarely let slip any secrets. For all I knew, she may have kept an army of lovers scattered about France. Ours was a purely functional arrangement For all that, she seemed genuinely concerned for my future.

"Will you go south," she said as we lay together in my modest lodgings two streets away from the Louvre, "to the Italian city-states? There is always work for mercenaries there. You could be like your fellow countryman, Sir John Hawkwood, and end your days with rich estates in the Romagna and Tuscany. Your grateful employers might erect an equestrian statue of you, all in white marble, and place it beside the fresco of Hawkwood in the Duomo in Florence. Wouldn't that be fine?"

I agreed that it would, though hardly likely. "Italy is one prospect," I admitted, "though I have another in mind."

"Where?" she asked, her eyes gleaming with an insatiable desire to know the thoughts and dreams of others, "east, perhaps, to Constantinople? The Greeks shower any man with gold if he brings them enough Turkish heads."

"Not so far east as that," I answered, "Herr Hartmann used to speak of a war brewing in the Kingdom of Bohemia. I have a mind to go there."

She frowned. "Bohemia? A godless place, full of heathens and heretics. The country is nothing but mountains and forests and barren waste. You would hate it. No, you must not go to Bohemia, John. A mercenary captain cannot afford to follow his conscience."

For once, she failed to see into a man's heart and divine the truth. Constanza assumed that I wished to ride east to fight the so-called heretics, inspired by Jan Hus to take up arms against the tyranny of the church. God knows how she would have reacted if I told her I dreamed of joining the heretics, and leading them in a glorious anti-crusade against the church.

She gave me further advice, on how I should take greater care of my lands at Rougemont-sur-Seine, and do more to win the King's favour. Since rejoining the army I had performed no brave deeds, accidentally or otherwise. My concern was to keep a whole skin and survive the war with enough money to forge my own career.

All my plans were brought crashing down thanks to the actions of one man: my old lord Thomas, Duke of Clarence.

Henry's greatest mistake in France was to return to England with his bride and leave Clarence in a position of command. Perhaps filial love blinded him to the duke's faults, his rampant envy and ambition. Or maybe he pitied Clarence and wished to give him an opportunity to win the glory he so desperately craved.

Whatever the truth, Clarence was given command of four thousand men and ordered to lead a chevauchée into Anjou and Maine. His instructions were to wreak as much havoc as possible, burn and pillage and despoil in the old style, render the lands waste and scare the people into accepting Henry as their rightful King. Clarence's ultimate aim was to seize Angers, the provincial capital of Anjou, and gain control of the entire region.

I might have stayed out of it. The Duke of Exeter would have kept me and my fledgling company in Paris, where he needed good men to keep the volatile city in order. We never knew when the citizens might take into their heads to rise up in revolt, and the presence of armed men at every barracks and street corner was the best way of keeping the mob quiet.

Constanza had other ideas. "Offer your sword to Clarence," she urged, "with the King out of the country, it is the only way to win fame and glory."

For such a chilly woman, who never spoke of love or even hinted at it, she took a great deal of interest in my affairs. I believe she regarded me as a project, a challenge to keep her wits sharp when she had nothing else to do. After all, if she could take such inferior clay as John Page and turn it into gold, what might she not achieve?

"Fame and glory I can do without," I lied, "but wealth is different. Wealth, and land, and more castles to call my own."

"Then serve with Clarence," she said, "he will have good memories of you. If nothing else, it will add to your reputation as a fighting soldier, and attract more men to your banner."

She knew how to play on my vanity. I agreed, and rode out with the Duke of Exeter and a hundred hobelars to join Clarence's muster at Bernay.

We invaded Anjou in the early spring, fourteen hundred and twenty-one years after the birth of Christ, and twenty-seven years after mine. I was in the prime of youth and strength, with a company of hobelars under my command, and my new banner fluttering overhead. The seamstress of Melun had made a beautiful new pennon from the raw materials I gave her, and the red wolf's head once again rippled over the fields of France.

I was tempted to think my task was done, that I had redeemed my father's name and reputation. This was hopelessly premature. As yet I had won no victories in my own right, gained no lands save one poor and unprofitable barony, inspired no troubadours to sing ballads of the Wolf-Cub and his exploits.

Our army pushed further into the fair green province of Anjou, ancestral homeland of the Plantagenets. Everything seemed possible. In time my fame would grow to eclipse that of my father. One day I would return to England, full of years and honours, to set up a splendid tomb in his memory. His bones would be removed from under the black oak near Steventon, and re-interred as befitted a Christian and a soldier.

All these dreams came to ruin, thanks to the murderous folly of Clarence.

31.

The Duke was in a hurry to secure Angers, and force-marched his troops across the River Huisne at Pont-de-Gennes, east of Le Man. We met with no resistance, and were able to swing south-west to another river crossing at the Loire. Within days of departing from Bernay, Angers was in our grasp.

At this crucial moment, Clarence hesitated. Our scouts and foraging parties reported that Angers was strongly held, and he dithered over whether to press on and lay siege, or fall back to some convenient bastion.

His captains, among them the Earl of Salisbury and Sir Gilbert Umfraville, nephew of Sir Robert, gave him conflicting advice. As a mere knight banneret, I ranked too low to offer an opinion, but was all for pushing on to Angers. King Henry would not have hesitated, regardless of the strength of the garrison.

The duke, however, was not his brother. "We will fall back," he said at last, after several hours of head-scratching and bitter argument, "and consider what is best to be done."

What is best to be done. It was a phrase full of ill omen, and reflected the uncertainty of his mind. You know only too well, O Sultan, how a general must be decisive, and allow no time for doubt to creep into the hearts of his officers. The furrowed brows and dark looks on the faces of men like Umfraville and Salisbury, both far abler soldiers than their chief, filled me with anxiety.

The army turned around and made camp at Beaufort-en-Vallée. Our men would have marched a great deal faster had we known that an enemy host was advancing west from Tours, to block our line of retreat back to Normandy.

A word on the enemy. Desperate for allies after the loss of Normandy and Paris, the beleaguered Dauphin had begged for help from Scotland. The Scots, those red-shanked robbers, always keen to thrust a dagger between England's shoulders, agreed to send ten thousand of their best fighting men to France under the command of the Earl of Buchan and the Earl of Wigtown.

About half these men, along with a few hundred French, were now encamped at a village near Baugé, east of the River Couasnon. Our army at Beaufort, cheerfully ignorant of the approaching doom, was some eight miles south-west of the river.

Clarence had just sat down to dinner in his pavilion when Sir Gilbert Umfraville galloped into camp at the head of a foraging party.

As was his habit, the duke had invited his nobles and some favoured knights to share the meal. Despite my lowly status, I was also invited. A few shreds of popular fame still clung to me, and it turned out that every nobleman present had read The Siege of Rouen. They treated me with genial contempt. Exeter, for instance, called me the Infant Chaucer, which I took as a compliment of sorts.

We dined in our armour, in case of a sudden call to arms. I was tearing the leg off a roast capon when Sir Gilbert barged into the pavilion, rank with sweat and dust. He wasn't one to stand on ceremony, and gasped out his news without waiting for permission to speak.

"The enemy, Your Grace," he panted, "they are up in force west of the Couasnon, barely an hours' march away."

Clarence, whose narrow features were already flushed with too much wine, shot to his feet. The burst of excited chatter from his nobles died away as he wiped his mouth.

"How many?" he demanded. His entire body quivered, like a hound about to be unleashed on a fox, and there was a gleam in his eyes that made my heart skip.

Sir Gilbert paused for breath. He and his uncle were hard-headed Border knights, superb fighters and strangers to any notion of mercy or compassion. Both were thoroughly hated by the Scots, whom they raided and slaughtered with impunity.

Scottish vengeance on the Umfravilles was fast approaching. "Some five or six thousand, Your Grace," he replied, "I saw the banners of Buchan and Wigtown, and de Lafayette, the Constable of France. Mostly Scottish knights and men-at-arms, with a few French."

"We are outnumbered," said Exeter, "and they have blocked our path into Normandy. No matter. I say we retreat south, cross the Loire at some convenient point, and circle back to our own territory. If Buchan and Lafayette choose to follow, we can wait for them on ground of our own choosing."

There was a murmur of agreement. I was relieved at Exeter's calm good sense, and the support he had from his peers.

All save Clarence, whose voice was the only one that counted. "Retreat?" he exclaimed in a tone of high-pitched indignation, "and allow the Dauphin to boast that his men caused the banners of England to fly before them? Never!"

A baffled silence fell over the pavilion. This was Clarence's moment, of course, the one he had waited and prayed for ever since Agincourt. God had handed him a chance to win a victory at last and even the score with his brother.

Salisbury was the first to recover. "Your Grace," he said, barely containing his impatience, "we only have fifteen hundred men-at-arms. The rest are archers. We could fight a defensive battle, behind lines of stakes and ditches, but..."

"To attack would be sheer folly," rasped Sir Gilbert, "we may as well cut our own throats, and save the Scots the trouble."

His northern bluntness made no impression on Clarence, who didn't seem to hear him. "If we ride north, now," he said excitedly, "with all speed, we could take them unawares and cut them up in their tents. In the confusion, they won't realise how few we are."

"Come, Sir Gilbert," he cried when this met with further silence, "these are Border tactics, are they not? The swift raid, the sudden dash, and then away again before the enemy knows what hit him!"

"The last time such a thing was attempted in the north country, Your Grace," Sir Gilbert replied quietly, "was at Otterburn, where Harry Hotspur tried to ambush the Scots as they lay in camp. We all know how that ended. Hotspur was taken captive, and his men scattered and slain."

"Just so," said Lord Roos, "any talk of a head-on assault against superior numbers is madness. We should withdraw at once. Let the Dauphin claim his empty victory, and to hell with his boasts."

Clarence, the stubborn dolt, would not listen to reason. "I am in command here," he yelled, his voice shrill again, with more than a touch of petulance, "and my orders *will* be obeyed! We *will* ride out and attack the enemy. Does any man here challenge my authority?"

Not one of them spoke up. Less through fear of Clarence, I suspect, than the King, who had placed his brother in charge of the army as a mark of confidence and trust. Any challenge to Clarence was a challenge to Henry.

No man present, whatever his rank or degree, cared to defy the victor of Agincourt, and the butcher of Caen and Montereau.

"Salisbury," said Clarence after a long pause, "I believe a number of our archers are still out foraging. Gather up the strays, and bring the entire force of archers north in support as soon as possible. Meantime I will lead our men-at-arms to Baugé."

"Yes, Your Grace," mumbled Salisbury, staring at the floor. Clarence was deaf to his sullen tone, and blind to the expressions on the faces around him.

"Come, gentlemen," the duke bellowed, his face ruddy with drink and excitement, "to the greater glory of England, and the confusion of our enemies!"

"To your company, Sir John," Salisbury ordered me as we dispersed. I bowed and hurried out of the pavilion, wishing I could take horse and ride as far and as fast away as possible.

I found my men at dinner, seated on the grass near our tents. "Up," I cried, "fetch your horses. Ralf, get Odo."

Odo was my destrier, named after the horse I had lost, slain by Sir Roland's cut-throats on the road near Louviers. My men scrambled for their mounts, tethered in a little wood nearby.

Of them all, only Pepin the cook would be left behind. He raised his flask of cheap red wine in an ironic salute, and lay flat on his back to enjoy the warm spring sunshine. I envied the villain, and had to suppress an urge to kick his fat *derrière*.

Trumpets screamed through the camp, summoning our knights and men-at-arms to their duty. Like the nobles, they were already in armour, and had only to wait for their squires to fetch weapons and horses.

The golden pards and blood-red cross of England were to the fore as the long column of horsemen, splendid in burnished steel, thundered out of the camp. Clarence set a furious pace, and hundreds of racing hoofs churned up a great cloud of dust that formed a dirty yellow haze in the air. The long line of horsemen streamed away over the hill, heading for the river crossing near Baugé.

Salisbury sent outriders to bring in the foragers, which gave our archers time to deploy at a more leisurely pace. Few of them looked keen to follow in the wake of the men-at-arms, and engage a much larger host lurking somewhere over the horizon to the north.

Solid, dependable Ralf, who I had made my standard bearer, jogged up with Odo. "Are we going to fight, my lord?" he asked, and for once there was a twinge of anxiety in his soft voice.

"We are," I replied shortly. He was frightened, but I couldn't help that. My own fear was enough to cope with, and my hands shook as they tightened the girths of my saddle.

It took the best part of an hour for our foragers to return. Salisbury was beside himself with impatience, and cursed the stragglers in terms that would have made a whore blush. He was another of King Henry's hard, capable captains, much like Warwick and Exeter and the Umfravilles. Any one of them would have made a better commander than Clarence, and avoided the disaster that was fast unfolding.

When our entire force was gathered, Salisbury led us north along the same road as Clarence. Our archers were all mounted, and for a time I dared to hope that we may reach the battlefield in time to rescue the duke from his folly.

We rode hard, half-blinded by dust swirling up from the road, and rapidly covered the eight miles between our camp and Baugé. Salisbury only called a halt when he sighted the roofs and spires of the town, north-east of the Loire.

I nudged my destrier forward to get a better view of the river. There was only one bridge, built of stone and wide enough for two, maybe three horsemen to ride abreast. South-west of the bridge, on our side of the Loire, was a small village.

The breath caught in my throat when I saw Clarence's vanguard, strung out along the road leading to the bridge. In his haste, the duke had failed to keep his men together, and now they were dangerously stretched out in loose formation.

"Where in hells are the enemy?" I heard Salisbury mutter, straining his eyes in the direction of Baugé.

He must have had poor eyesight. "There, my lord," I cried, pointing at the bridge. The sun glinted off a mass of lances and spears gathered on the northern side. Among the forest of bright pennons I made out the lilies of France and the saltire of Scotland.

The main force of our men-at-arms were bunched together at the southern side of the bridge. Clarence's standard was among them, and Salisbury cursed as they milled about like a flock of sheep. Clouds of white-fletched arrows rained down on them, loosed by a few hundred Scottish archers strung along the opposite bank.

"Don't just stand there!" Salisbury raged, "pull your men back, you fool, out of range!"

No-one objected to the insult. Clarence was piling error upon error. Having charged ahead so eagerly and abandoned his archers, he was now struck with indecision, and exposed his men to a murderous hail of missiles while he dithered, uncertain whether to attack or retreat. The stubby, powerful darts punched through steel and layers of leather and flesh, nailed men to their saddles or sent them tumbling to earth in a tangle of limbs.

In fairness, the duke had reason to hesitate. North of the bridge the ground rose slightly, and the enemy had placed their men-at-arms at the top of the slope. They were dismounted, and presented a glittering hedge of steel points. Our men would have to tackle them if we wished to force passage to the town.

"This is Buchan's work," growled Salisbury, "he knows his business well. Too well, damn him. Clarence must not cross the bridge!"

He looked around, and crooked his finger at me. "Sir John, ride down and advise His Grace to withdraw. Immediately. Tell him I will not advance another step. The archers will deploy here, and cover his retreat if the enemy pursue. Go!"

I was about to prick in my spurs, when a distant squall of bugles sounded across the plain.

This time Salisbury's curses were fit to turn the air black. Clarence had made his decision, and taken his men across the bridge.

Whatever his faults, he lacked not for courage. It might have been the king himself charging at the head of his knights, a slim figure in silvery plate, the sunlight reflecting off his ducal coronet. He held his sword aloft like a marshal's baton, while above him the pards of England snapped and flickered in the wind as though alive.

Sounds glorious, does it not? The stuff of ballads. If I have achieved sixty years on this earth, it is because I appreciate the distinction between romance and reality. Clarence, alas, never did.

Salisbury made the sign of the cross. "Christ save His Grace," he murmured, "for I cannot."

Thus far, O Sultan, I have spoken much of siegecraft but little of pitched battles. The battlefield tactics of my countrymen have not changed a great deal in a hundred years, though our captains in France are now being forced to adopt new methods. In my youth, however, the old ways were still the best.

Englishmen prefer to ride to battle but fight on foot. Our archers are deployed in V-shaped wedges, protected to the front by rows of stakes and on their flanks by companies of dismounted men-at-arms. The latter wield glaives, halberds, battle-axes, shortened lances and other such butcher's tools, and their task is to carve in pieces those enemy troops that manage to survive the arrow-storm.

This has been the English way of war for over a century. It served us well on many battlefields, from Halidon Hill to Crécy and Poitiers, Auberoche, Najéra and Agincourt. At Baugé Clarence chose to throw away our proven strategy, and replace it with a mounted charge on a narrow front, uphill, against a more numerous enemy that had ample time to prepare.

Even the meanest wit could predict the result. The duke crashed headlong into the fence of pole-arms, relying on the sheer weight of his horse and armour to force a gap.

The Scottish foot refused to yield ground. His sword flashed as it struck right and left, and then he was swallowed up in the throng.

Clarence's knights thundered up the slope in his wake. Some of their impetus was lost, thanks to the incline, and their charge failed to pierce the enemy ranks. War-shouts and the clatter of steel echoed across the field, mingled with the frightful shrieks of wounded horses. Battle was joined in earnest. No chivalric warfare this, the mock combat of the tourney, but war to the death.

The blur of knightly heraldry was spattered with the bright gush of blood. I saw blades rise and fall, savage strokes given and taken, bones crushed, helmets cleaved like parchment, bright blood spattered over the road. A horse tried to crawl away from the melée, trailing blood and dung. His back legs were broken, and trailed uselessly behind him as the poor beast's forelegs scrabbled for purchase.

"They make no headway, my lord," said one of Salisbury's knights, "we must go to their aid."

The earl rounded on him. "What would you have me do, fool?" he snarled, "take our hobelars across the bridge, and throw them onto the French pikes?"

He ripped off his gauntlet and gnawed a knuckle, caught in an agony of indecision. There was still time for him to quit the field and save the archers.

Honour forbade him. Almost every other English nobleman of any consequence had charged over the bridge with Clarence - Sir Gilbert Umfraville, Lord Roos, the earls of Huntingdon and Somerset, and many others.

These were Salisbury's peers, as well as friends and kinsmen. The ties of honour and family demanded he make some attempt to rescue them.

"Page," he shouted, "take your company down to the village, and drive off those arbalesters on the opposite bank. Bold, Hersy, Heyward, you as well."

The latter were men-at-arms, each in command of a troop of hobelars. All told, we numbered some sixty men, barely a third of the crossbowmen on the other side of the river. Our war bows   had a longer range, and we could pick them off from distance.

I goaded Odo into a trot, down the gentle rise towards the village, surrounded by an orchard and rows of hedges. There was ample cover for our men to dismount and advance to the river without being spotted by the enemy.

"Ralf," I said, "wait here, while I take the men forward. You must not lose the standard, do you hear me? If the day goes against us, get off the field. I would not have it fall into enemy hands."

Ralf nodded, his face sickly pale, and I slid off Odo and looked for somewhere to tether him while the rest of my company dismounted.

We were on a square patch of green, perhaps used by the villagers for summer fairs and markets. It was a deceptively peaceful spot, the din of battle muffled by the woodland between us and the river.

"There has been fighting here, my lord," remarked one of my archers, "look to the church."

A little stone church lay on the edge of the green. The door had been stoved in, and the glass in the arched windows shattered. There was some further evidence of a brief skirmish - no bodies, but a couple of discarded shields, a dented bascinet, and some rust-coloured smears of blood on the steps.

I hesitated, chewing my lip. Had the French stationed a company of troops to hold the village? If so, where were they now? Perhaps Clarence's vanguard had driven them off before moving on to the bridge.

"Follow," I ordered, and cautiously approached the church, sword in hand. The rest of the archers under their captains loped through the trees towards the riverside.

I used my sword to thrust open the broken door, which lay ajar on its hinges. It creaked inward, and I stepped quickly through the arch, aware of what a perfect target I made for anyone hidden inside.

The interior of the church was cool, and well-lit by the narrow windows set high in the walls flanking the nave.

My feet almost slipped on a greasy pool of blood. The flagstones were awash with the stuff, all the way up to the altar on its dais at the northern end. More than a dozen men lay strewn over the floor. Their jupons bore the silver fleur-de-lis of France.

I wrinkled my nose against the stench of death and looked down at the nearest body. His neck was laid open by the downward stroke of some vicious chopping weapon, a halberd or pole-axe.

The French had held the church, that much seemed clear. Our men had cleared them out, and slain a few in the melée. I pictured the desperate struggle for possession of the church, the outnumbered defenders striving to hold the door against the English. The crash of breaking glass, the screams, the oaths, the flow of blood across consecrated ground. The final slaughter.

"My lord!" An archer's voice, half-strangled by panic, broke into my thoughts.

"My lord, the French are here!"

The true test of any officer is his conduct in the presence of immediate danger. I have always been one to act in a crisis, thank God, rather than goggle and ask foolish questions while the world collapses around me.

Even as I ran outside, the earth quaked underfoot, and the rumble of distant thunder filled the air.

Hoofbeats. I looked to the river, fearing the enemy had found another crossing and sent horsemen to drive away our archers.

"No, my lord," cried the archer who had alerted me, "to your left, on the ridge!"

Behind the village was a steep rise. I bit down on a curse as I glimpsed the flash of steel on the ridge, lance-points and helms.

The summit of the ridge filled with rank after rank of horsemen. Where had they come from? For one insane moment, I wondered if the French had employed a magician to raise soldiers from the earth.

The answer was simple enough. Salisbury had cursed the Earl of Buchan, the Franco-Scots commander, for knowing his business too well, and so he did. While Clarence blundered over the bridge and wasted his best men in a futile attack against the Scottish foot, Buchan kept half his army in reserve, concealed behind the ridge. Perhaps the speed of Clarence's advance had taken them by surprise, hence the presence of

French soldiers in the church.

Now, with the duke's company embroiled on the northern bank, and our archers divided, Buchan threw his reserve into the fray.

"Mount," I yelled at my men, as though they needed telling, "retreat, back to the earl!"

The ominous thunder rolled closer as I fumbled with the reins of my destrier, tied to a tree on the fringes of the orchard. Odo shied away and tossed his huge head, panicked by the noise, and I had the devil's own job to calm him.

Men fled past, desperate to get to their horses before the enemy reached the village. There was no question of making a stand. Without the protection of stakes and men-at-arms, our archers were helpless against the armoured giants on horseback bearing down on them.

Some credit must go to de Lafayette, the Constable of France. He commanded the reserve, and led them in an irresistible storm-charge down the steep rise. The horsemen flooded into the narrow lanes and encircled the village.

I finally managed to get Odo under control, and had one leg hooked over the saddle when a scream of agony made him rear and hurl me to the ground. I landed heavily on my side, and was about to curse Odo for the witless son of a carthorse when another scream erupted behind me.

"My lord! My lord, in God's name, help me!"

Ralf's voice. I twisted onto my front and saw him engaged with two Scottish men-at-arms. He crouched behind his shield as they hacked and battered at him and tried to rip the wolf banner from his grasp.

Stung into action, I forgot Odo and scrambled towards the fight. The attention of the Scots was on Ralf, and they didn't see me until I was upon them.

I aimed a two-handed cut at the nearest Scotsman's leg. My blade sheared through a gap in his leg-armour and the mail beneath. Hot red blood spurted from the wound, and his yell of pain was muffled inside the heavy steel cask of a closed bascinet.

His mace, which he had raised to smash in Ralf's skull, fell from his hand and missed my head by inches. I sidestepped and hacked again at his leg. More blood spat forth and he keeled over in the saddle, clinging with both hands to the reins. His horse staggered and whinnied in fright, while his comrade tried to ride around him to get at me.

He had forgotten Ralf. My groom wasn't much of a fighter, but had enough presence of mind to draw his dagger and stab at the Scotsman's visor.

His clumsy thrust scraped harmlessly against the steel. It was enough to distract his target, and give me time to duck under the wounded man's horse. While I cowered under its belly, the other Scot swung at Ralf with his axe.

Ralf caught the blow on his shield, but the heavy blade split the wood and bowled him clean out of the saddle. My precious banner spiralled to earth. Enraged, I rushed at the Scot and stabbed at his horse's eyes, heedless of the laws of chivalry.

He chose the wiser part of valour, wheeled his mount and galloped away. His injured comrade also fled, blood pouring from the gash I had opened in his leg.

There was no time to catch my breath. The enemy were everywhere, steel-clad riders hunting our fugitive archers through the village and the orchard.

I plunged my sword back into its sheath and dragged Ralf to his feet. "Can you ride?" I yelled into his ear. He looked at me with mazed eyes, blinked, and gave a brief nod.

Ralf's rouncy had bolted, but Odo stood nearby, quietly

nuzzling at the grass, oblivious to the noise and bloodshed. He was strong enough to carry the weight of two men, so I grabbed my standard and pushed Ralf towards him.

Thanks to de Lafayette, we made good our escape from the village. The Constable was solely concerned with Clarence, and recalled his men from their pursuit of the archers. They turned away and rode in force to the southern end of the bridge, sealing off the duke's only means of escape.

From my vantage point on the hill above the village, I watched the slow death of our vanguard. Clarence and his nobles fought back-to-back in a steadily dwindling circle around their banners, with the duke's standard planted firmly in the centre.

Salisbury's banner moved away from field, back down the highway towards Beaufort. He had given up the battle for lost, and would not stay to witness his friends die.

"God aid them," said Ralf, who had slid down from Odo's broad back, "they make a brave end."

Tears streamed down our faces. We and the rest of the little band of survivors on the hill could do nothing to help the doomed Englishmen beyond the bridge. That knowledge made us weep, along with the stark, hopeless courage of their last stand.

Long after the battle was done, several Scottish nobles claimed the honour of slaying Clarence. I was too far away to see who finally struck him down, but did see the ducal coronet, wet with royal blood, raised in triumph on the end of a Scottish pike.

It was swiftly joined by his severed head, impaled on a second pike. The jeers and hoots of the enemy drifted across the field, while we cursed and shook our fists in vain at them.

After decades of defeat and humiliation at English hands,

the Franco-Scots were in the mood for revenge. All but a handful of our men were cut down, still fighting, and the names of Lord Roos, Sir Gilbert Umfraville and the Count de Tancarville among the roll-call of our slain. The earls of Huntingdon and Somerset, as well as a few others, were disarmed and led away as prisoners.

Baugé was a black day for England, possibly the worst defeat we ever suffered in France. Like most disasters in war, it could have been easily avoided, had Clarence listened to the advice of better men. Pride, envy and the childish rivalry with his eldest brother compelled him to his doom.

"What now, my lord?" asked Ralf when the slaughter was done.

It was near dusk by now. Grim shadows slanted across the land. The sound of singing could be heard from the direction of Baugé, where our enemies rejoiced in their unexpected victory.

Most of our hobelars had fled south to rejoin Salisbury. Only the survivors of my company, and a few other stragglers, remained on the hill.

Twelve of my men still lived. The others were slain in the village when de Lafayette sprang his ambush.

I had a choice. Rejoin Salisbury, who would probably try and make his way back to the capital, and take refuge behind its walls until King Henry returned to France with reinforcements. Or I could forget my duty, break my indenture, and ride away in search of a greater destiny. In the wake of the defeat at Baugé, with our army dispersed and in full retreat, I would seldom have a better opportunity.

It would mean starting again, with no money. My war-chest was still in Paris, guarded by six mercenaries I had hired for the task.

I thought quickly, and came to a decision.

"Follow me, if you wish," I told my men, "or else go where you will. I leave it to your conscience."

"What of you, my lord?" asked Ralf.

"Follow," I replied, "and find out."

With that, I put spurs to Odo's flanks and rode away.

A tremendous sense of freedom washed over me as I set my face, not towards Paris or Normandy, but the distant east.

***

Phrantzes laid down his pen, yawned, and knuckled his eyes.

"Is that the end?" he croaked, reaching for the cup of watered wine at his elbow.

John Page sat with his back to the wall, arms folded, staring out of the window at the turrets and roofs of Constantinople. He had barely moved from this spot, save to stretch his limbs and relieve himself, for the past three days.

He massaged his throat. "For now," he replied, his voice no less hoarse, "I have little more to say of my time in France."

For three days he had recited his tale, and talked for long hours while Phrantzes scribbled. The stack of parchment on the table, covered in the former imperial courtier's neat, precise hand, was the fruit of their labours.

All that remained was to deliver their work to the Sultan, and pray he was sufficiently entertained by it to spare their lives.

"How long?" said Phrantzes after he had drank two cupfuls of wine, "even if he doesn't kill us this time, how long will he suffer us to live?"

He propped his head in his hands and started to weep. "I have to see my wife again, and my little ones. God in Heaven, what torments are they being exposed to?"

298

"Your wife is very beautiful," said Page, "so I expect the Sultan will put her in his harem. Have no fear. She will come to no harm there. Nothing fatal, at any rate."

His brutal tone shocked Phrantzes out of his tears, as it was meant to. The little man trembled with rage, and might have launched himself at Page if footsteps hadn't sounded in the corridor outside.

Both men fell silent as the door glided open, and the same stocky, middle-aged Sipahi officer of three days ago stood framed in the entrance.

He waited for a moment, fists planted on his hips, his eyes carefully scrutinising the prisoners.

"You are done?" he asked Phrantzes in Greek.

Phrantzes laid his hand flat on top of the stack of parchment. "Yes...sir," he replied carefully, "my companion has given an account of the French wars. We hope your master finds it to his taste."

The officer smirked. "Of course you do, Master Phrantzes. If he does not, your heads will decorate the city walls."

He snapped his fingers, and the same mousy clerk in the skull-cap and black robe crept under his arm into the cell. Without looking at either prisoner, the clerk gathered up the documents and scuttled out.

Phrantzes resumed his tears when the prison door slammed shut. Page closed his eyes and whistled another marching song of his youth.

They were left alone for an entire week. In that time they saw no-one save the Turkish guards who pushed their meals through the door twice a day and emptied their waste bucket.

Two men, living in close confinement with the shadow of the executioner's blade hanging over them, are like to run mad.

Phrantzes might have done so, but for John Page's quiet composure.

"We live in the moment," he said, "one moment at a time. There is no past, no future. Such things are myths, created by men to feed our delusions of importance."

"Spare me your halfwit philosophy," Phrantzes said bitterly, "I wish to pray. Only in prayer do I find any comfort."

Page shrugged. "Pray, then, if it helps. Pray all you like."

After seven days of increasingly strained conversation and ever-longer silences, the Sipahi returned.

Phrantzes quailed when he saw the cluster of armed men at the officer's back, and the broad tulwar hanging from his belt.

"His Sacred and Imperial Majesty," the Sipahi announced, "Emperor, Sultan of Sultans, Khan of Khans, Commander of the Faithful, Successor of the Prophet and Lord of the Universe, has listened to the tale of the infidel Sir John Page, knight of England."

There was a look of sulky disappointment on the officer's jowly features. "The Sultan was intrigued by it. At times delighted, at others repelled. After much thought, he has decided on a stay of execution."

Phrantzes went limp with relief, and even Page seemed to relax slightly.

"His Imperial Majesty grants you another three days," said the officer, "three more days to save your lives."

END

AUTHOR'S NOTE

John Page, author of The Siege of Rouen, was a real person.
Other than his poem, which survives in a single manuscript
partially incorporated into a fifteenth century chronicle, we
know very little about him. In the poem he claims to have been
an eye-witness to the siege of Rouen (1418-19), but gives no
other clue to his identity. There was a Prior of Bernewell
named John Page alive during this era, though it is unclear why
he should have been present at a siege in France. Several
English soldiers of the same name are listed on the surviving
muster rolls of Henry V's army for the Normandy campaign,
and it is possible the poet was one of these men.

The John Page who gave the account of his life to George
Phrantzes, former secretary and confidante to the doomed

Emperor Constantine XI, makes two claims: one, to have penned The Siege of Rouen, and secondly, to be the bastard son of Thomas Page, a mercenary captain who enjoyed some brief fame in the latter years of Edward III's reign.

The outlaw chaplain of Lindfield, Robert Stafford alias Frere Tuk or Tuck, was also real. He is named in the court records for the years 1417 and 1429, where the clerk records that Stafford took the 'unusual name' of Frere Tuk as an alias. It is unclear whether he invented the name for himself, or was inspired by the character of Friar Tuck in the Robin Hood ballads. He and his band of outlaws appear to have had some grudge against the foresters of Surrey and Sussex, and committed a great number of forest offences, much as described in Page's account. Stafford/Tuk was still alive in 1429, and there is no record of him ever being punished for his crimes.

Page evidently had a vivid imagination, and it is down to the reader how much of his account should be believed. For instance, there is no record of a failed attempt by the English to undermine the walls of Rouen, or of Henry engaging a French knight in single combat in the mines (though he did so later, at the siege of Meulan). Either these incidents went unrecorded, or Page was indulging in a little artistic licence to strengthen his personal association with the King. Neither is there any proof that Henry had a part in the murder of the Duke of Burgundy, though Burgundy's removal certainly helped the English cause in France.

Whatever lies or half-truths he chose to tell, Page's description of Henry V, the famous victor of Agincourt, has the ring of truth. Far from the attractive hero of Shakespeare, Henry was in reality a ruthless pragmatist who justified the most extreme actions on the grounds of doing God's work. The account of his massacre of male citizens at Caen is only mentioned in one other source, a Venetian chronicle, but Henry was perfectly capable of such an act: we know he ordered similar massacres at Agincourt and Montereau. The scourge of God, as he called himself, was a stranger to mercy. He was also one of the ablest soldier-kings England ever produced, and Page is clearly torn between admiration of Henry's military prowess, and repugnance at his cruelty.

It should be remembered that, at the time of writing, Page was in fear of his life. His task was to keep the Ottoman sultan, Mehmed the Conqueror, entertained for as long as possible. The moment he failed, his neck was forfeit. The same fate would befall his fellow prisoner, George Phrantzes. In such circumstances, a little exaggeration of the truth is perhaps to be expected.

It is known that Phrantzes was eventually ransomed and retired to the monastery of Tarchaneiotes in Corfu. He makes no mention of John Page in his writings - possibly he wanted to forget his association with such a dubious character. The details of Page's career are unrecorded in any other source.

The next volume of Page's memoirs, written under duress in the days after the sack of Constantinople in 1453, deal with his service in the heretical armies of the Hussites, and their wars against the Holy Roman Emperor...

16350070R00172

Printed in Great Britain
by Amazon